J 741.597 Ang
Angleberger, Tom
Doorways to danger

$12.99
on1257552607

WITHDRAWN

W9-ALN-816
3 4028 10210 5252
HARRIS COUNTY PUBLIC LIBRARY

DISNEP

DOORWAYS
TO
DANGER

Facebook: **facebook.com/idwpublishing**
Twitter: **@idwpublishing**
YouTube: **youtube.com/idwpublishing**
Instagram: **@idwpublishing**

ISBN: 978-1-68405-780-1

24 23 22 21   1 2 3 4

Cover Art by
Jeff Harvey

Cover Colors by
Valentina Pinto

Letters by
Amauri Osorio

Design by
Nathan Widick

SPECIAL THANKS TO
Eugene Paraszczuk, Julie Dorris,
Jodi Hammerwold, Roberto Santillo,
and Carlotta Quattrocolo
for their invaluable assistance.

DOORWAYS TO DANGER. JUNE 2021. FIRST PRINTING. © 2021 Disney Enterprises, Inc. All Rights Reserved. IDW Publishing, a division of Idea and Design Works, LLC. Editorial offices: 2765 Truxtun Road, San Diego, CA 92106. The IDW logo is registered in the U.S. Patent and Trademark Office. Any similarities to persons living or dead are purely coincidental. With the exception of artwork used for review purposes, none of the contents of this publication may be reprinted without the permission of Idea and Design Works, LLC. Printed in KOREA.

IDW Publishing does not read or accept unsolicited submissions of ideas, stories, or artwork.

DISNEY PUBLISHING WORLDWIDE
Global Magazines, Comics and Partworks

PUBLISHER
Lynn Waggoner

EXECUTIVE EDITOR
Carlotta Quattrocolo

EDITORIAL TEAM
Bianca Coletti (Director, Magazines)
Guido Frazzini (Director, Comics)
Stefano Ambrosio (Executive Editor)
Camilla Vedove (Senior Manager, Editorial Development)
Behnoosh Khalili (Senior Editor)
Julie Dorris (Senior Editor)
Mina Riazi (Assistant Editor)
Gabriela Capasso (Assistant Editor)

DESIGN
Enrico Soave (Senior Designer)

ART
Ken Shue (Vp, Global Art),
Roberto Santillo (Creative Director)
Marco Ghiglione (Creative Manager)
Manny Mederos (Senior Iillustration Manager)
Stefano Attardi (Illustration Manager)

PORTFOLIO MANAGEMENT
Olivia Ciancarelli (Director)

BUSINESS & MARKETING
Mariantonietta Galla (Senior Manager, Franchise)
Virpi Korhonen (Editorial Manager)

IDW PUBLISHING

PUBLISHER
Nachie Marsham

EVP OF OPERATIONS
Rebekah Cahalin

VP OF SALES
Blake Kobashigawa

EDITOR-IN-CHIEF
John Barber

EDITORIAL DIRECTOR, ORIGINALS
Mark Doyle

EDITORIAL DIRECTOR GRAPHIC NOVELS AND COLLECTIONS
Justin Eisinger

DIRECTOR, SPECIAL PROJECTS
Scott Dunbier

SR. MARKETING DIRECTOR
Anna Morrow

DIRECTOR OF DESIGN & PRODUCTION
Tara McCrillis

SR. DIRECTOR OF MANUFACTURING OPERATIONS
Shauna Monteforte

IDW FOUNDERS
Ted Adams and Robbie Robbins

WRITTEN BY
TOM ANGLEBERGER

DEDICATED TO
CHARLIE ANGLEBERGER
WHOSE VAULT FULL OF MCDUCK HISTORY
AND TREASURE TROVE OF STORY IDEAS
BROUGHT THIS BOOK TO LIFE

ART BY
JEFF HARVEY

COLORS BY
VALENTINA PINTO

ASSISTANT EDITORS
RILEY FARMER
GABRIELA CAPASSO

EDITORS
DENTON J. TIPTON
JULIE DORRIS AND
ELIZABETH BREI

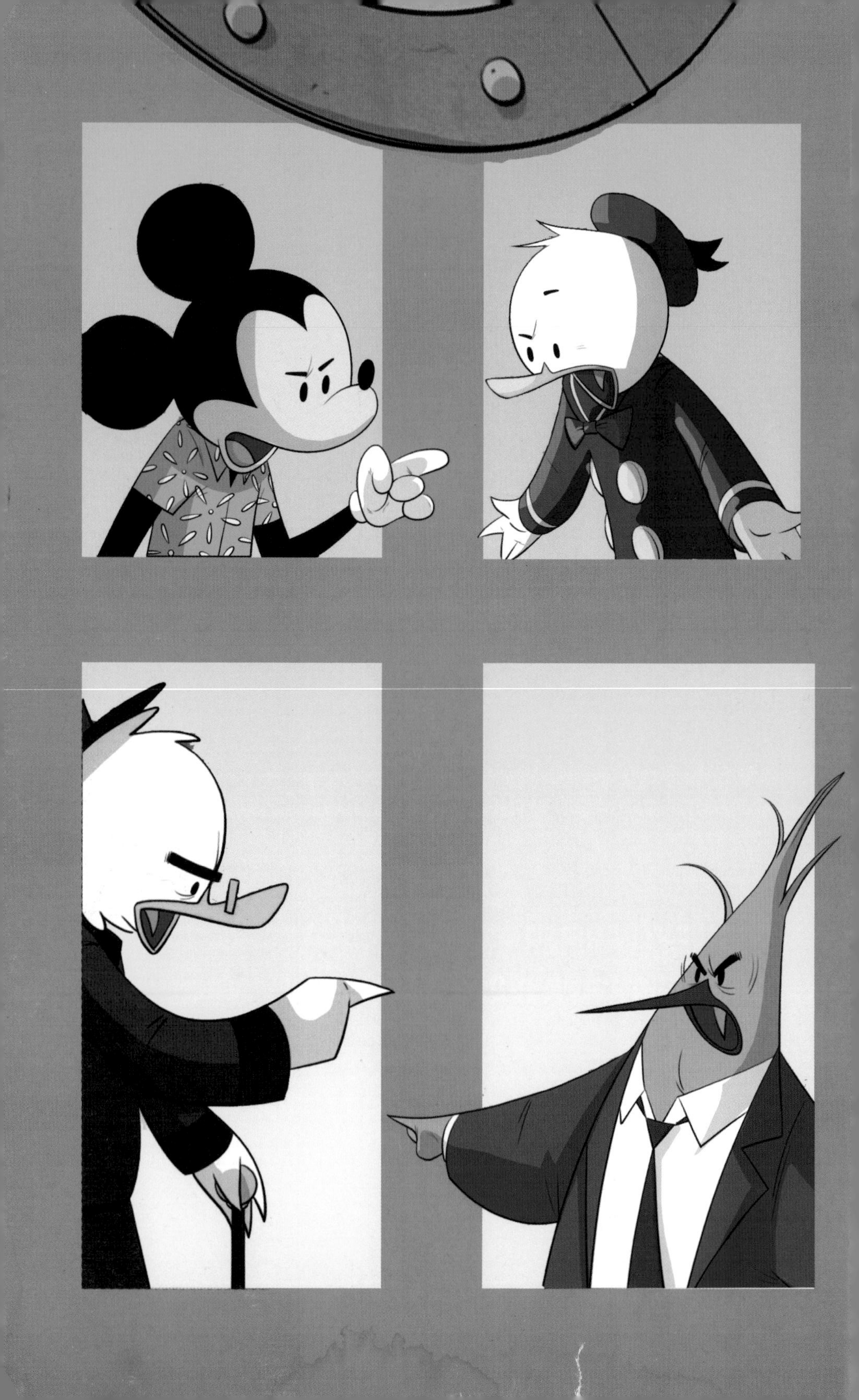

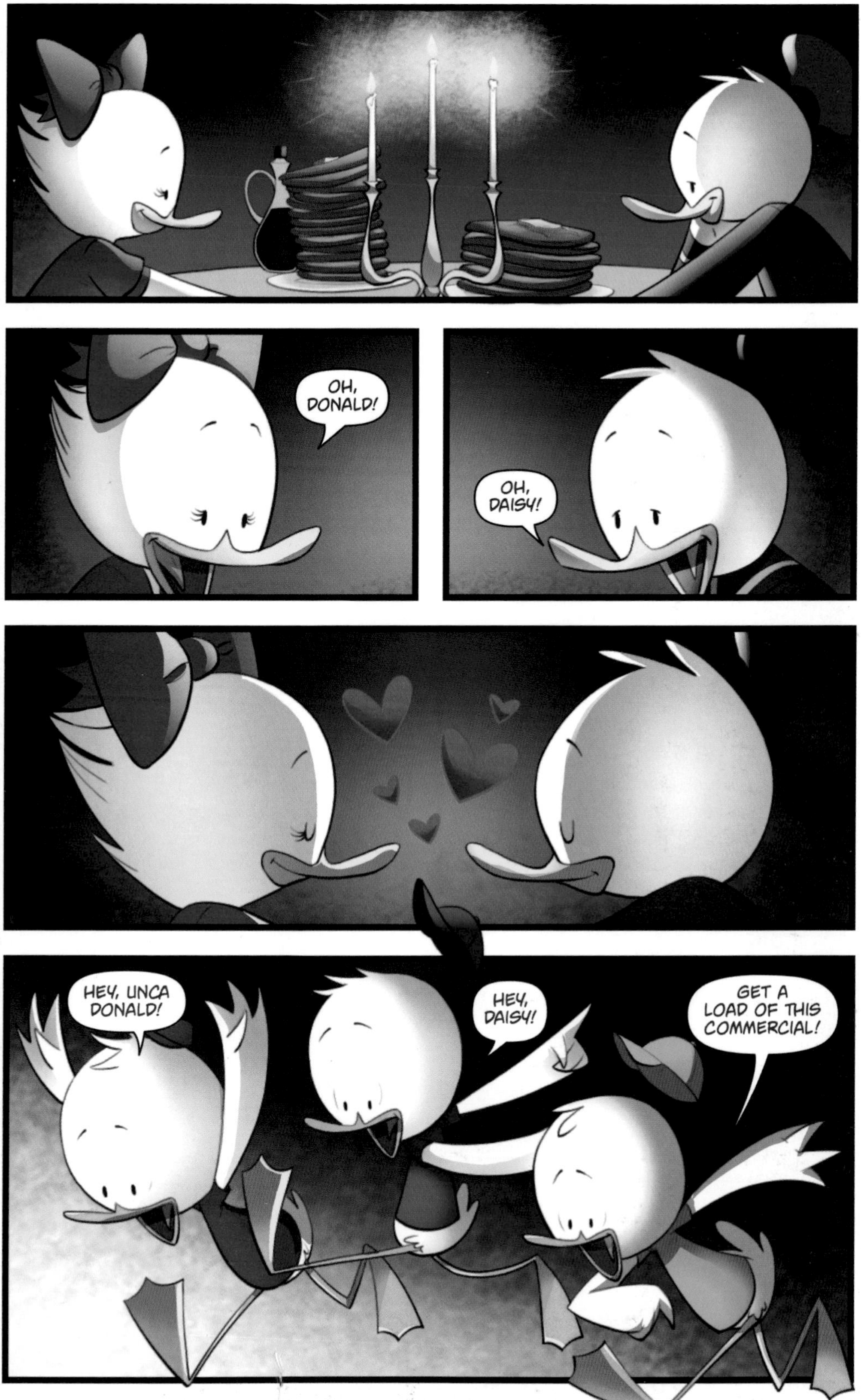
OH, DONALD!
OH, DAISY!
HEY, UNCA DONALD!
HEY, DAISY!
GET A LOAD OF THIS COMMERCIAL!

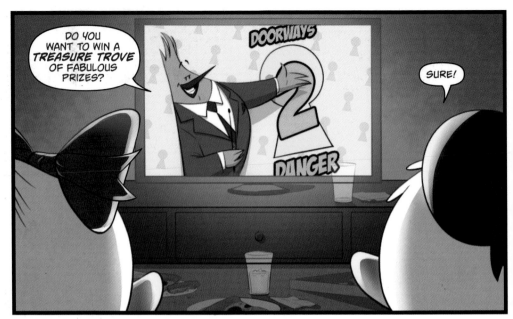

DO YOU WANT TO WIN A *TREASURE TROVE* OF FABULOUS PRIZES?

SURE!

I'M JAY BLUEJAY, HOST OF *DOORWAYS TO DANGER.* AND I WANT TO GIVE *YOU* THE MOST *FABULOUS PRIZES...*

I'LL TAKE 'EM!

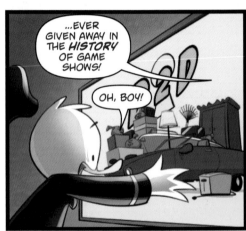

...EVER GIVEN AWAY IN THE *HISTORY* OF GAME SHOWS!

OH, BOY!

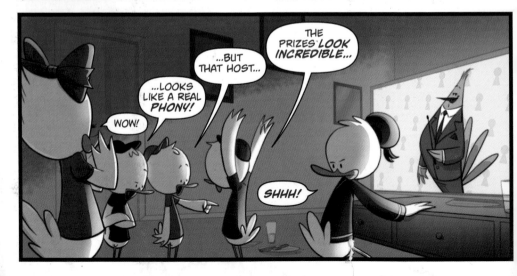

THE PRIZES *LOOK INCREDIBLE...*

...BUT THAT HOST...

...LOOKS LIKE A REAL *PHONY!*

WOW!

SHHH!

ON THIS THRILLING ADVENTURE SHOW, PAIRS OF CONTESTANTS WILL TRAVEL TO *EXOTIC LOCATIONS*...

...AND FACE *CRAZY CHALLENGES*...

...THE *FIVE DOORWAYS TO DANGER!*

...AS THEY RACE TO FIND THE KEYS TO...

D2D

THIS DOESN'T LOOK LIKE A GAME SHOW...

...IT LOOKS LIKE A REAL *ADVENTURE!*

AND THAT DOOR LOOKS *FAMILIAR*...

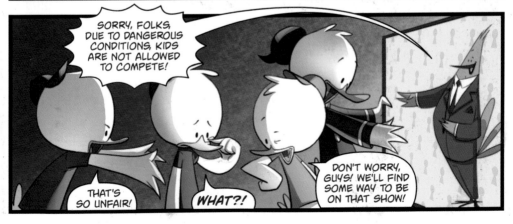

SORRY, FOLKS, DUE TO DANGEROUS CONDITIONS, KIDS ARE NOT ALLOWED TO COMPETE!

THAT'S SO UNFAIR!

WHAT?!

DON'T WORRY, GUYS! WE'LL FIND SOME WAY TO BE ON THAT SHOW!

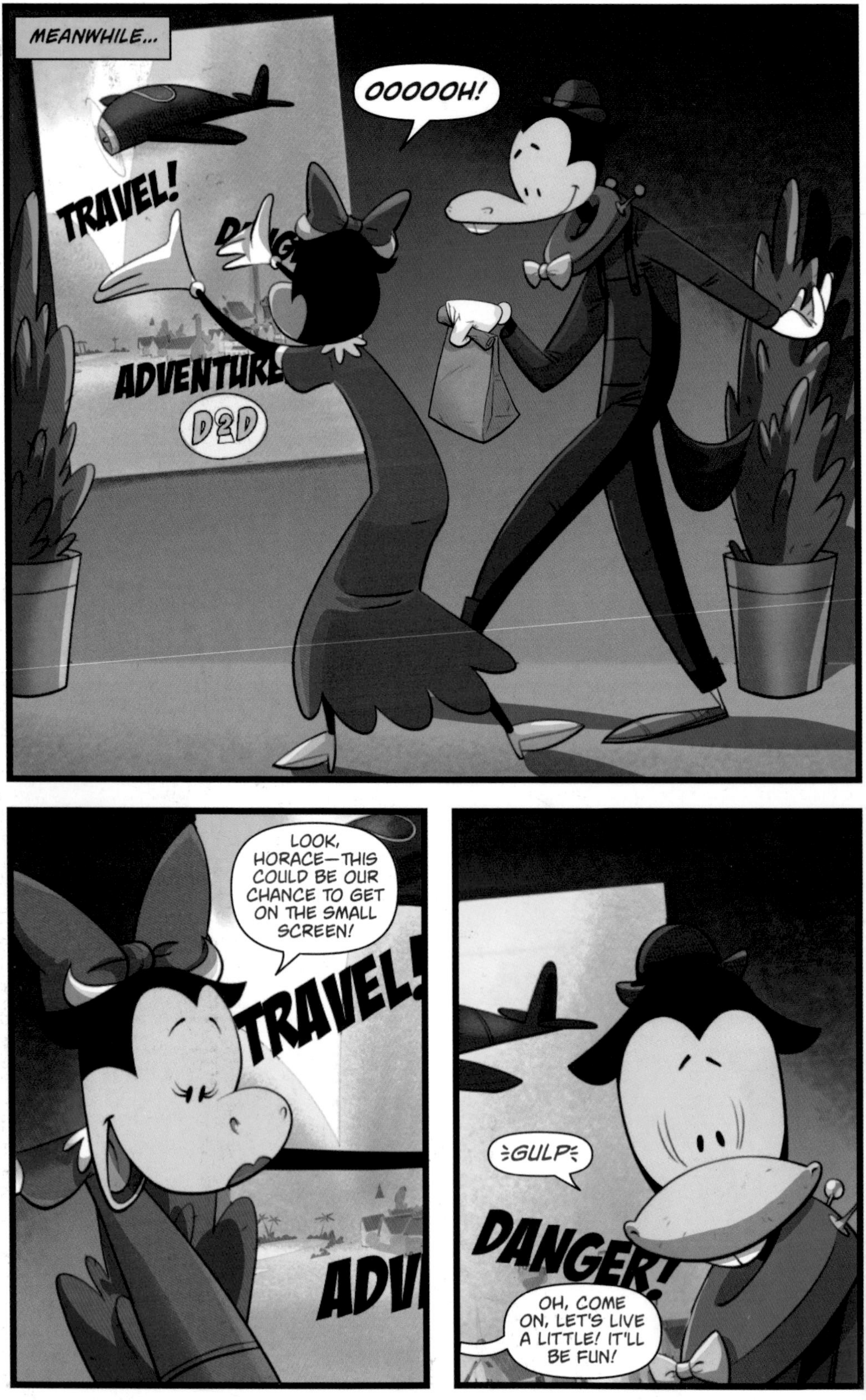
MEANWHILE...
OOOOOH!
TRAVEL!
ADVENTURE
D2D
LOOK, HORACE—THIS COULD BE OUR CHANCE TO GET ON THE SMALL SCREEN!
TRAVEL!
ADV
GULP
DANGER!
OH, COME ON, LET'S LIVE A LITTLE! IT'LL BE FUN!

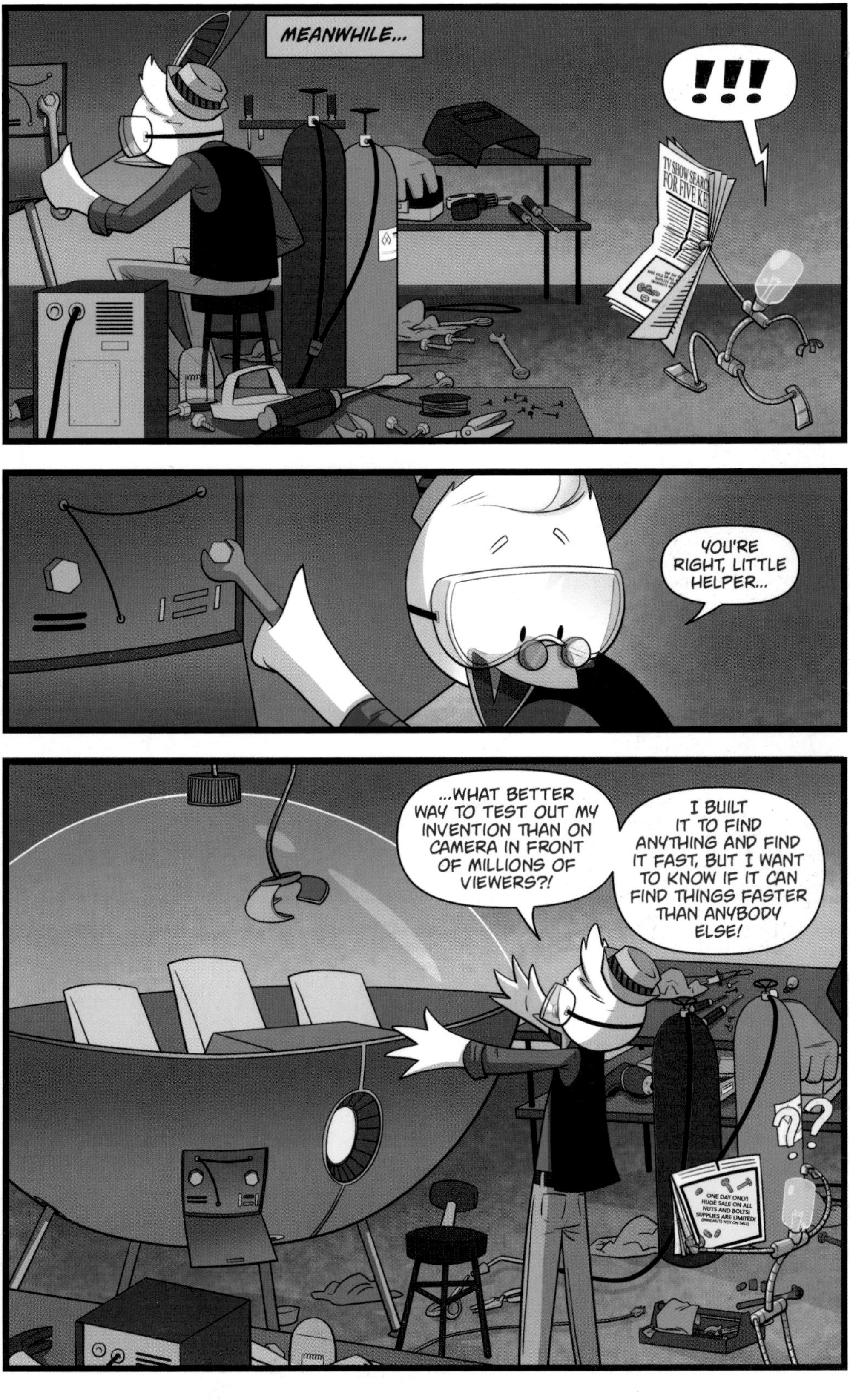
MEANWHILE...
!!!
YOU'RE RIGHT, LITTLE HELPER...
...WHAT BETTER WAY TO TEST OUT MY INVENTION THAN ON CAMERA IN FRONT OF MILLIONS OF VIEWERS?!
I BUILT IT TO FIND ANYTHING AND FIND IT FAST, BUT I WANT TO KNOW IF IT CAN FIND THINGS FASTER THAN ANYBODY ELSE!
?
ONE DAY ONLY! HUGE SALE ON ALL NUTS AND BOLTS! SUPPLIES ARE LIMITED!
(WINGNUTS NOT ON SALE)

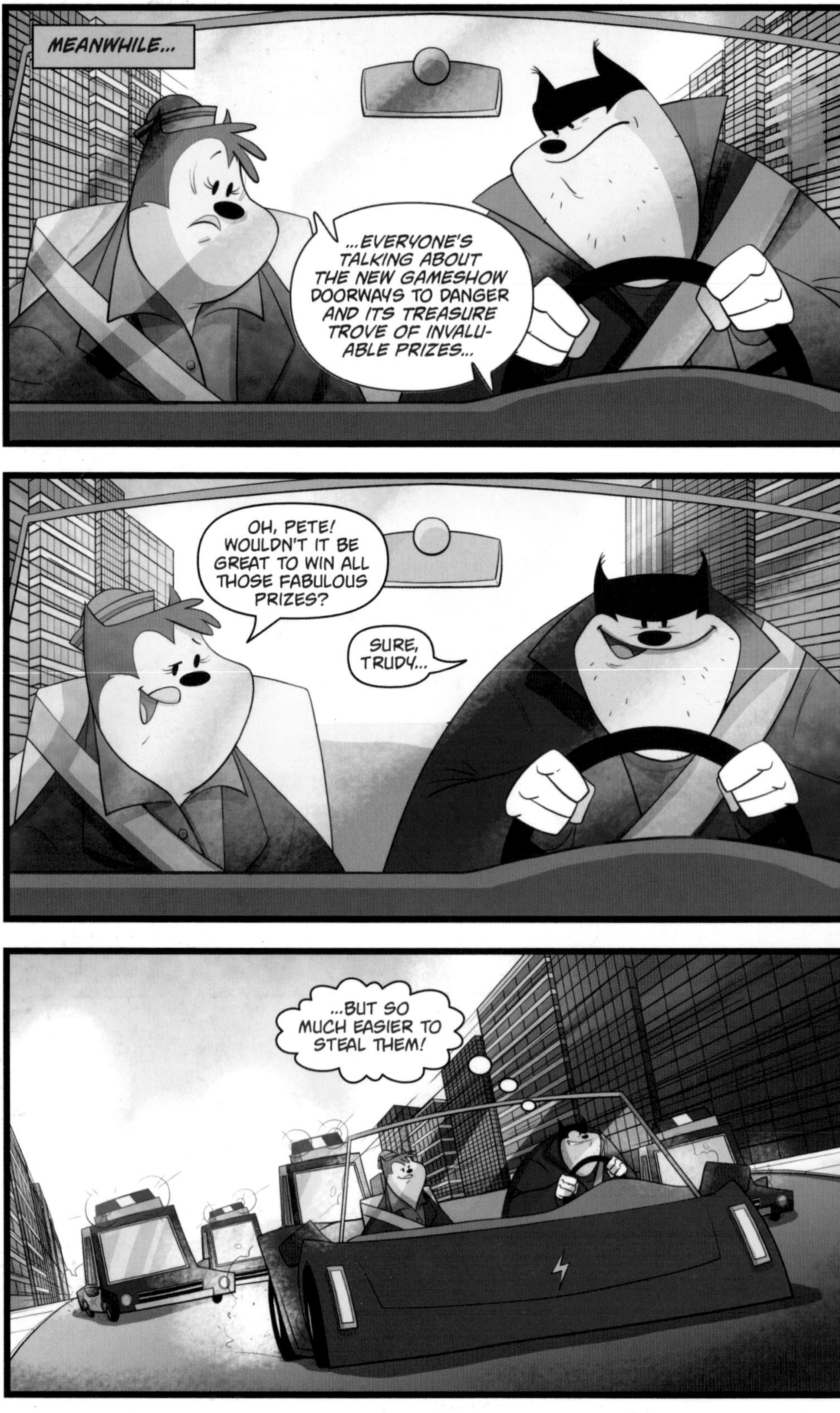
MEANWHILE...
...EVERYONE'S TALKING ABOUT THE NEW GAMESHOW DOORWAYS TO DANGER AND ITS TREASURE TROVE OF INVALU-ABLE PRIZES...
OH, PETE! WOULDN'T IT BE GREAT TO WIN ALL THOSE FABULOUS PRIZES?
SURE, TRUDY...
...BUT SO MUCH EASIER TO STEAL THEM!

ENTER THE D2D ADVENTURE!

BE ON TV! WIN FABULOUS PRIZES!

LOOK AT THAT, MICK! LET'S ENTER! WE MIGHT WIN A NEW CAR... OR A TOASTER... OR A CAR WITH A BUILT-IN TOASTER... OR—

RING RING

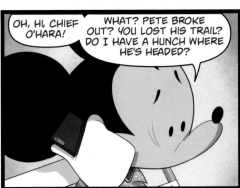

OH, HI, CHIEF O'HARA!

WHAT? PETE BROKE OUT? YOU LOST HIS TRAIL? DO I HAVE A HUNCH WHERE HE'S HEADED?

YEAH, CHIEF, I'VE GOT A REAL GOOD HUNCH!

LET'S GET ON THAT SHOW, GOOFY... I THINK WE'VE GOT A COUPLE OF PRIZES TO BAG!

OH, BOY! THIS IS GONNA BE FAB-YOO-LOUS!

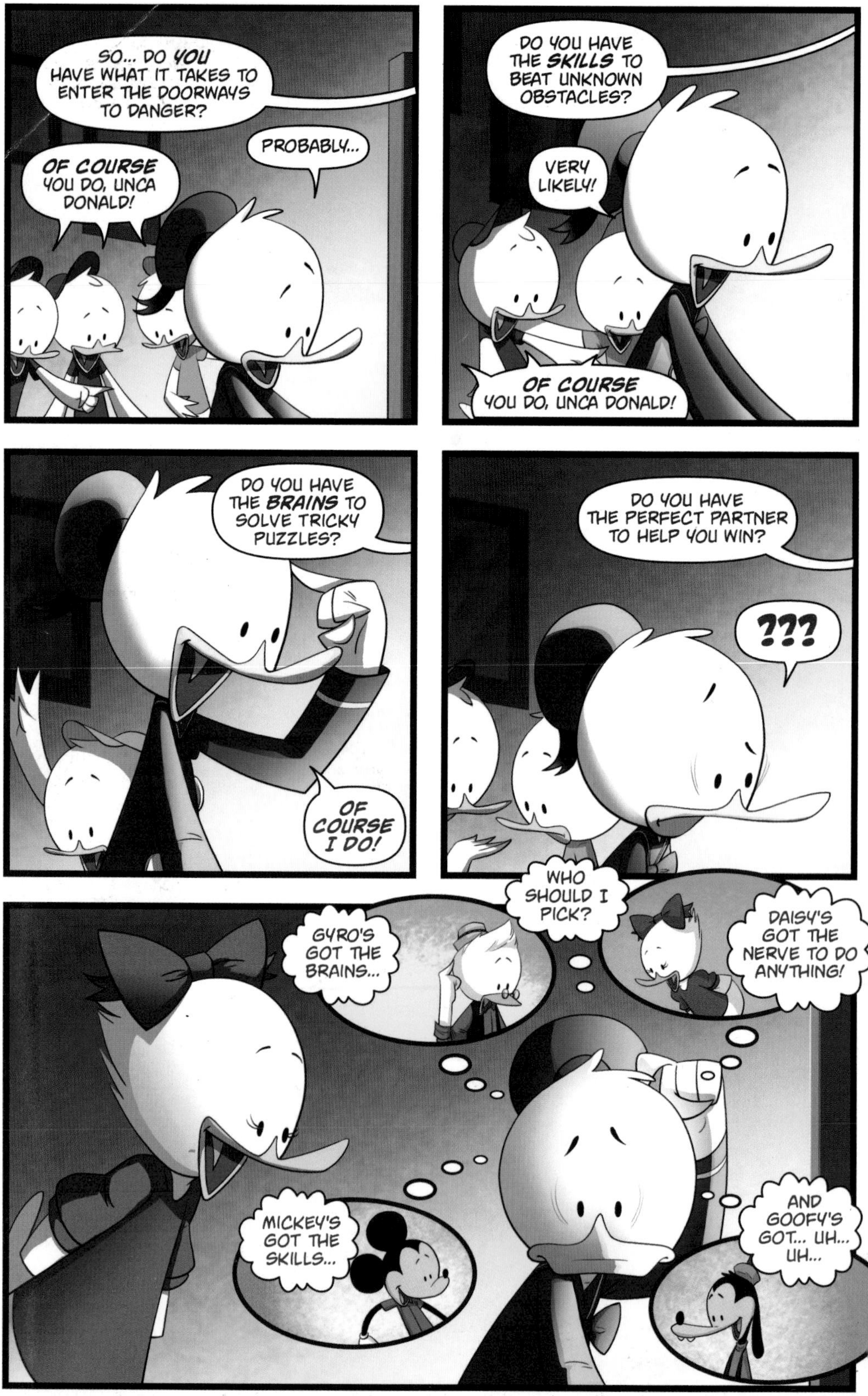
SO... DO YOU HAVE WHAT IT TAKES TO ENTER THE DOORWAYS TO DANGER?
PROBABLY...
OF COURSE YOU DO, UNCA DONALD!
DO YOU HAVE THE SKILLS TO BEAT UNKNOWN OBSTACLES?
VERY LIKELY!
OF COURSE YOU DO, UNCA DONALD!
DO YOU HAVE THE BRAINS TO SOLVE TRICKY PUZZLES?
OF COURSE I DO!
DO YOU HAVE THE PERFECT PARTNER TO HELP YOU WIN?
???
WHO SHOULD I PICK?
GYRO'S GOT THE BRAINS...
DAISY'S GOT THE NERVE TO DO ANYTHING!
MICKEY'S GOT THE SKILLS...
AND GOOFY'S GOT... UH... UH...

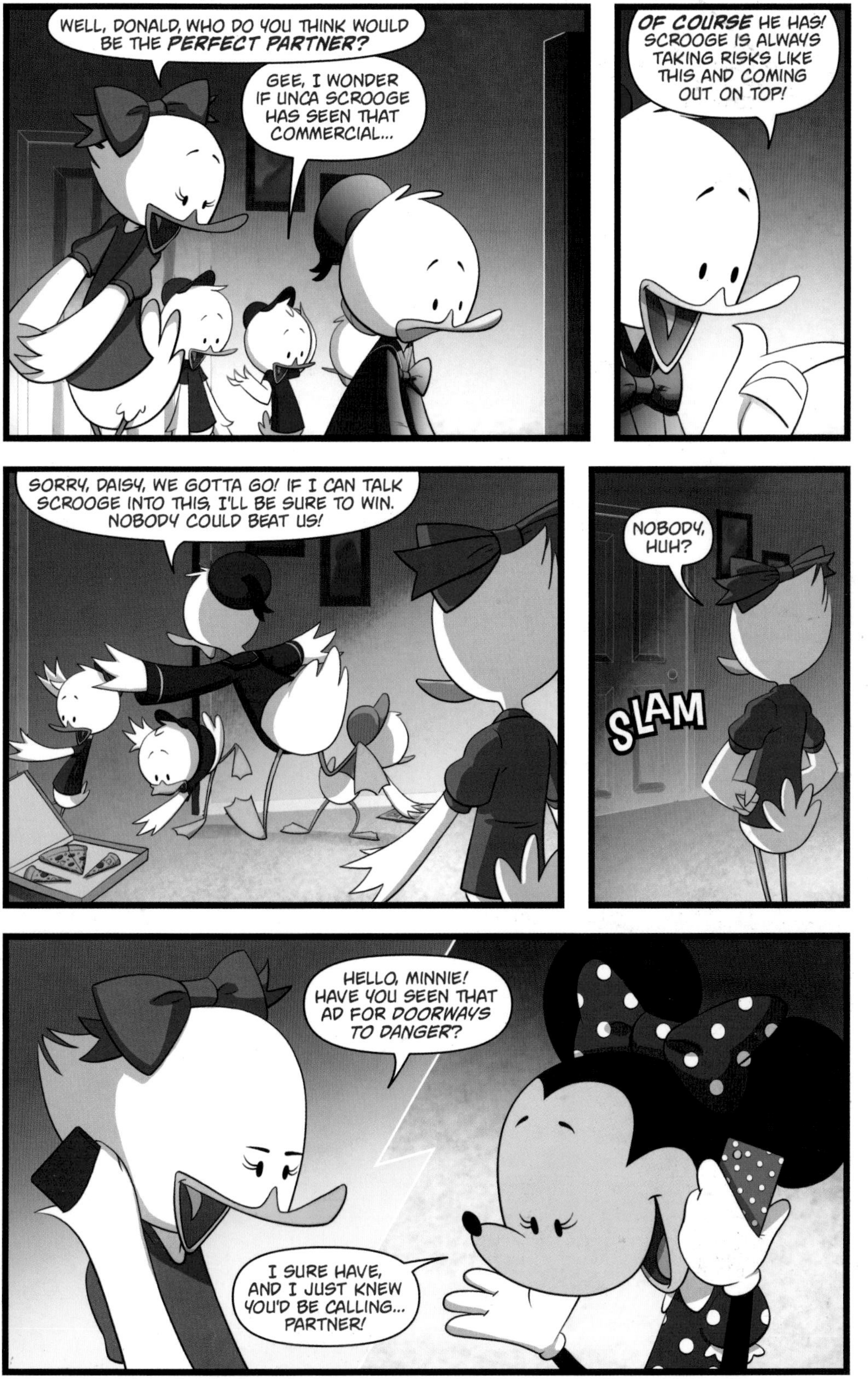
WELL, DONALD, WHO DO YOU THINK WOULD BE THE *PERFECT PARTNER?*
GEE, I WONDER IF UNCA SCROOGE HAS SEEN THAT COMMERCIAL...
OF COURSE HE HAS! SCROOGE IS ALWAYS TAKING RISKS LIKE THIS AND COMING OUT ON TOP!
SORRY, DAISY, WE GOTTA GO! IF I CAN TALK SCROOGE INTO THIS, I'LL BE SURE TO WIN. NOBODY COULD BEAT US!
NOBODY, HUH?
SLAM
HELLO, MINNIE! HAVE YOU SEEN THAT AD FOR *DOORWAYS TO DANGER?*
I SURE HAVE, AND I JUST KNEW YOU'D BE CALLING... PARTNER!

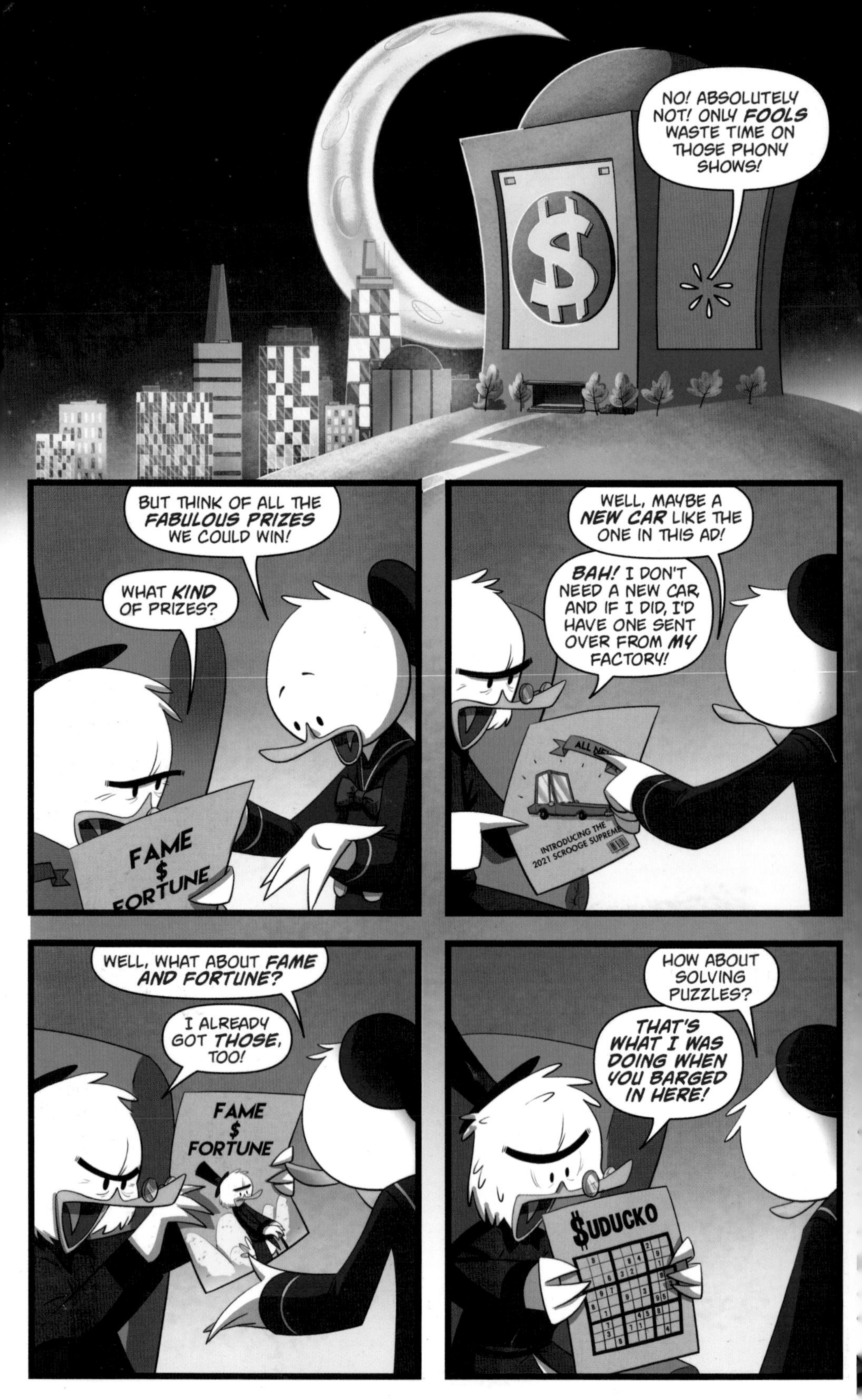
NO! ABSOLUTELY NOT! ONLY FOOLS WASTE TIME ON THOSE PHONY SHOWS!
BUT THINK OF ALL THE FABULOUS PRIZES WE COULD WIN!
WHAT KIND OF PRIZES?
FAME $ FORTUNE
WELL, MAYBE A NEW CAR LIKE THE ONE IN THIS AD!
BAH! I DON'T NEED A NEW CAR, AND IF I DID, I'D HAVE ONE SENT OVER FROM MY FACTORY!
INTRODUCING THE 2021 SCROOGE SUPREME
WELL, WHAT ABOUT FAME AND FORTUNE?
I ALREADY GOT THOSE, TOO!
FAME $ FORTUNE
HOW ABOUT SOLVING PUZZLES?
THAT'S WHAT I WAS DOING WHEN YOU BARGED IN HERE!
$UDUCKO

HEY, UNCA SCROOGE!

BETTER LOOK AT THIS...

...BEFORE YOU SAY NO!

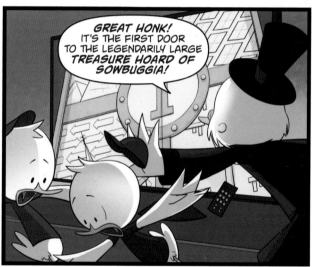

GREAT HONK! IT'S THE FIRST DOOR TO THE LEGENDARILY LARGE *TREASURE HOARD OF SOWBUGGIA!*

THE TREASURE *WHAT OF WHEREBUGGIA?*

THE TREASURE HOARD OF SOWBUGGIA!

THE LOST RICHES OF *KING JAXTO THE AWFUL!*

IT'S ALL HERE IN THE CHAPTER ON *LOST TREASURES!*

JUNIOR WOODCHUCK'S GUIDE

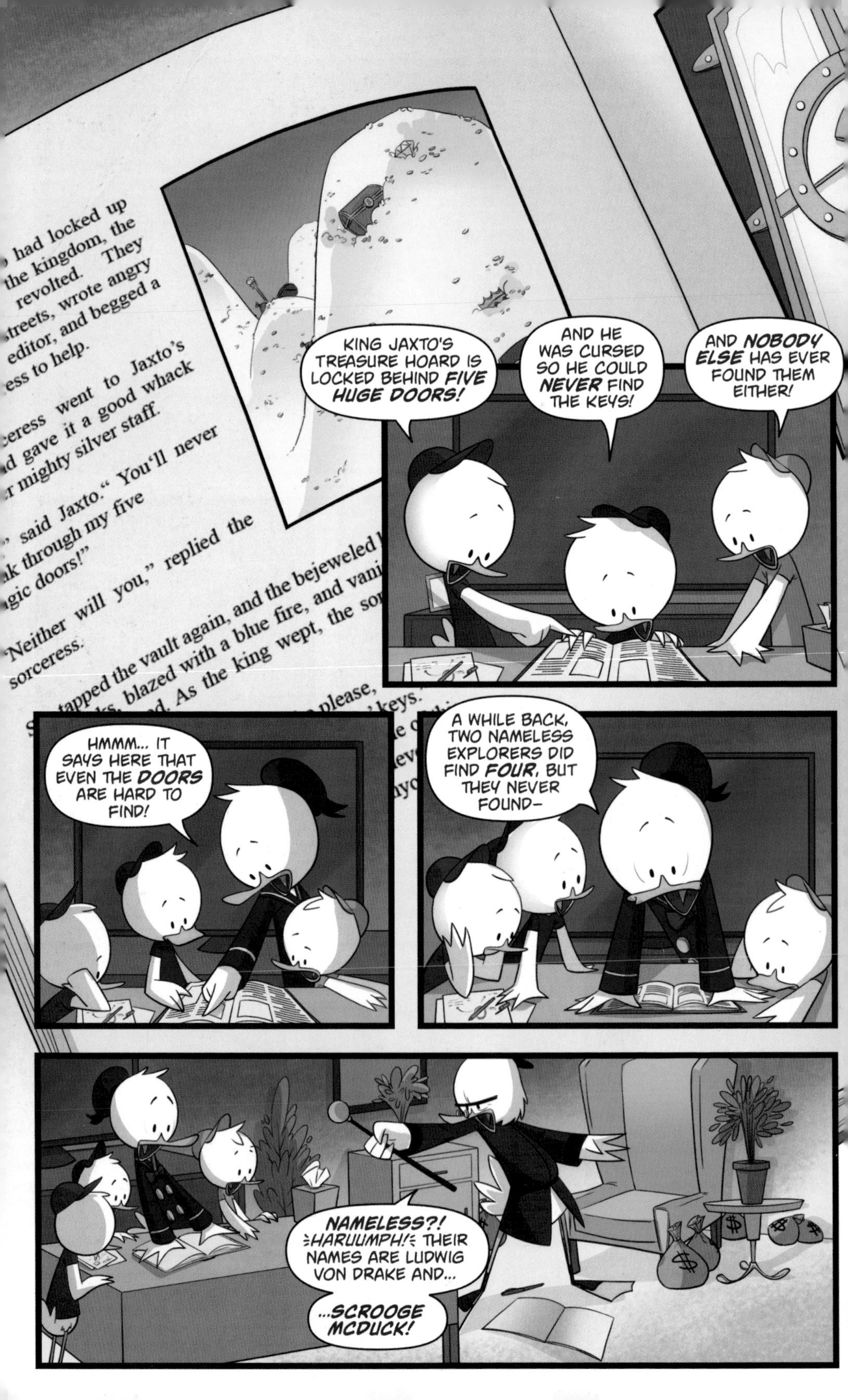
KING JAXTO'S TREASURE HOARD IS LOCKED BEHIND FIVE HUGE DOORS!
AND HE WAS CURSED SO HE COULD NEVER FIND THE KEYS!
AND NOBODY ELSE HAS EVER FOUND THEM EITHER!
HMMM... IT SAYS HERE THAT EVEN THE DOORS ARE HARD TO FIND!
A WHILE BACK, TWO NAMELESS EXPLORERS DID FIND FOUR, BUT THEY NEVER FOUND—
NAMELESS?! HARUUMPH! THEIR NAMES ARE LUDWIG VON DRAKE AND...
...SCROOGE MCDUCK!

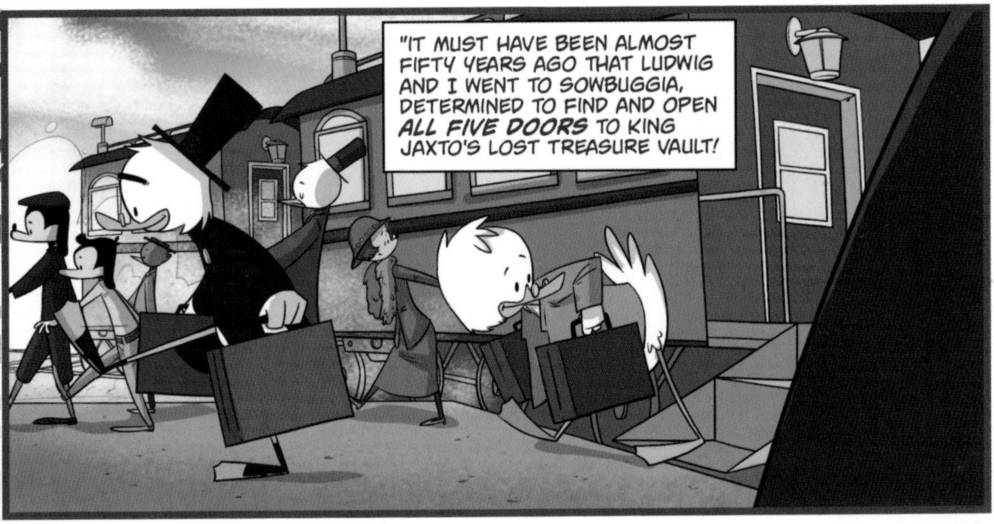
"IT MUST HAVE BEEN ALMOST FIFTY YEARS AGO THAT LUDWIG AND I WENT TO SOWBUGGIA, DETERMINED TO FIND AND OPEN ALL FIVE DOORS TO KING JAXTO'S LOST TREASURE VAULT!

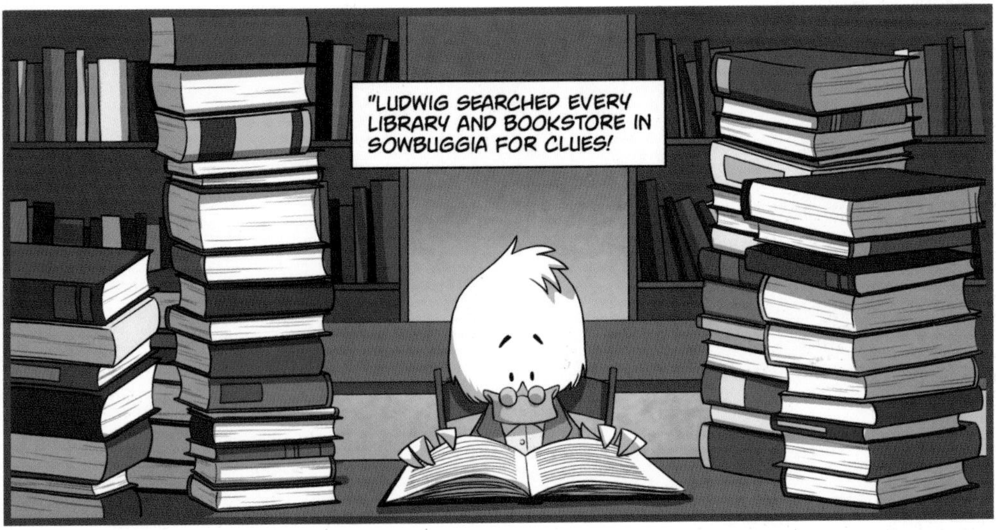
"LUDWIG SEARCHED EVERY LIBRARY AND BOOKSTORE IN SOWBUGGIA FOR CLUES!

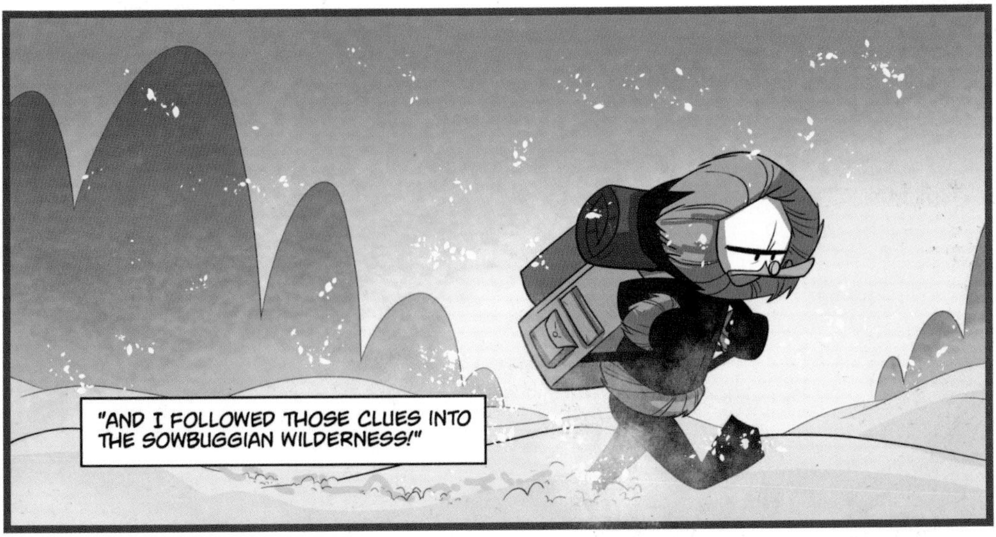
"AND I FOLLOWED THOSE CLUES INTO THE SOWBUGGIAN WILDERNESS!"

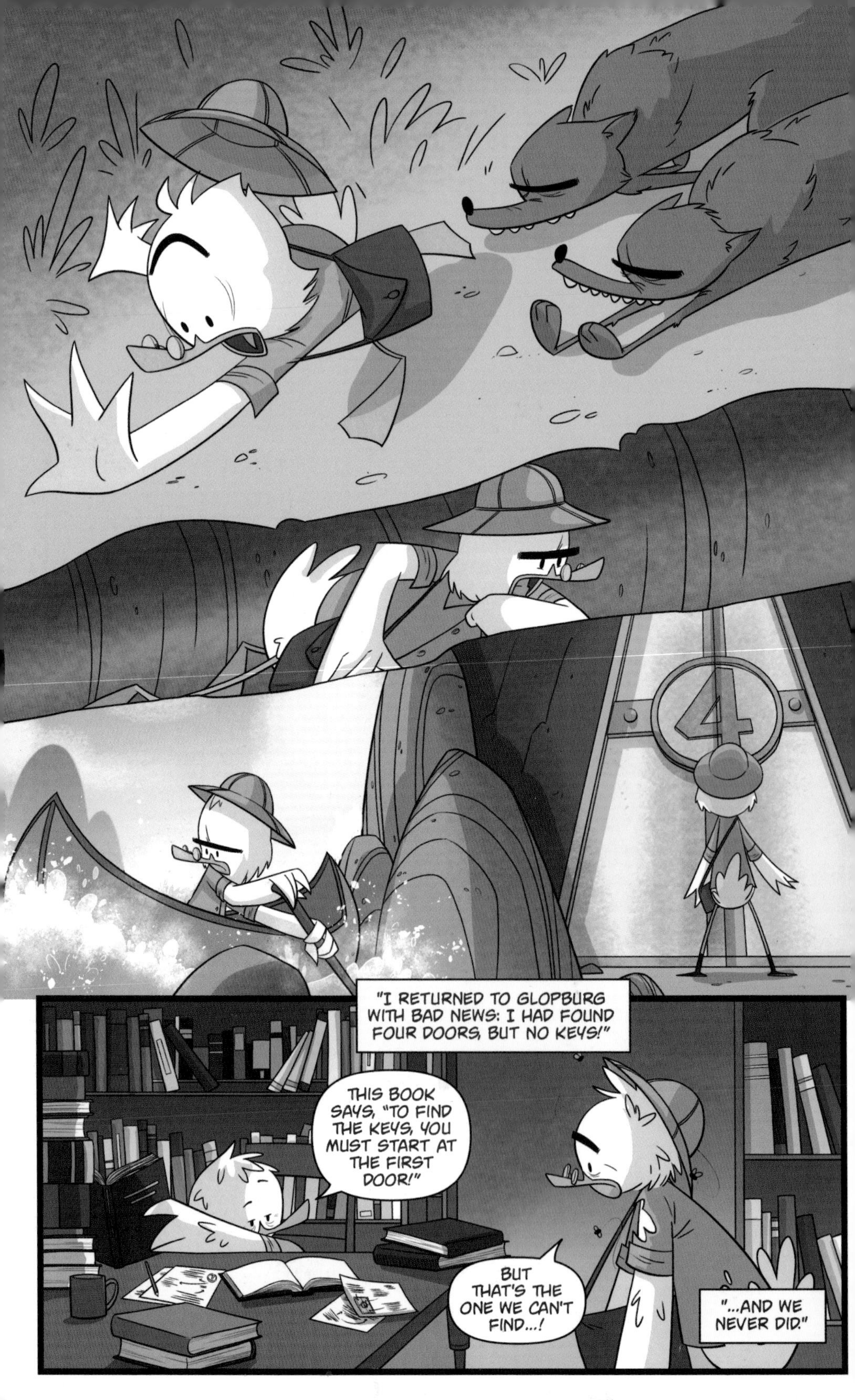
"I RETURNED TO GLOPBURG WITH BAD NEWS: I HAD FOUND FOUR DOORS, BUT NO KEYS!"
THIS BOOK SAYS, "TO FIND THE KEYS, YOU MUST START AT THE FIRST DOOR!"
BUT THAT'S THE ONE WE CAN'T FIND...!
"...AND WE NEVER DID."

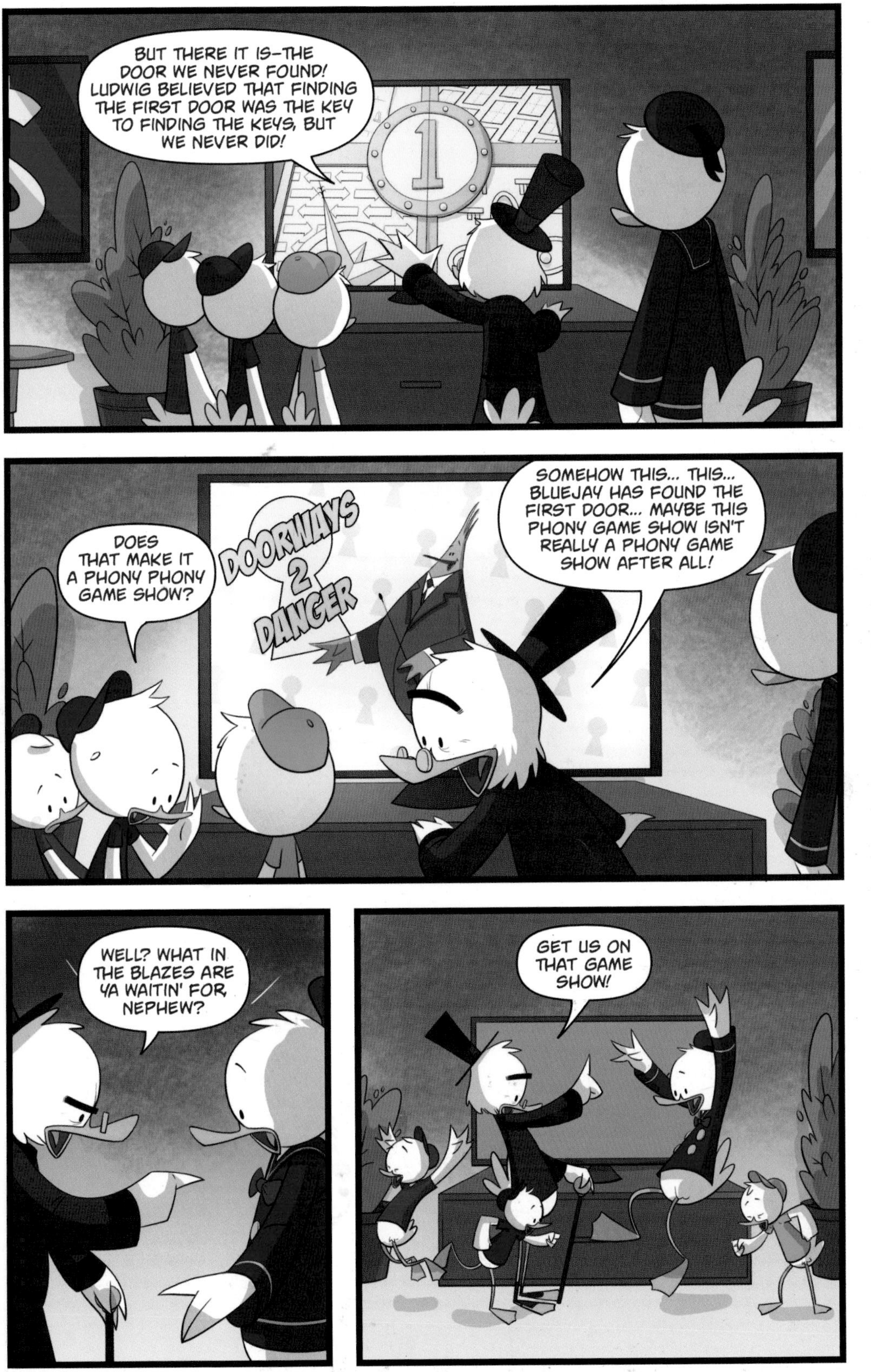
BUT THERE IT IS—THE DOOR WE NEVER FOUND! LUDWIG BELIEVED THAT FINDING THE FIRST DOOR WAS THE KEY TO FINDING THE KEYS, BUT WE NEVER DID!
1
DOORWAYS 2 DANGER
DOES THAT MAKE IT A PHONY PHONY GAME SHOW?
SOMEHOW THIS... THIS... BLUEJAY HAS FOUND THE FIRST DOOR... MAYBE THIS PHONY GAME SHOW ISN'T REALLY A PHONY GAME SHOW AFTER ALL!
WELL? WHAT IN THE BLAZES ARE YA WAITIN' FOR, NEPHEW?
GET US ON THAT GAME SHOW!

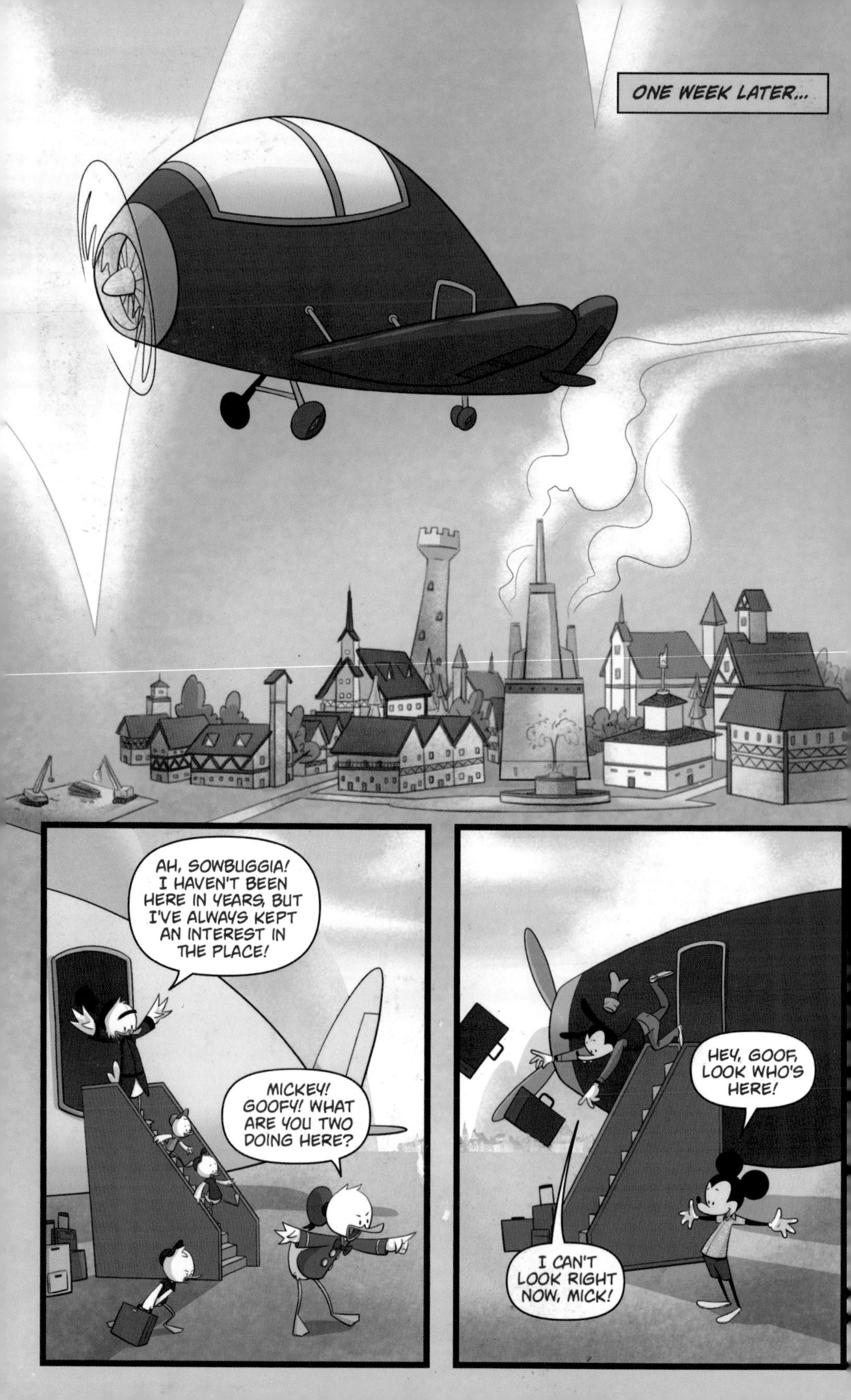
ONE WEEK LATER...
AH, SOWBUGGIA! I HAVEN'T BEEN HERE IN YEARS, BUT I'VE ALWAYS KEPT AN INTEREST IN THE PLACE!
MICKEY! GOOFY! WHAT ARE YOU TWO DOING HERE?
HEY, GOOF, LOOK WHO'S HERE!
I CAN'T LOOK RIGHT NOW, MICK!

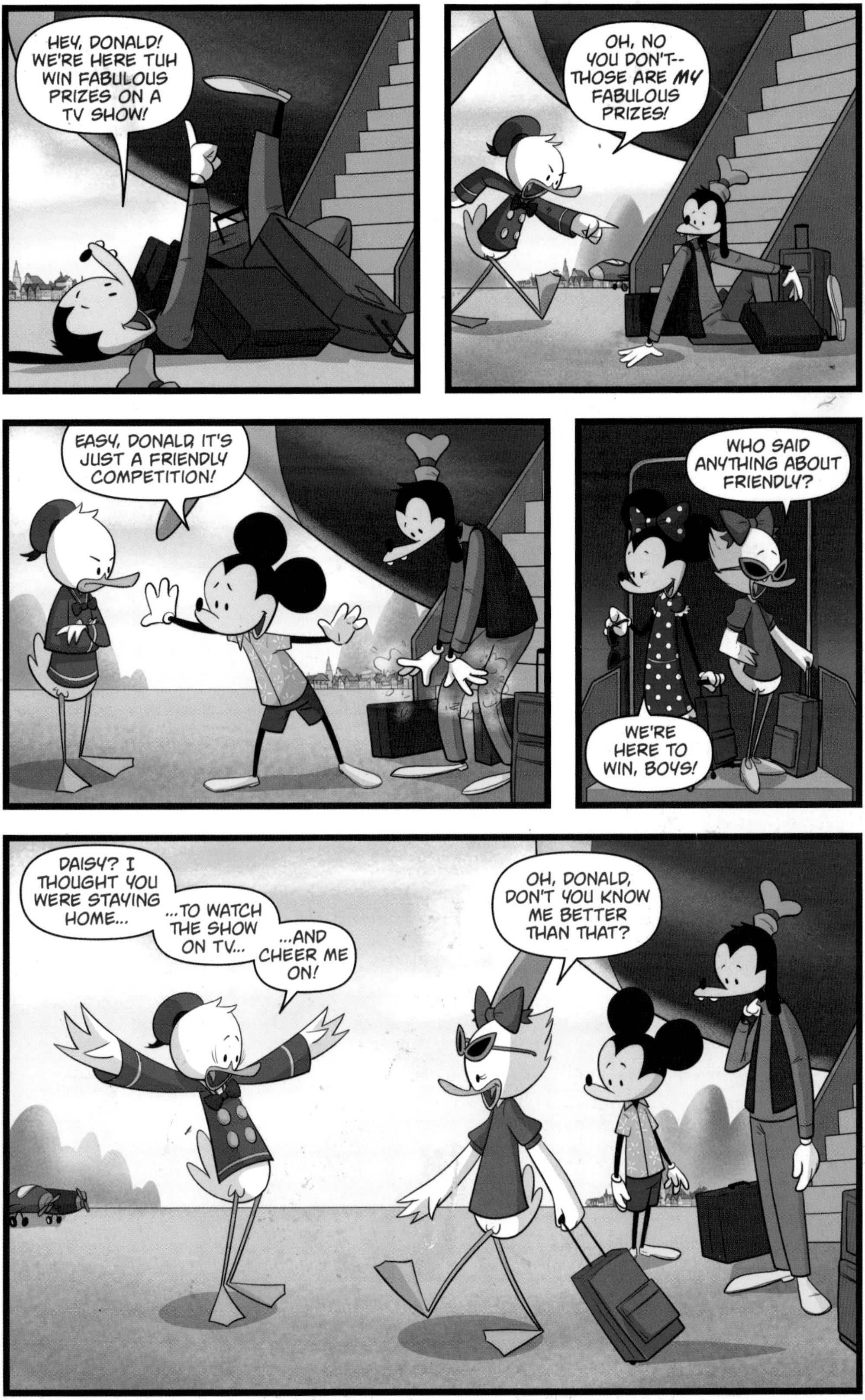
HEY, DONALD! WE'RE HERE TUH WIN FABULOUS PRIZES ON A TV SHOW!
OH, NO YOU DON'T-- THOSE ARE MY FABULOUS PRIZES!
EASY, DONALD IT'S JUST A FRIENDLY COMPETITION!
WHO SAID ANYTHING ABOUT FRIENDLY?
WE'RE HERE TO WIN, BOYS!
DAISY? I THOUGHT YOU WERE STAYING HOME...
...TO WATCH THE SHOW ON TV...
...AND CHEER ME ON!
OH, DONALD, DON'T YOU KNOW ME BETTER THAN THAT?

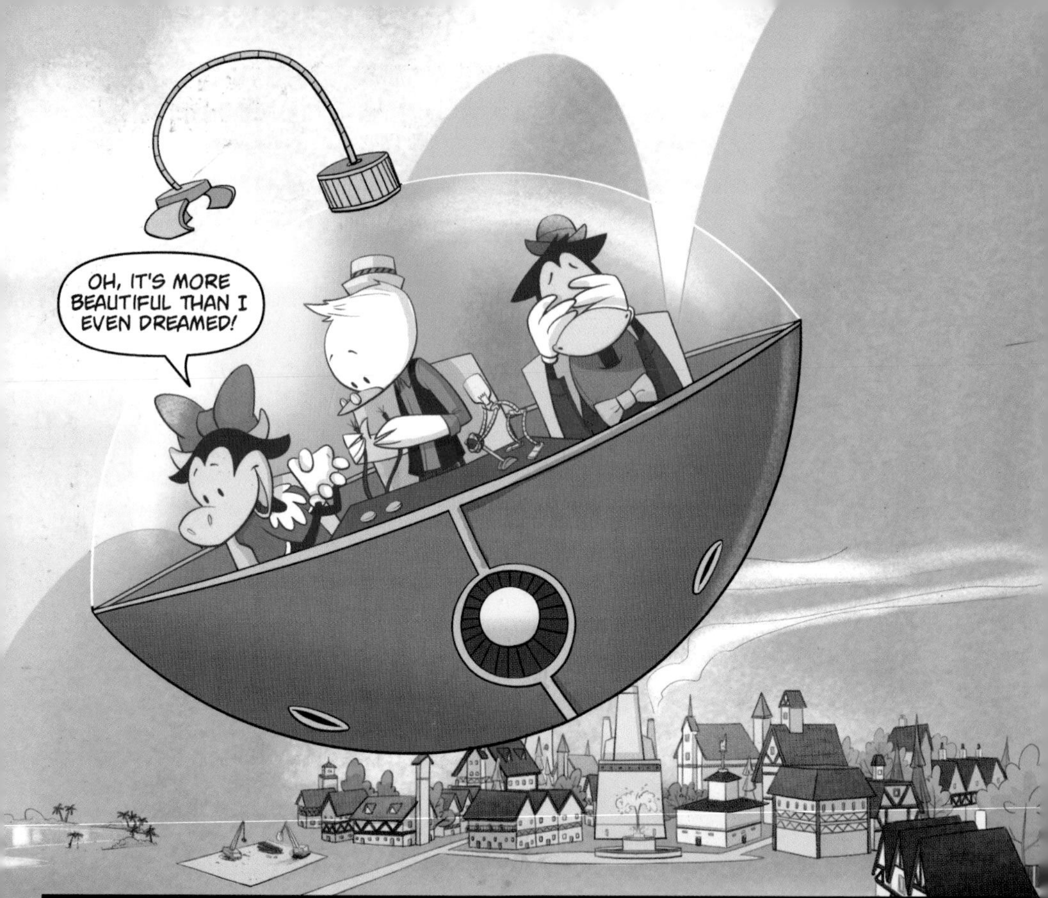
OH, IT'S MORE BEAUTIFUL THAN I EVEN DREAMED!

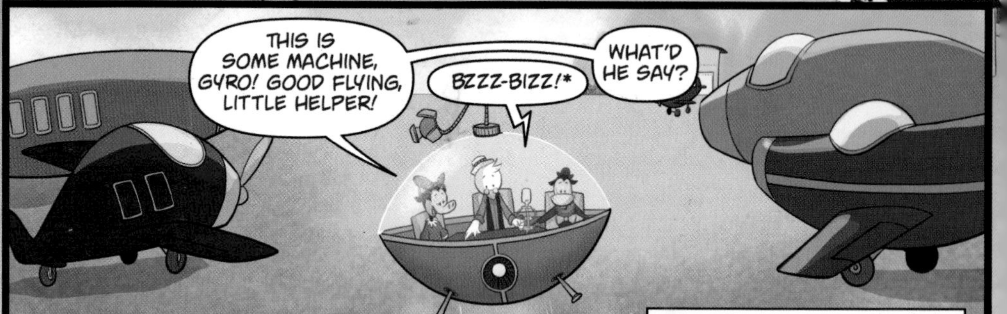
THIS IS SOME MACHINE, GYRO! GOOD FLYING, LITTLE HELPER!
BZZZ-BIZZ!*
WHAT'D HE SAY?
*OH, I WASN'T FLYING... IT FLIES ITSELF!

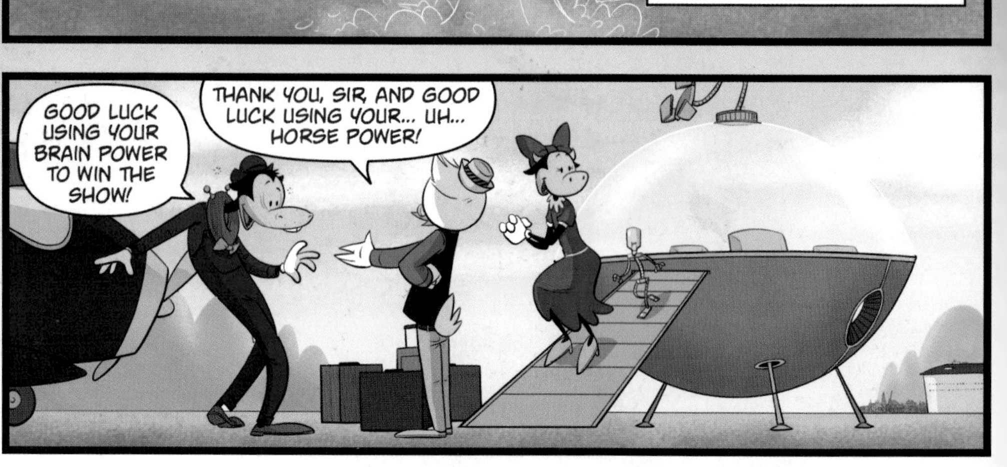
GOOD LUCK USING YOUR BRAIN POWER TO WIN THE SHOW!
THANK YOU, SIR, AND GOOD LUCK USING YOUR... UH... HORSE POWER!

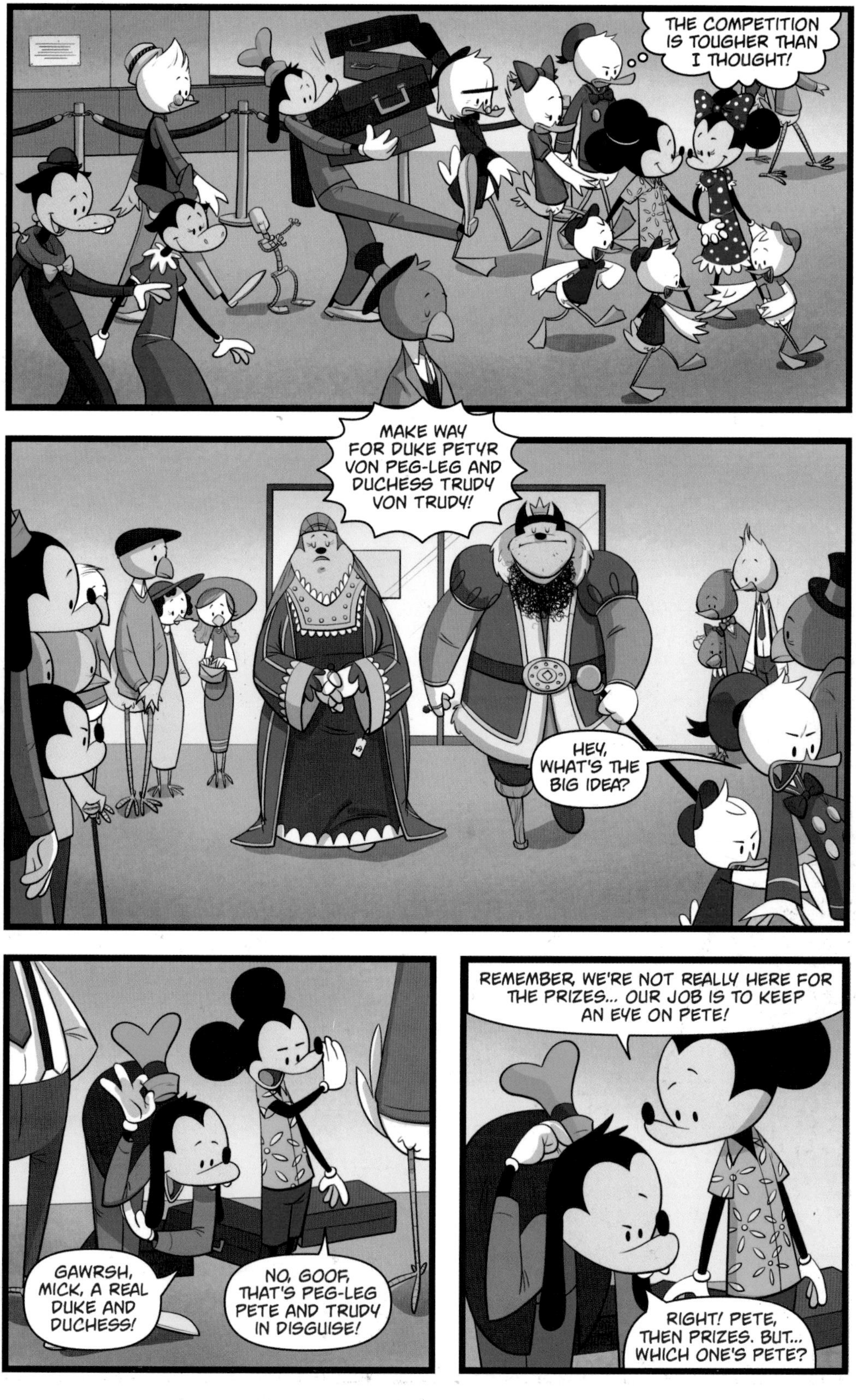
THE COMPETITION IS TOUGHER THAN I THOUGHT!
MAKE WAY FOR DUKE PETYR VON PEG-LEG AND DUCHESS TRUDY VON TRUDY!
HEY, WHAT'S THE BIG IDEA?
GAWRSH, MICK, A REAL DUKE AND DUCHESS!
NO, GOOF, THAT'S PEG-LEG PETE AND TRUDY IN DISGUISE!
REMEMBER, WE'RE NOT REALLY HERE FOR THE PRIZES... OUR JOB IS TO KEEP AN EYE ON PETE!
RIGHT! PETE, THEN PRIZES. BUT... WHICH ONE'S PETE?

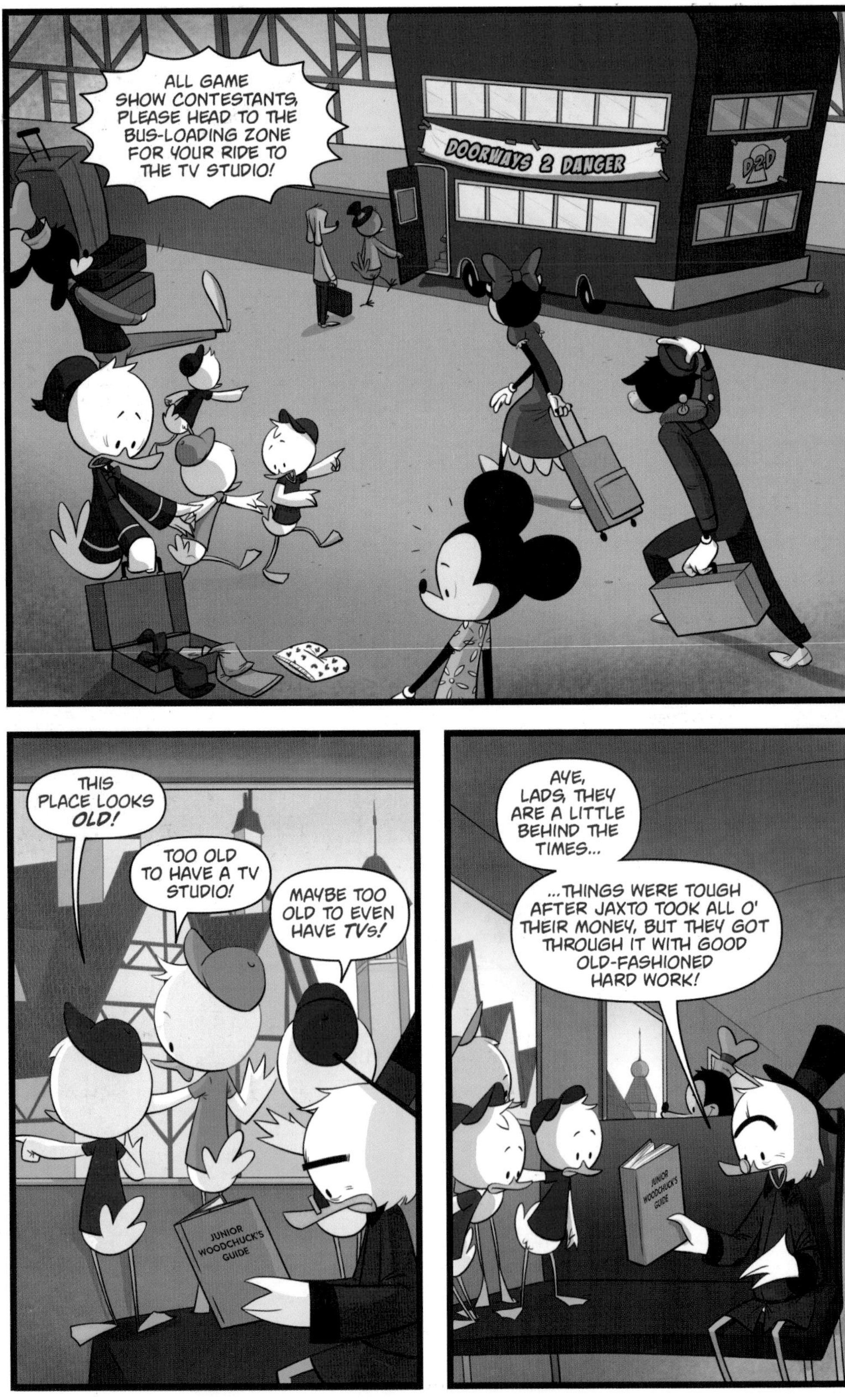
ALL GAME SHOW CONTESTANTS, PLEASE HEAD TO THE BUS-LOADING ZONE FOR YOUR RIDE TO THE TV STUDIO!
DOORWAYS 2 DANGER
D2D
THIS PLACE LOOKS *OLD!*
TOO OLD TO HAVE A TV STUDIO!
MAYBE TOO OLD TO EVEN HAVE *TV*s!
JUNIOR WOODCHUCK'S GUIDE
AYE, LADS, THEY ARE A LITTLE BEHIND THE TIMES...
...THINGS WERE TOUGH AFTER JAXTO TOOK ALL O' THEIR MONEY, BUT THEY GOT THROUGH IT WITH GOOD OLD-FASHIONED HARD WORK!
JUNIOR WOODCHUCK'S GUIDE

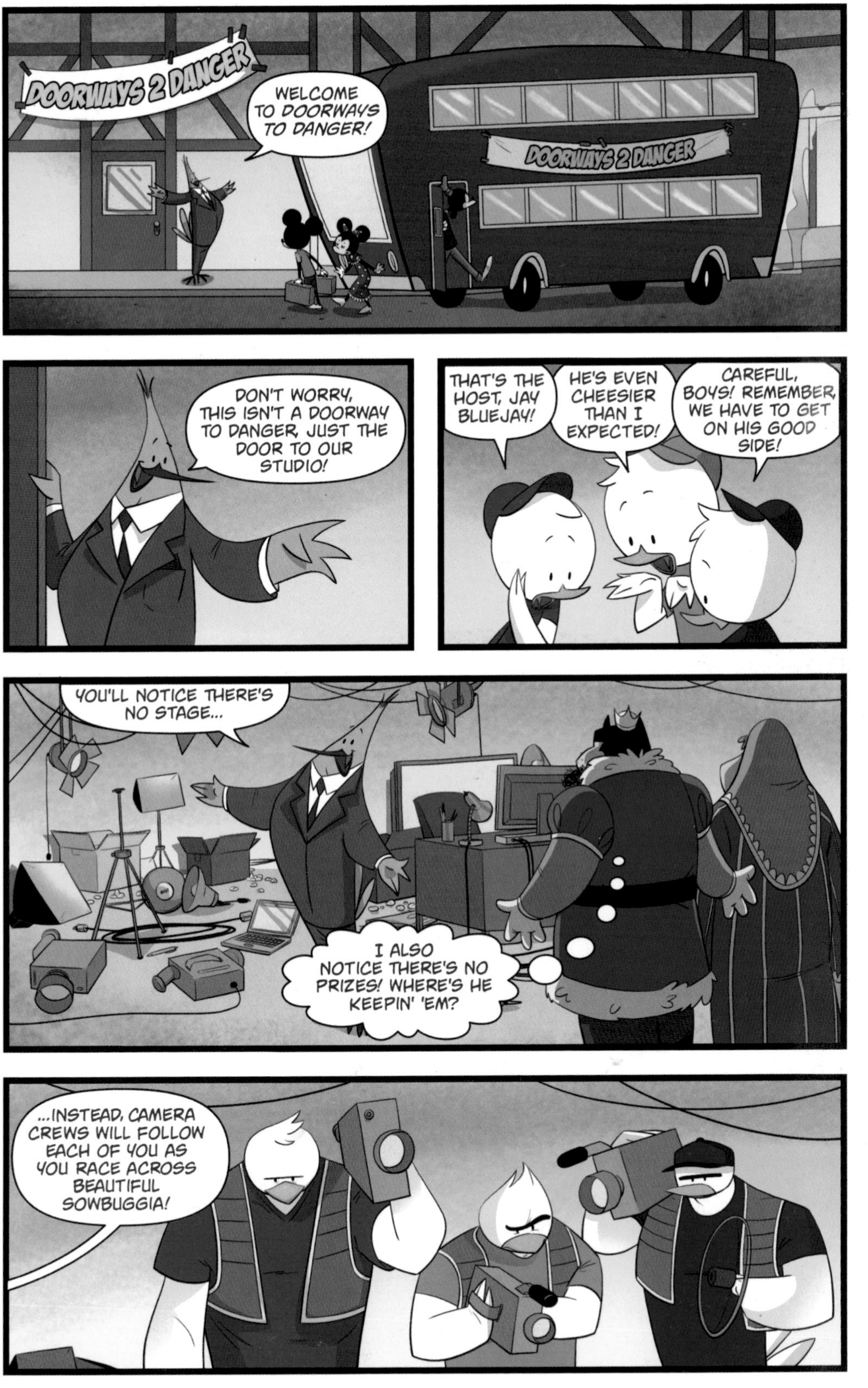
DOORWAYS 2 DANGER
WELCOME TO DOORWAYS TO DANGER!
DOORWAYS 2 DANGER
DON'T WORRY, THIS ISN'T A DOORWAY TO DANGER, JUST THE DOOR TO OUR STUDIO!
THAT'S THE HOST, JAY BLUEJAY!
HE'S EVEN CHEESIER THAN I EXPECTED!
CAREFUL, BOYS! REMEMBER, WE HAVE TO GET ON HIS GOOD SIDE!
YOU'LL NOTICE THERE'S NO STAGE...
I ALSO NOTICE THERE'S NO PRIZES! WHERE'S HE KEEPIN' 'EM?
...INSTEAD, CAMERA CREWS WILL FOLLOW EACH OF YOU AS YOU RACE ACROSS BEAUTIFUL SOWBUGGIA!

EVEN I DON'T KNOW WHERE YOU'LL GO AS YOU SEARCH FOR THE FIVE HIDDEN KEYS TO THE FIVE AMAZING DOORS!
SOWBUGGIA
AFTER I START EACH ROUND, TEAMS WILL SPREAD OUT TO SEARCH FOR THE CLOSEST KEY.
HOW WILL WE KNOW WHERE TO LOOK?
YOU WON'T! THE KEYS COULD BE ANYWHERE, SO YOU HAVE TO LOOK EVERYWHERE!
BUT, EACH KEY SHOULD BE WITHIN ONE MILE OF THE DOOR IT UNLOCKS. SO YOU'LL HAVE TO MOVE FAST!
THE FIRST TEAM TO GRAB THAT KEY AND GIVE IT TO ME WINS A FABULOUS PRIZE!
GLOPBURG
STOLHANDIA
NORASDORF
THE LAST TEAM TO REACH THE KEY'S LOCATION GOES TO A DIFFERENT DOOR, THE EXIT DOOR!
SOWBUGGIA
THEN I'LL USE THE KEY TO UNLOCK THE DOOR, AND THE REMAINING TEAMS WILL HEAD TO THE NEXT ROUND THROUGH THE DOORWAYS TO DANGER!

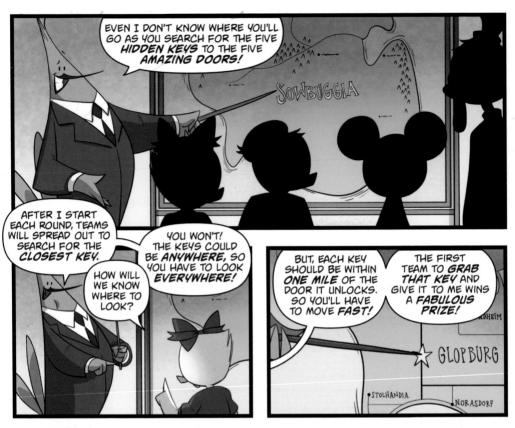

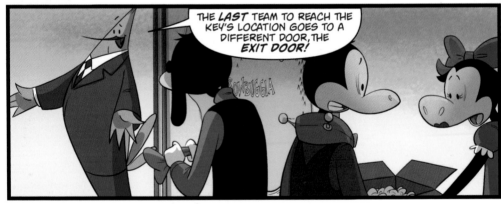

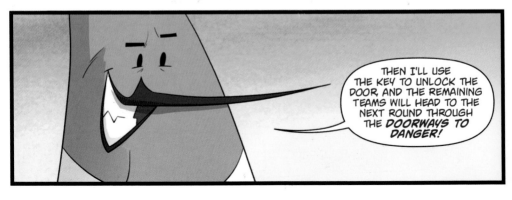

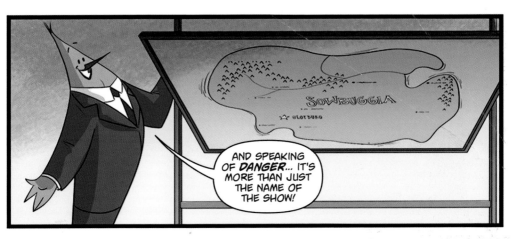

AND SPEAKING OF **DANGER**... IT'S MORE THAN JUST THE NAME OF THE SHOW!

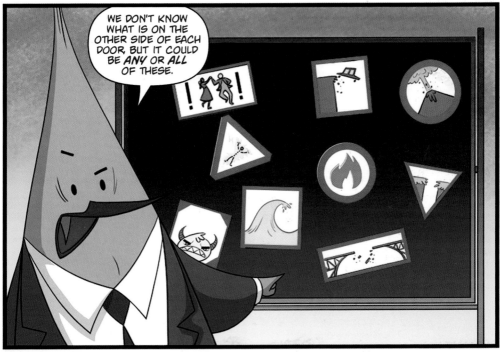

WE DON'T KNOW WHAT IS ON THE OTHER SIDE OF EACH DOOR, BUT IT COULD BE **ANY** OR **ALL** OF THESE.

I CAN'T SWIM!

I'M GOING TO JOIN ONE OF THE ANGRY MOBS!

I'M ALLERGIC TO MONSTERS!

I'M AFRAID OF HEIGHTS!

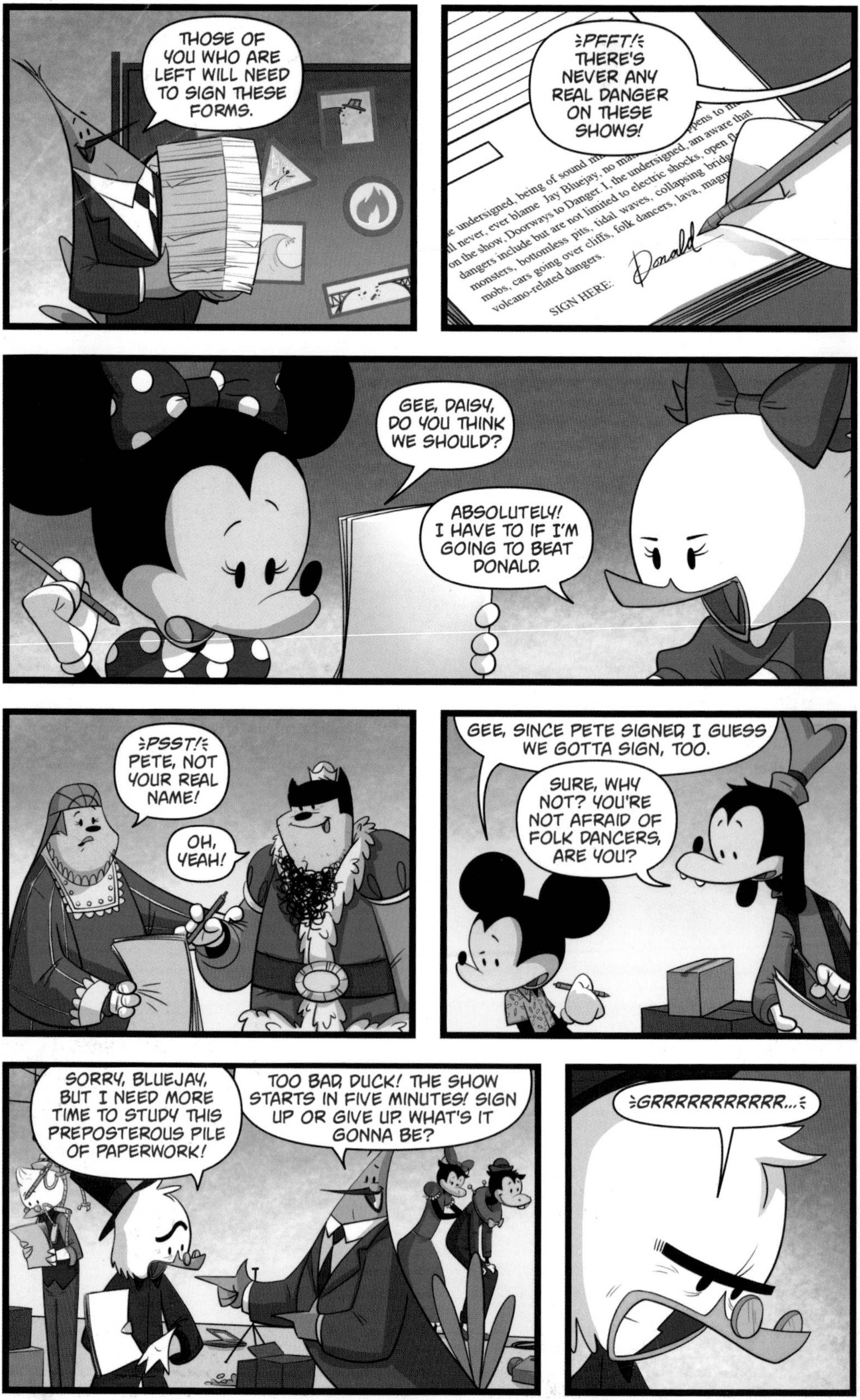

THOSE OF YOU WHO ARE LEFT WILL NEED TO SIGN THESE FORMS.
≥PFFT!≤ THERE'S NEVER ANY REAL DANGER ON THESE SHOWS!
e undersigned, being of sound m
ll never, ever blame Jay Bluejay, no ma
on the show, Doorways to Danger I, the undersigned, am aware that
dangers include but are not limited to electric shocks, open fl
monsters, bottomless pits, tidal waves, collapsing brid
mobs, cars going over cliffs, folk dancers, lava, magm
volcano-related dangers.
SIGN HERE:
Donald
GEE, DAISY, DO YOU THINK WE SHOULD?
ABSOLUTELY! I HAVE TO IF I'M GOING TO BEAT DONALD.
≥PSST!≤ PETE, NOT YOUR REAL NAME!
OH, YEAH!
GEE, SINCE PETE SIGNED I GUESS WE GOTTA SIGN, TOO.
SURE, WHY NOT? YOU'RE NOT AFRAID OF FOLK DANCERS, ARE YOU?
SORRY, BLUEJAY, BUT I NEED MORE TIME TO STUDY THIS PREPOSTEROUS PILE OF PAPERWORK!
TOO BAD, DUCK! THE SHOW STARTS IN FIVE MINUTES! SIGN UP OR GIVE UP. WHAT'S IT GONNA BE?
≥GRRRRRRRRRR...≤

YOU BOYS STAY OUT OF TROUBLE. ONCE THE SHOW STARTS, I WON'T HAVE TIME TO WATCH YOU!

DON'T WORRY ABOUT US!

WE'RE WORRIED ABOUT YOU!

SEE, WE DON'T TRUST THAT J—

OKAY, KIDDIES, YOU NEED TO GO SIT IN THE STUDIO AUDIENCE!

NO WAY! WE WANNA BE ON THE SHOW, TOO!

SORRY, NO KIDS ALLOWED! IT'S A RULE.

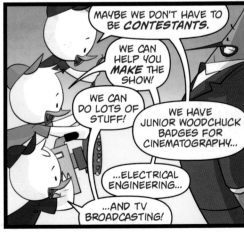

MAYBE WE DON'T HAVE TO BE CONTESTANTS.

WE CAN HELP YOU MAKE THE SHOW!

WE CAN DO LOTS OF STUFF!

WE HAVE JUNIOR WOODCHUCK BADGES FOR CINEMATOGRAPHY...

...ELECTRICAL ENGINEERING...

...AND TV BROADCASTING!

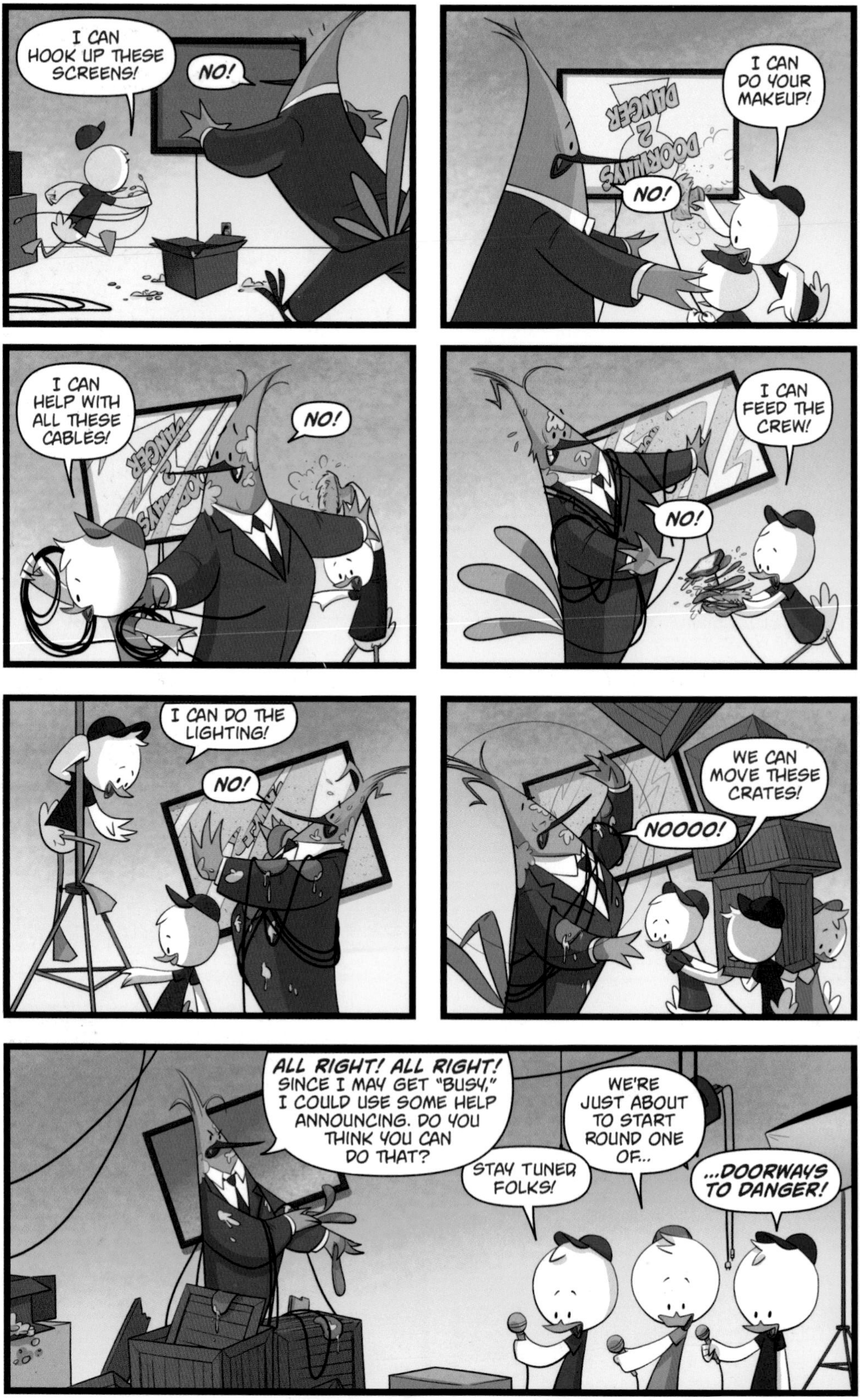
I CAN HOOK UP THESE SCREENS!
NO!
I CAN DO YOUR MAKEUP!
NO!
I CAN HELP WITH ALL THESE CABLES!
NO!
I CAN FEED THE CREW!
NO!
I CAN DO THE LIGHTING!
NO!
WE CAN MOVE THESE CRATES!
NOOOO!
ALL RIGHT! ALL RIGHT! SINCE I MAY GET "BUSY," I COULD USE SOME HELP ANNOUNCING. DO YOU THINK YOU CAN DO THAT?
STAY TUNED FOLKS!
WE'RE JUST ABOUT TO START ROUND ONE OF...
...DOORWAYS TO DANGER!

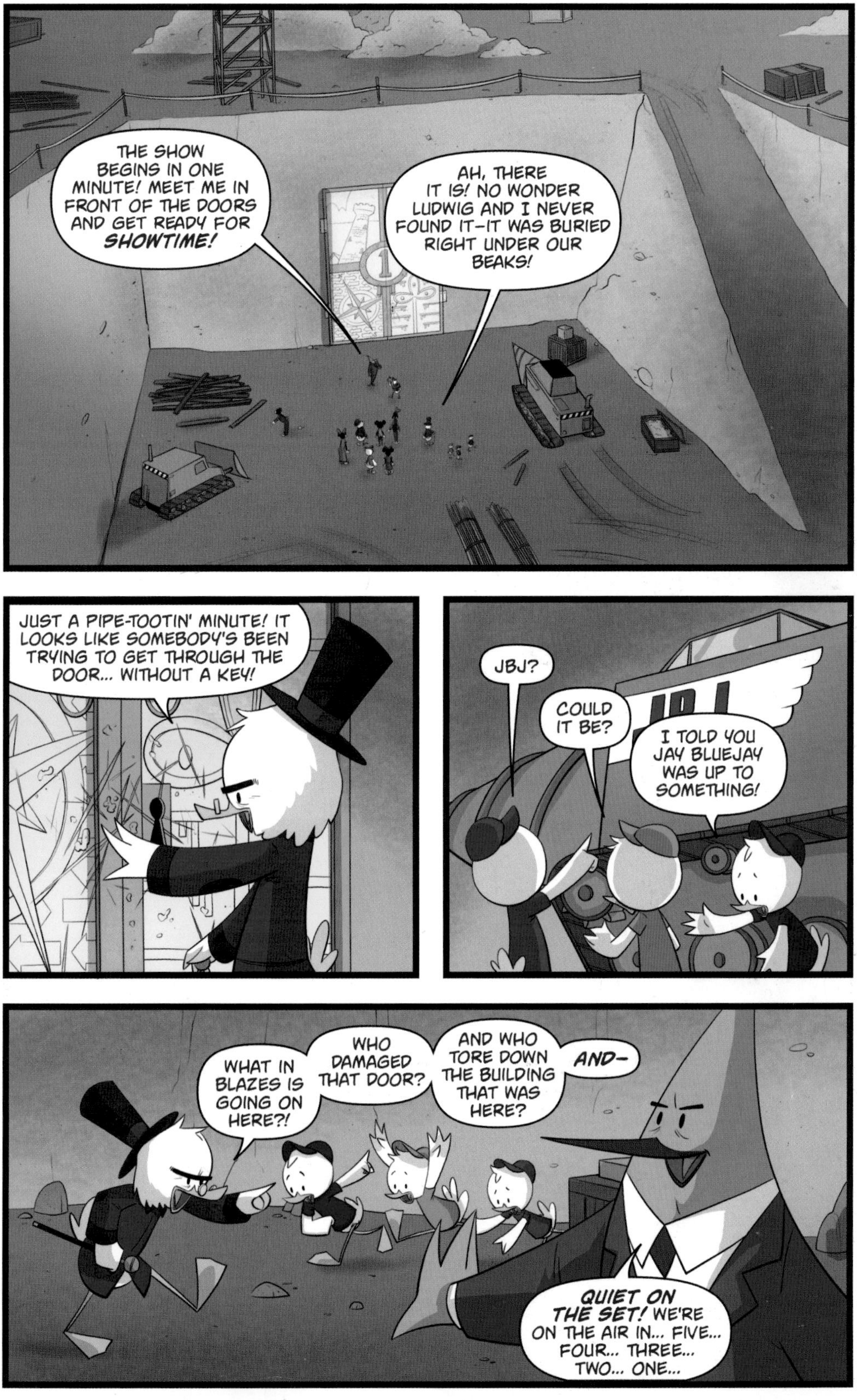
THE SHOW BEGINS IN ONE MINUTE! MEET ME IN FRONT OF THE DOORS AND GET READY FOR **SHOWTIME!**
AH, THERE IT IS! NO WONDER LUDWIG AND I NEVER FOUND IT—IT WAS BURIED RIGHT UNDER OUR BEAKS!
JUST A PIPE-TOOTIN' MINUTE! IT LOOKS LIKE SOMEBODY'S BEEN TRYING TO GET THROUGH THE DOOR... WITHOUT A KEY!
JBJ?
COULD IT BE?
I TOLD YOU JAY BLUEJAY WAS UP TO SOMETHING!
WHAT IN BLAZES IS GOING ON HERE?!
WHO DAMAGED THAT DOOR?
AND WHO TORE DOWN THE BUILDING THAT WAS HERE?
AND—
QUIET ON THE SET! WE'RE ON THE AIR IN... FIVE... FOUR... THREE... TWO... ONE...

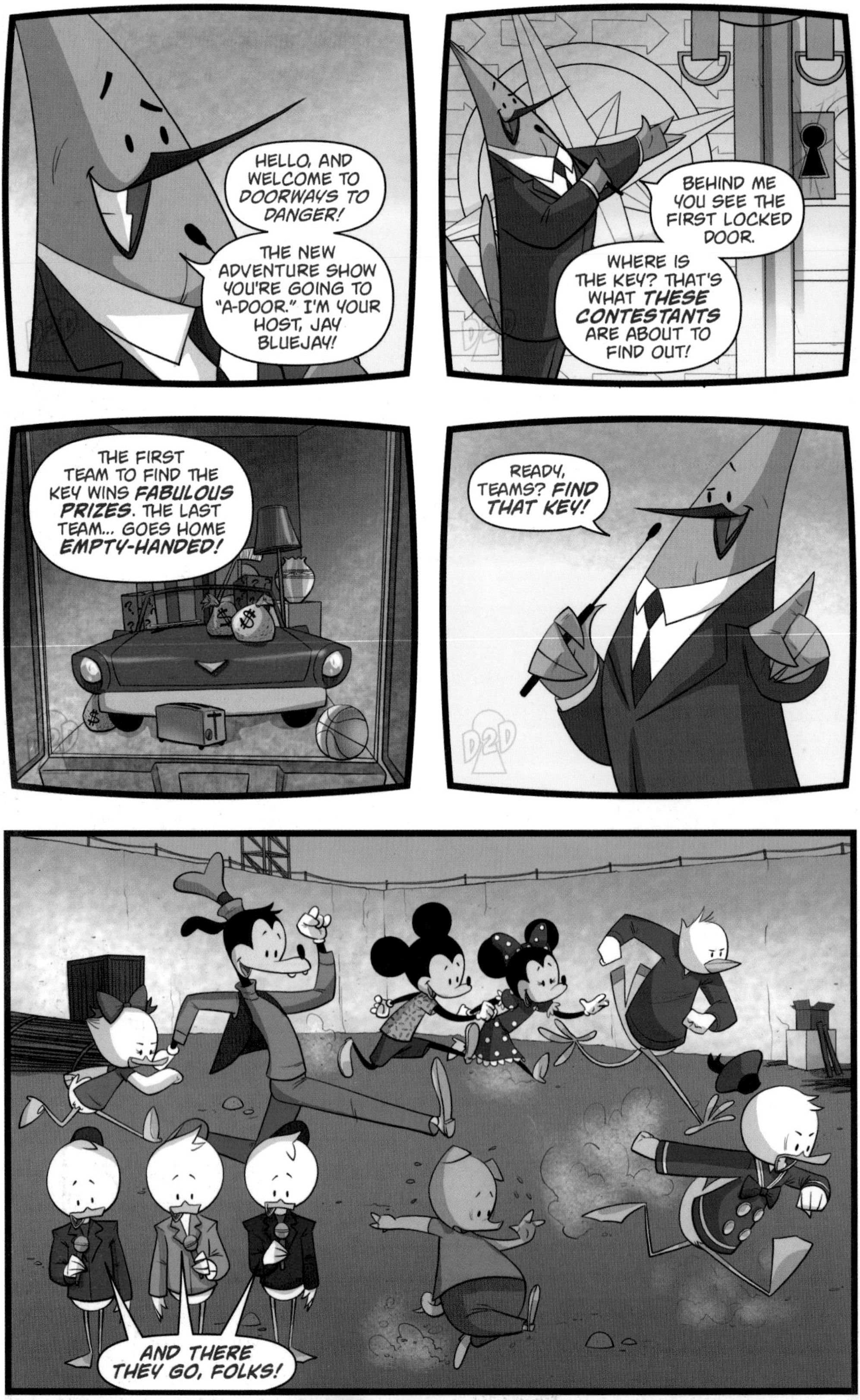

HELLO, AND WELCOME TO DOORWAYS TO DANGER!
THE NEW ADVENTURE SHOW YOU'RE GOING TO "A-DOOR." I'M YOUR HOST, JAY BLUEJAY!
D2D
BEHIND ME YOU SEE THE FIRST LOCKED DOOR.
WHERE IS THE KEY? THAT'S WHAT THESE CONTESTANTS ARE ABOUT TO FIND OUT!
D2D
THE FIRST TEAM TO FIND THE KEY WINS FABULOUS PRIZES. THE LAST TEAM... GOES HOME EMPTY-HANDED!
D2D
READY, TEAMS? FIND THAT KEY!
D2D
AND THERE THEY GO, FOLKS!

OKAY, NOW TO FIND THAT KEY!

EASY THERE, GOOF, WE CAN'T GET TOO FAR AHEAD OF... YOU KNOW WHO.

WHO?

NOW TO LOSE THIS CROWD AND DOUBLE BACK FOR THOSE PRIZES!

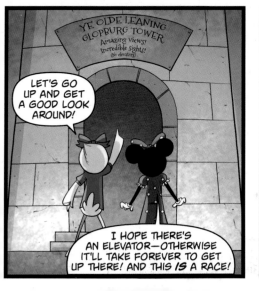

YE OLDE LEANING GLOPBURG TOWER
Amazing views!
Incredible sights!
(No elevator)

LET'S GO UP AND GET A GOOD LOOK AROUND!

I HOPE THERE'S AN ELEVATOR—OTHERWISE IT'LL TAKE FOREVER TO GET UP THERE! AND THIS *IS* A RACE!

NO NEED FOR *US* TO RUN. AS SOON AS I PRESS THIS BUTTON, THE *FIND-O-MATIC 3000* WILL FIND THE KEY FOR US.

?!

OF COURSE I PROGRAMMED IT CORRECTLY! DON'T YOU THINK I CAN SPELL K-E-Y?

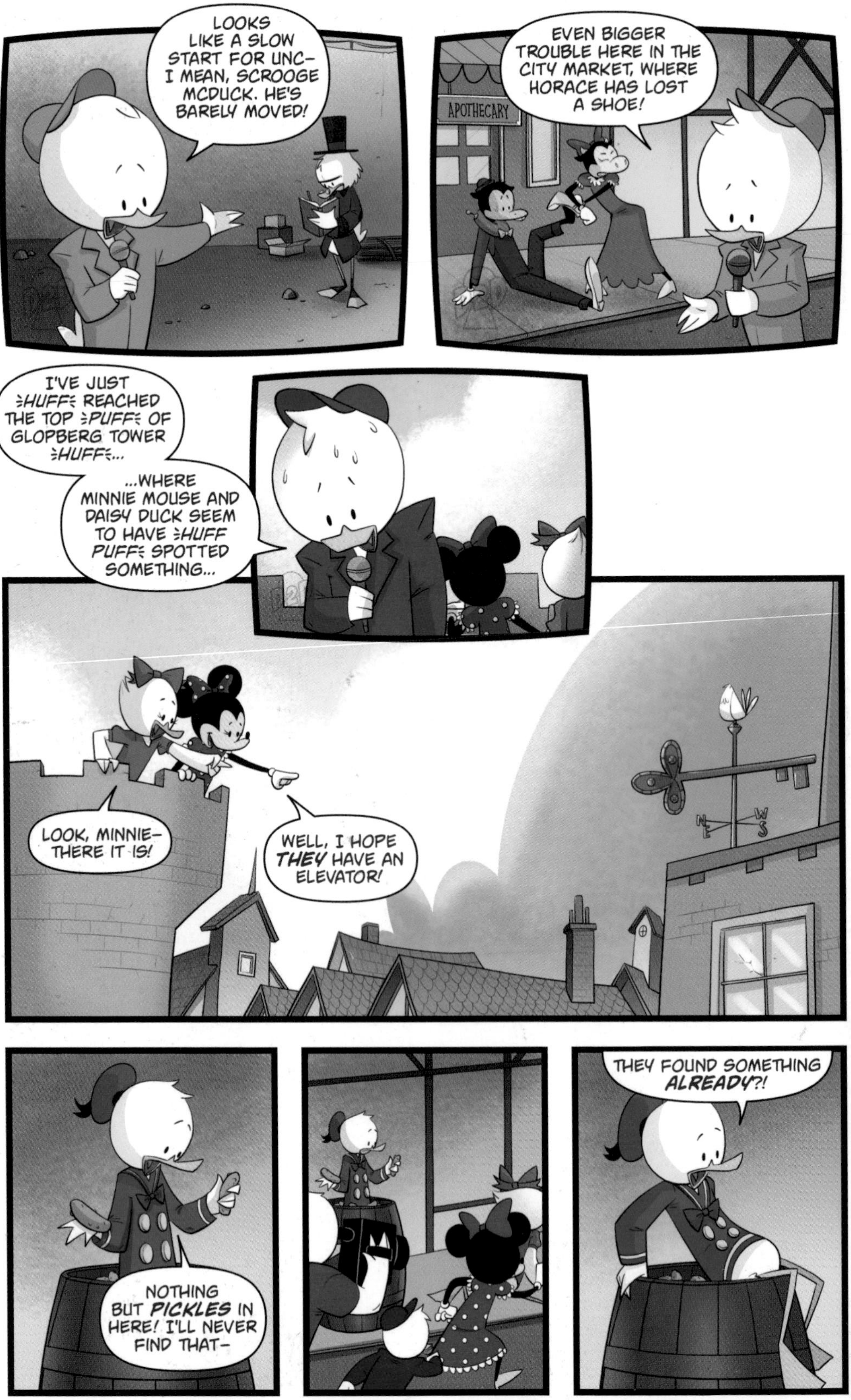
LOOKS LIKE A SLOW START FOR UNC— I MEAN, SCROOGE MCDUCK. HE'S BARELY MOVED!
APOTHECARY
EVEN BIGGER TROUBLE HERE IN THE CITY MARKET, WHERE HORACE HAS LOST A SHOE!
I'VE JUST HUFF REACHED THE TOP PUFF OF GLOPBERG TOWER HUFF...
...WHERE MINNIE MOUSE AND DAISY DUCK SEEM TO HAVE HUFF PUFF SPOTTED SOMETHING...
LOOK, MINNIE— THERE IT IS!
WELL, I HOPE *THEY* HAVE AN ELEVATOR!
NOTHING BUT *PICKLES* IN HERE! I'LL NEVER FIND THAT—
THEY FOUND SOMETHING *ALREADY*?!

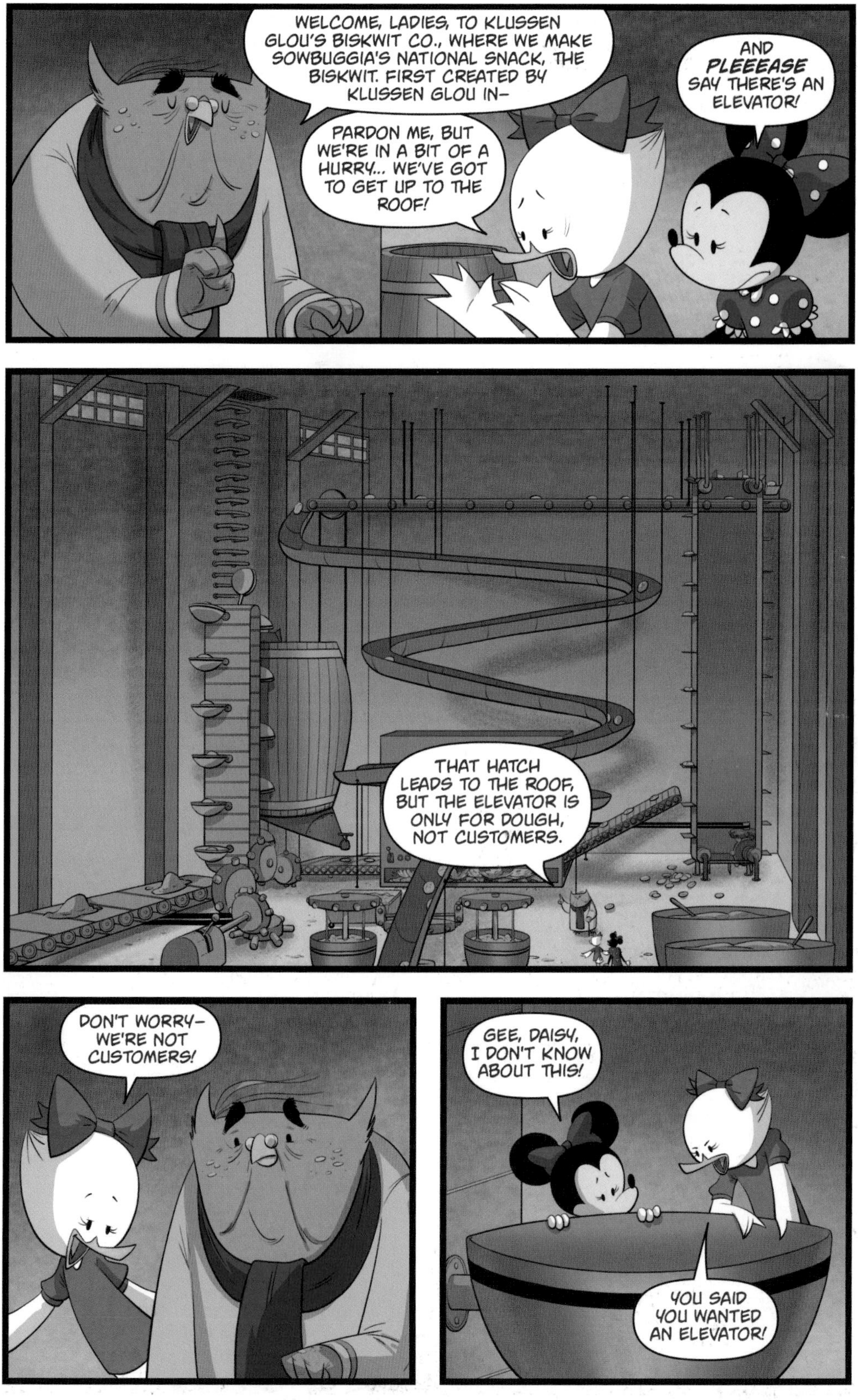
WELCOME, LADIES, TO KLUSSEN GLOU'S BISKWIT CO., WHERE WE MAKE SOWBUGGIA'S NATIONAL SNACK, THE BISKWIT. FIRST CREATED BY KLUSSEN GLOU IN–
PARDON ME, BUT WE'RE IN A BIT OF A HURRY... WE'VE GOT TO GET UP TO THE ROOF!
AND PLEEEASE SAY THERE'S AN ELEVATOR!
THAT HATCH LEADS TO THE ROOF, BUT THE ELEVATOR IS ONLY FOR DOUGH, NOT CUSTOMERS.
DON'T WORRY– WE'RE NOT CUSTOMERS!
GEE, DAISY, I DON'T KNOW ABOUT THIS!
YOU SAID YOU WANTED AN ELEVATOR!

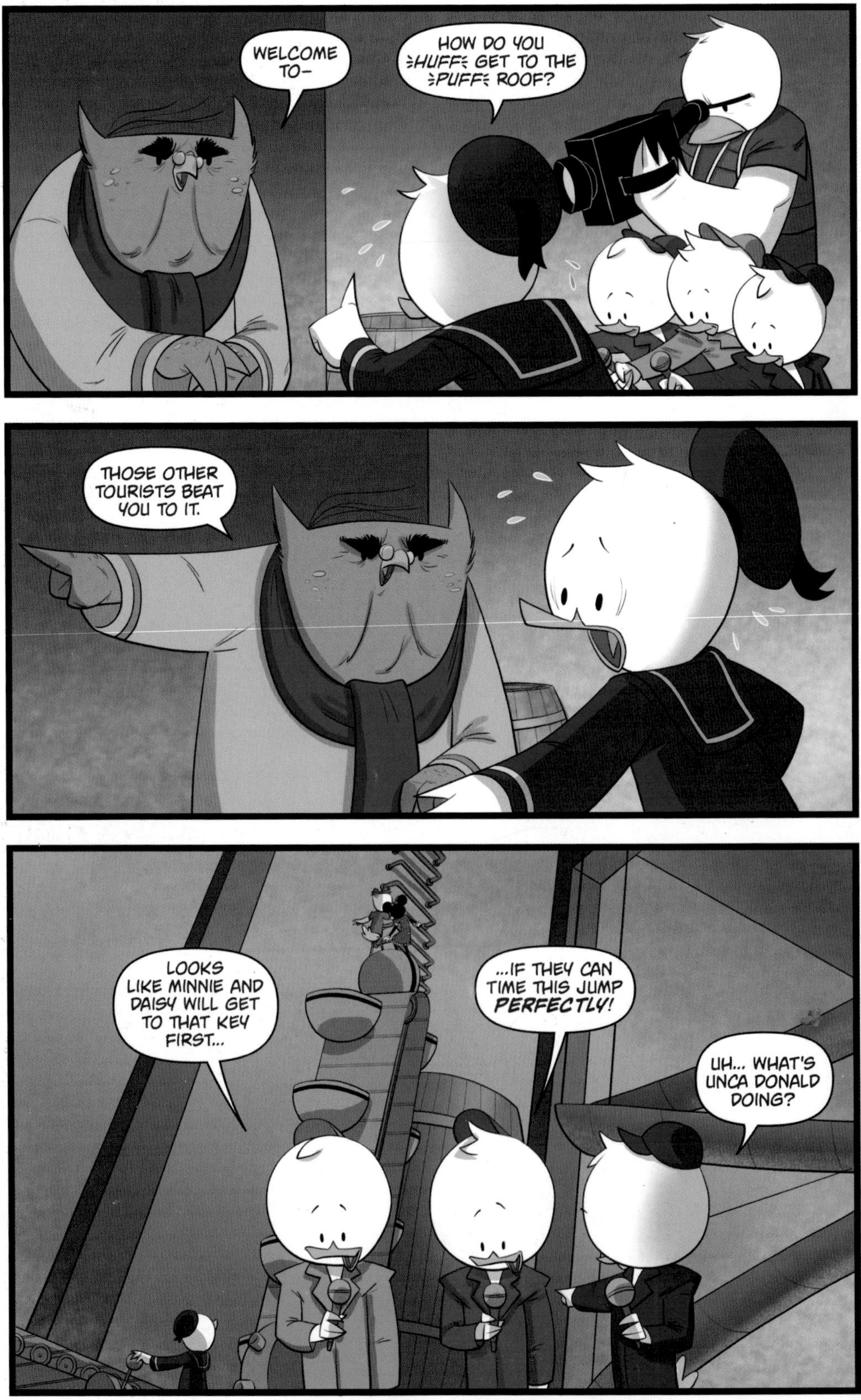
WELCOME TO-
HOW DO YOU *HUFF* GET TO THE *PUFF* ROOF?
THOSE OTHER TOURISTS BEAT YOU TO IT.
LOOKS LIKE MINNIE AND DAISY WILL GET TO THAT KEY FIRST...
...IF THEY CAN TIME THIS JUMP *PERFECTLY*!
UH... WHAT'S UNCA DONALD DOING?

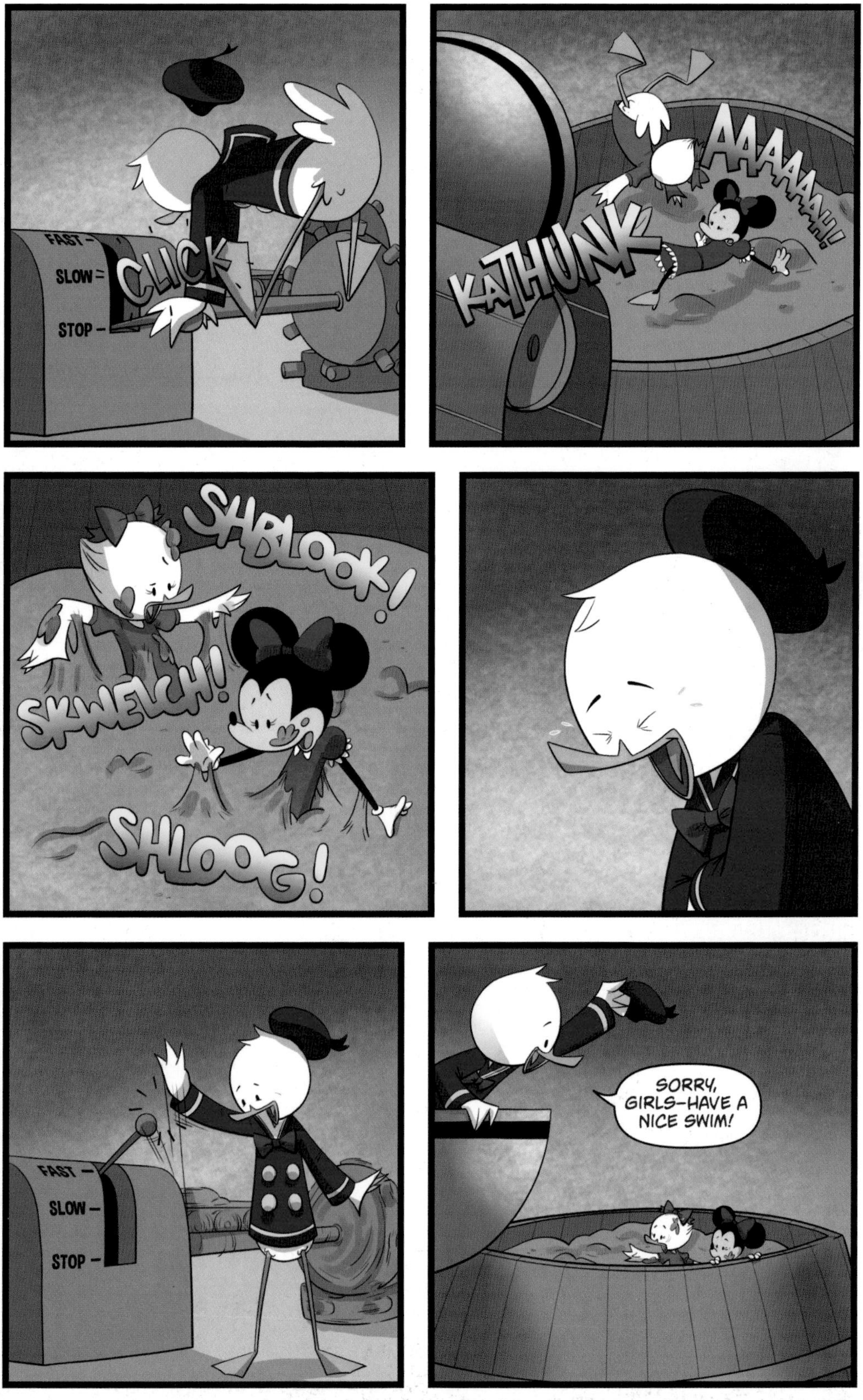
FAST
SLOW
STOP
CLICK
AAAAAAH!!
KATHUNK
SHBLOOK!
SKWELCH!
SHLOOG!
FAST
SLOW
STOP
SORRY, GIRLS—HAVE A NICE SWIM!

I GOT IT!

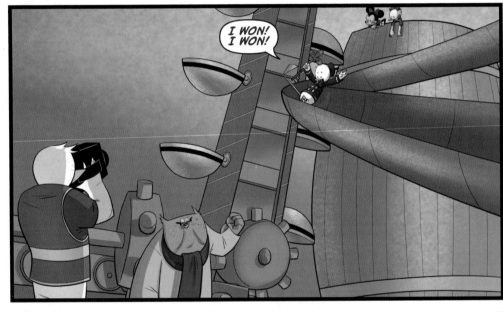

I WON! I WON!

I... UH... WON?

SORRY, UNCA DONALD.

YOUR PARTNER ISN'T HERE!

THE WINNERS ARE THE FIRST *TEAM* TO TOUCH THE KEY.

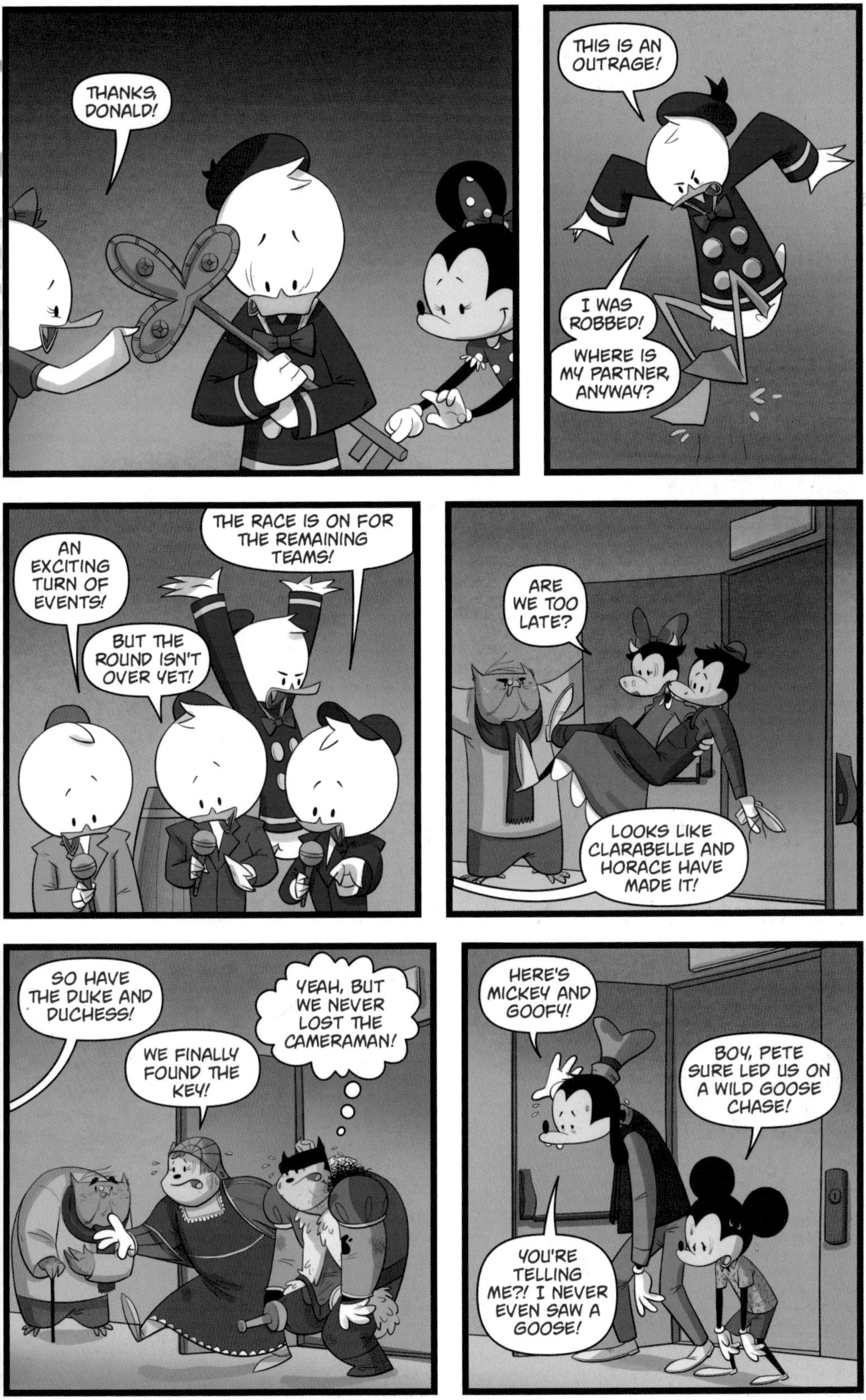
THANKS, DONALD!
THIS IS AN OUTRAGE!
I WAS ROBBED!
WHERE IS MY PARTNER, ANYWAY?
AN EXCITING TURN OF EVENTS!
THE RACE IS ON FOR THE REMAINING TEAMS!
BUT THE ROUND ISN'T OVER YET!
ARE WE TOO LATE?
LOOKS LIKE CLARABELLE AND HORACE HAVE MADE IT!
SO HAVE THE DUKE AND DUCHESS!
WE FINALLY FOUND THE KEY!
YEAH, BUT WE NEVER LOST THE CAMERAMAN!
HERE'S MICKEY AND GOOFY!
BOY, PETE SURE LED US ON A WILD GOOSE CHASE!
YOU'RE TELLING ME?! I NEVER EVEN SAW A GOOSE!

THAT JUST LEAVES TWO TEAMS.

WE'RE WAITING FOR DONALD'S PARTNER SCROOGE MCDUCK...

...AND GYRO AND LITTLE HELPER.

WHO WILL BE THE LAST TO MAKE IT?

AND WHO WILL GET KICKED OFF THE SHOW?

LOOK— HERE THEY COME NOW!

WHERE HAVE YOU BEEN?!

OH, JUST TAKING NOTES ON GLOPBURG'S GLORIOUS ARCHITECTURE...

THOSE CRUMMY OLD BUILDINGS?! WHAT ABOUT THE SHOW?! WHAT ABOUT THE FABULOUS GAME SHOW PRIZES?!

DON'T LET THE LITTLE PRIZES DISTRACT YOU FROM THE BIG ONE!

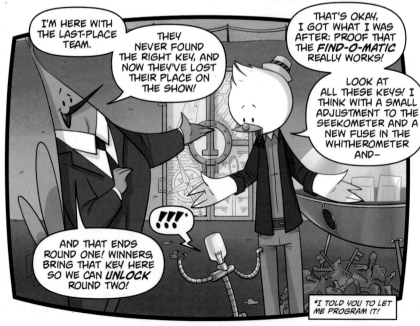

I'M HERE WITH THE LAST-PLACE TEAM.

THEY NEVER FOUND THE RIGHT KEY, AND NOW THEY'VE LOST THEIR PLACE ON THE SHOW!

THAT'S OKAY, I GOT WHAT I WAS AFTER: PROOF THAT THE *FIND-O-MATIC* REALLY WORKS!

LOOK AT ALL THESE KEYS! I THINK WITH A SMALL ADJUSTMENT TO THE SEEKOMETER AND A NEW FUSE IN THE WHITHEROMETER AND—

AND THAT ENDS ROUND ONE! WINNERS, BRING THAT KEY HERE SO WE CAN *UNLOCK* ROUND TWO!

!!!*

*I TOLD YOU TO LET ME PROGRAM IT!

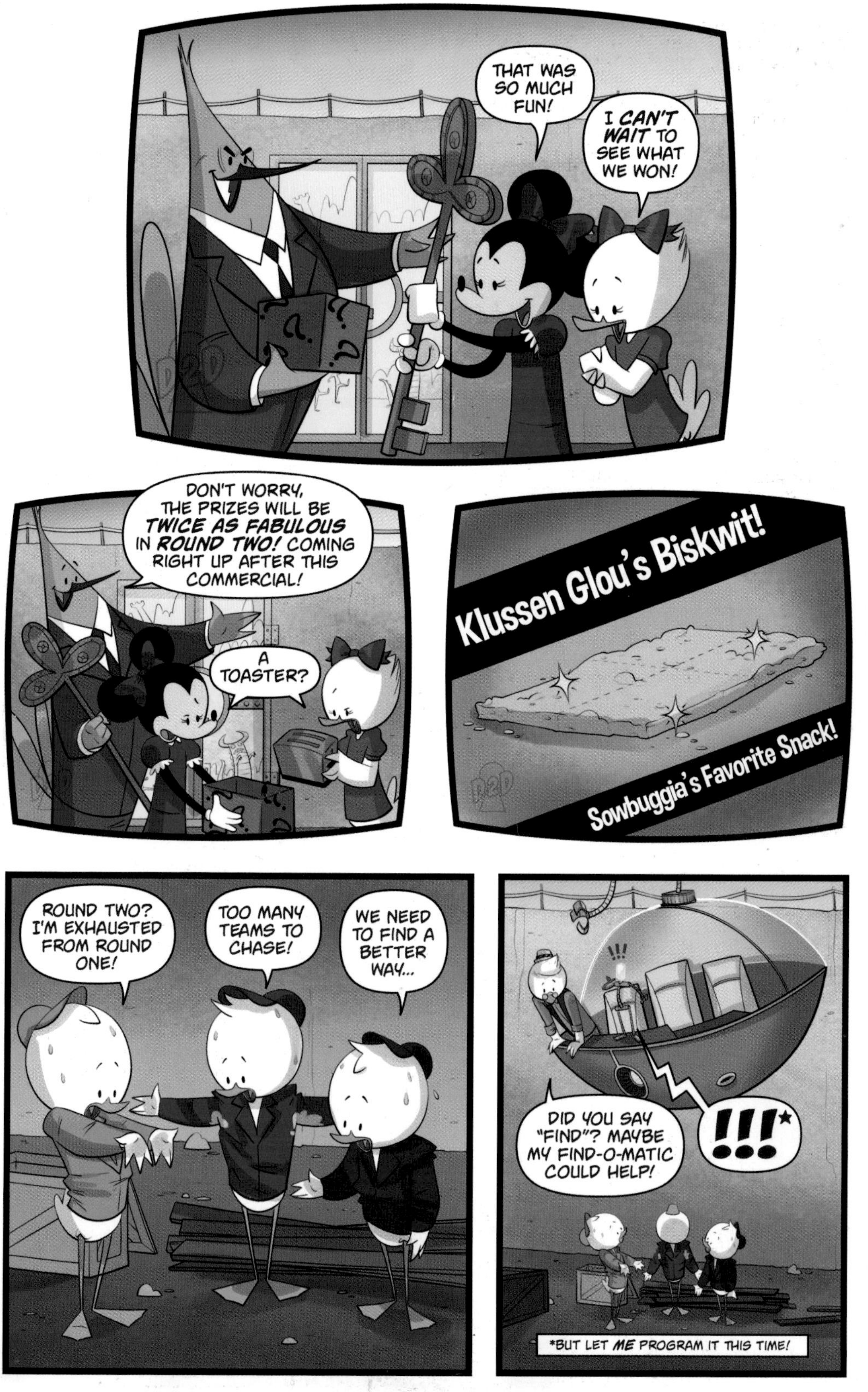
THAT WAS SO MUCH FUN!
I CAN'T WAIT TO SEE WHAT WE WON!
DON'T WORRY, THE PRIZES WILL BE TWICE AS FABULOUS IN ROUND TWO! COMING RIGHT UP AFTER THIS COMMERCIAL!
A TOASTER?
Klussen Glou's Biskwit!
Sowbuggia's Favorite Snack!
ROUND TWO? I'M EXHAUSTED FROM ROUND ONE!
TOO MANY TEAMS TO CHASE!
WE NEED TO FIND A BETTER WAY...
!!!
DID YOU SAY "FIND"? MAYBE MY FIND-O-MATIC COULD HELP!
!!!*
*BUT LET ME PROGRAM IT THIS TIME!

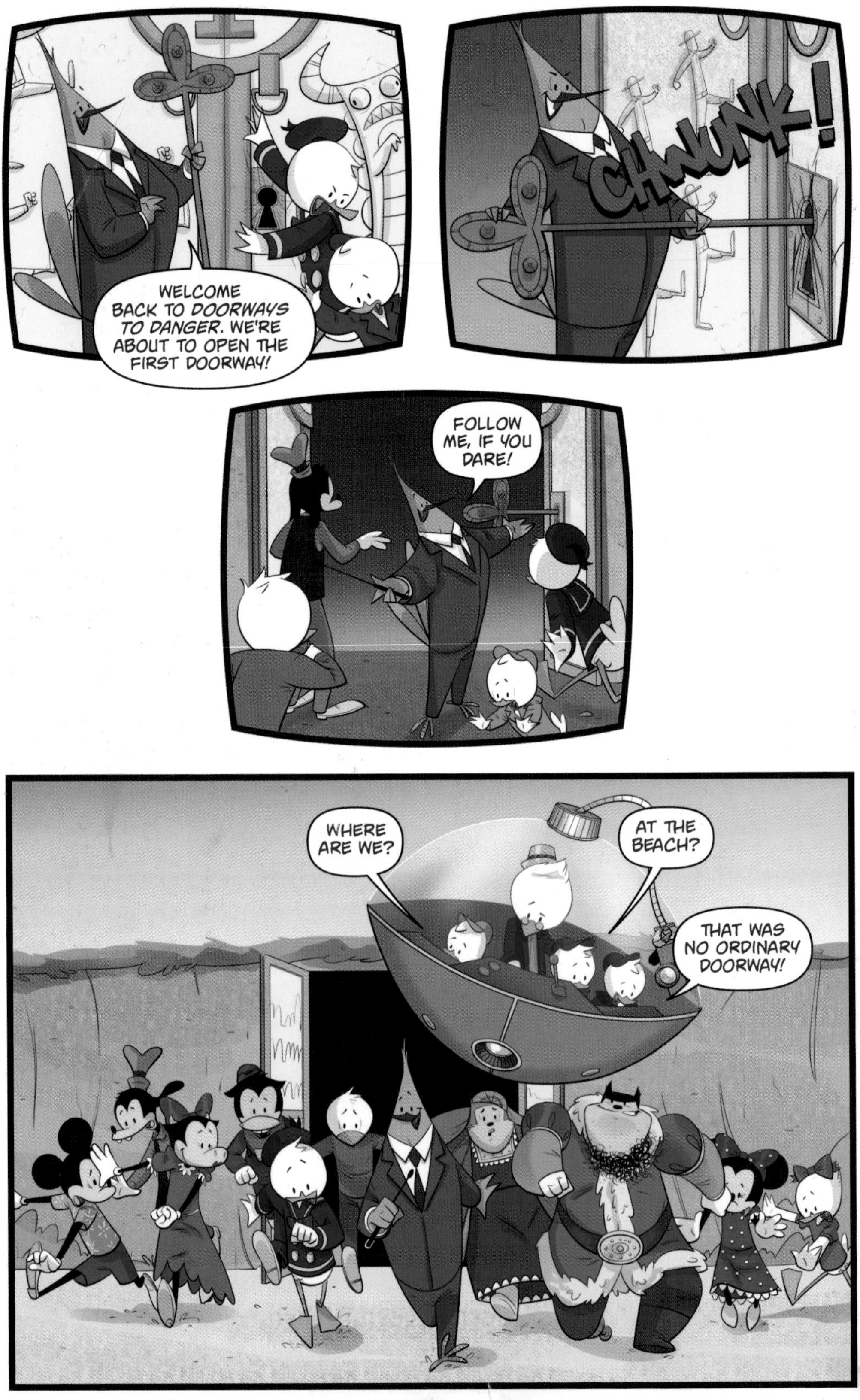
WELCOME BACK TO DOORWAYS TO DANGER. WE'RE ABOUT TO OPEN THE FIRST DOORWAY!
CHUNK!
FOLLOW ME, IF YOU DARE!
WHERE ARE WE?
AT THE BEACH?
THAT WAS NO ORDINARY DOORWAY!

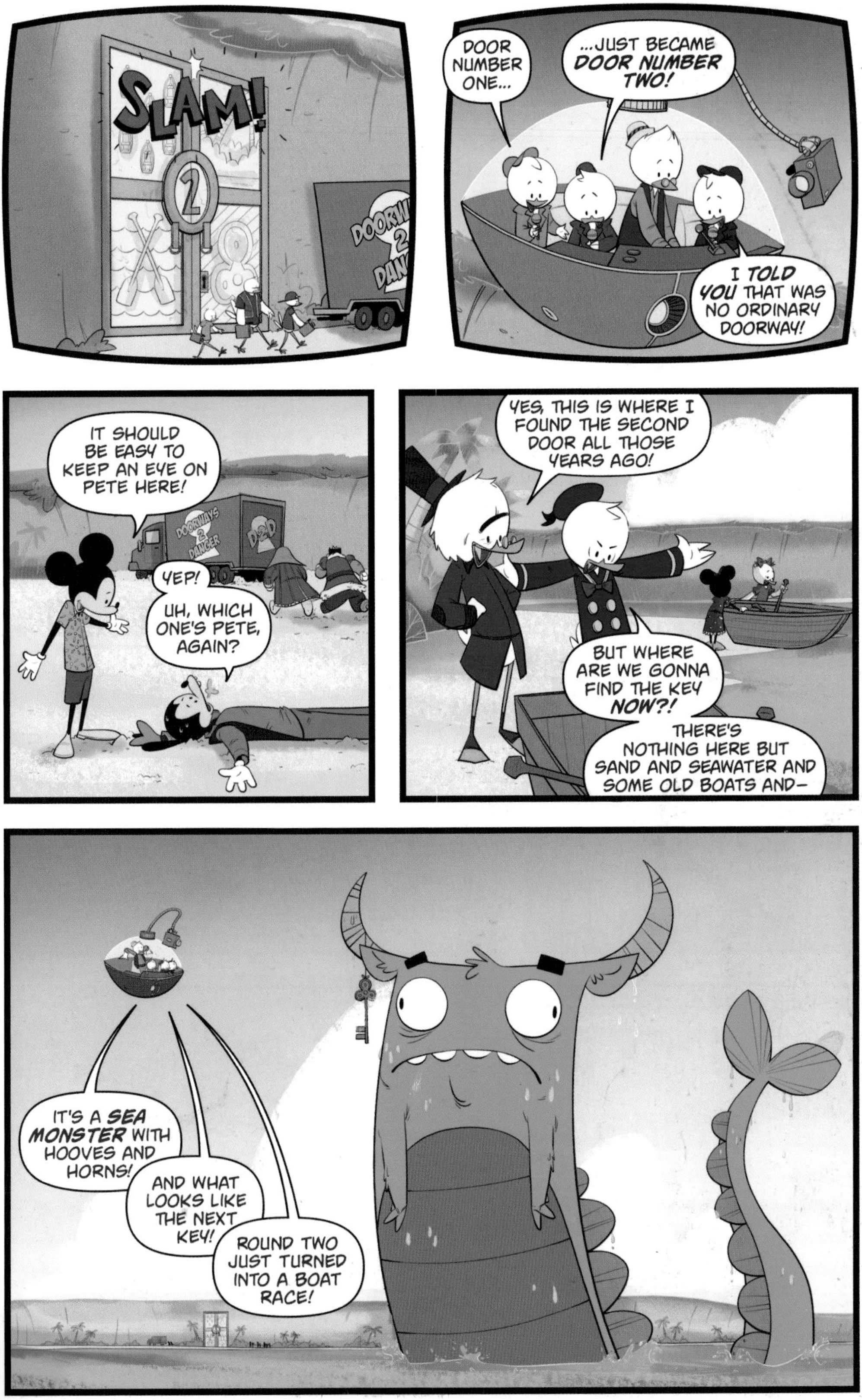
SLAM!
DOORWAYS 2 DANGER
DOOR NUMBER ONE...
...JUST BECAME DOOR NUMBER TWO!
I TOLD YOU THAT WAS NO ORDINARY DOORWAY!
IT SHOULD BE EASY TO KEEP AN EYE ON PETE HERE!
DOORWAYS 2 DANGER
D2D
YEP!
UH, WHICH ONE'S PETE, AGAIN?
YES, THIS IS WHERE I FOUND THE SECOND DOOR ALL THOSE YEARS AGO!
BUT WHERE ARE WE GONNA FIND THE KEY NOW?!
THERE'S NOTHING HERE BUT SAND AND SEAWATER AND SOME OLD BOATS AND–
IT'S A SEA MONSTER WITH HOOVES AND HORNS!
AND WHAT LOOKS LIKE THE NEXT KEY!
ROUND TWO JUST TURNED INTO A BOAT RACE!

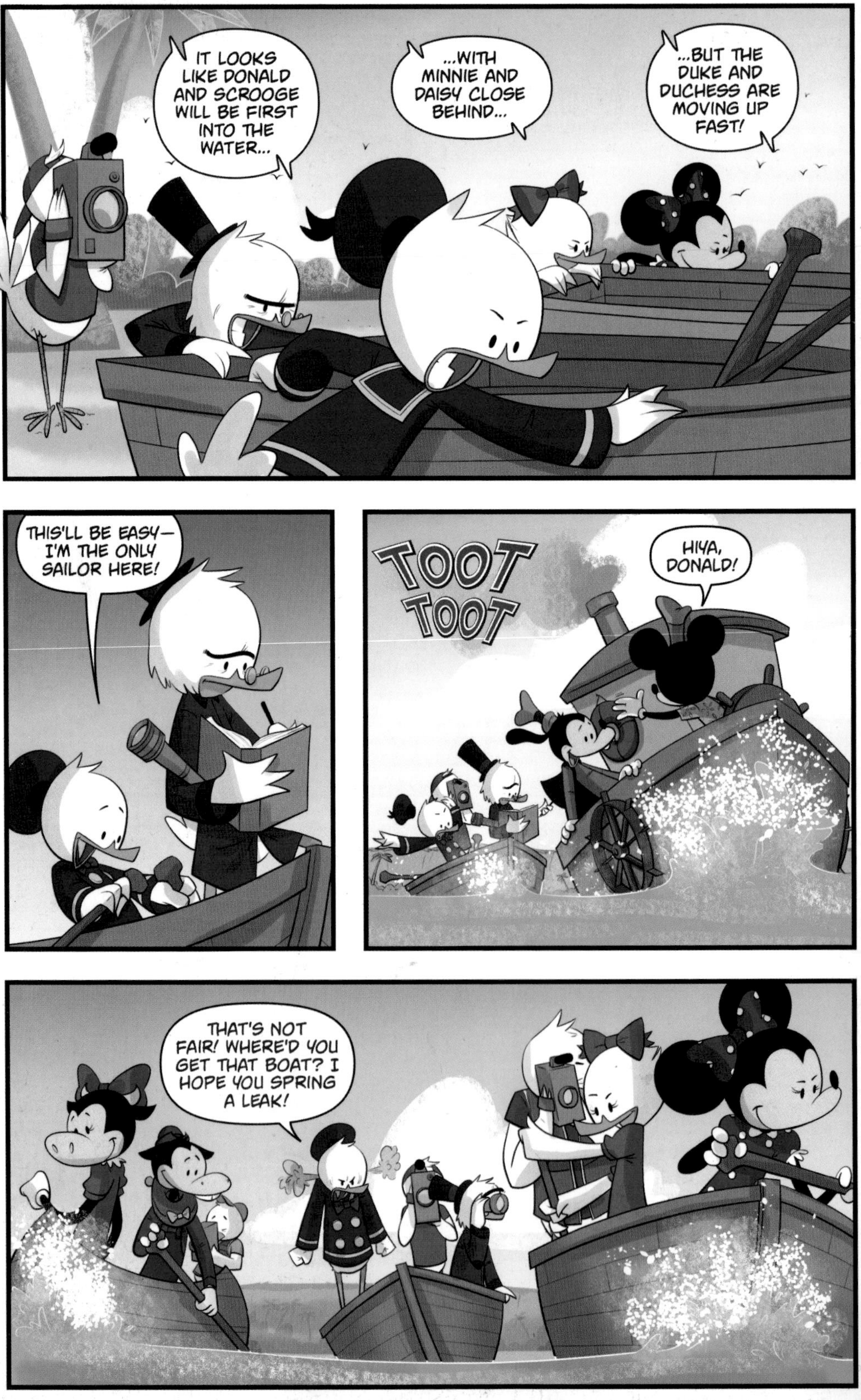
IT LOOKS LIKE DONALD AND SCROOGE WILL BE FIRST INTO THE WATER...
...WITH MINNIE AND DAISY CLOSE BEHIND...
...BUT THE DUKE AND DUCHESS ARE MOVING UP FAST!
THIS'LL BE EASY— I'M THE ONLY SAILOR HERE!
TOOT TOOT
HIYA, DONALD!
THAT'S NOT FAIR! WHERE'D YOU GET THAT BOAT? I HOPE YOU SPRING A LEAK!

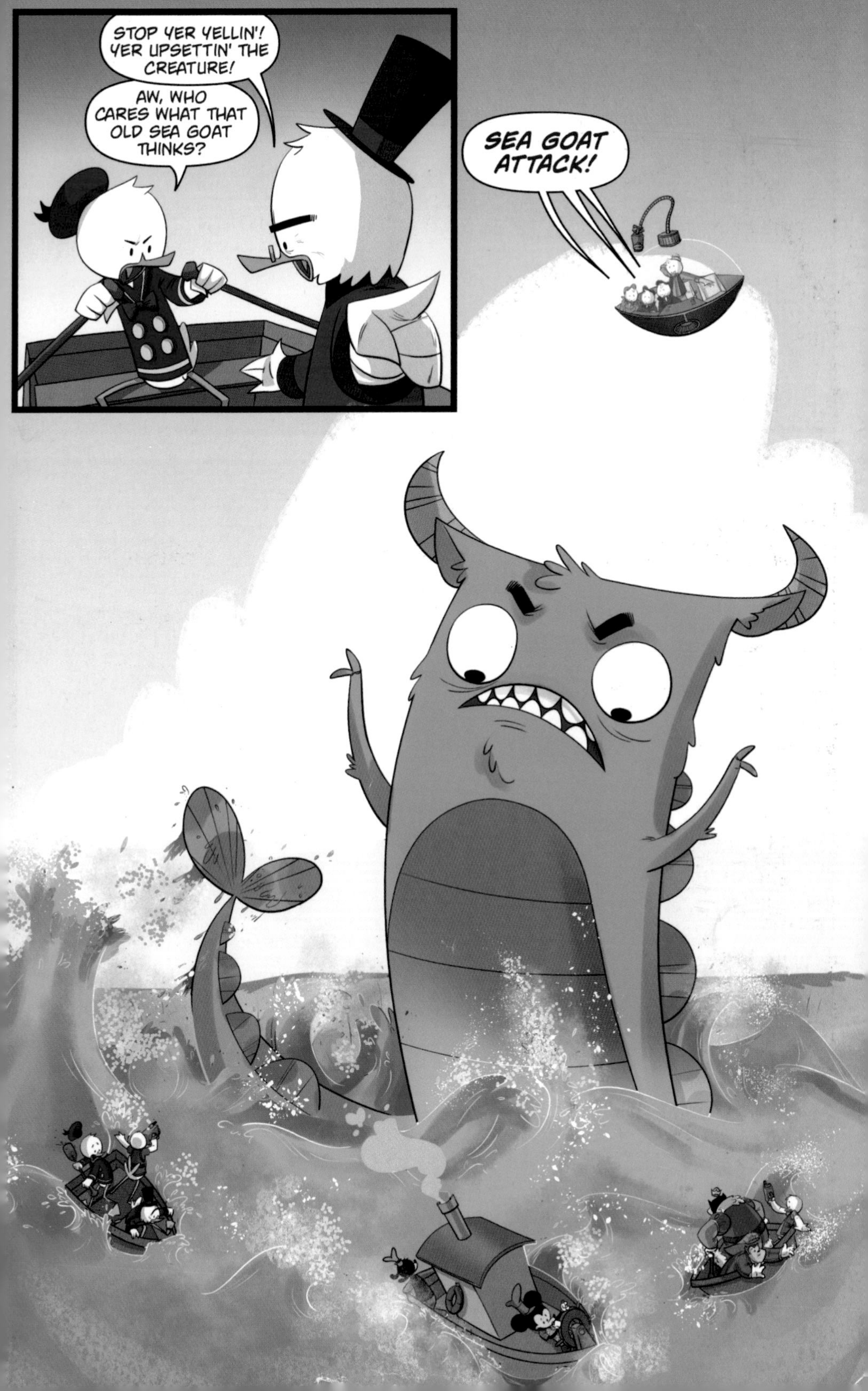
STOP YER YELLIN'! YER UPSETTIN' THE CREATURE!
AW, WHO CARES WHAT THAT OLD SEA GOAT THINKS?
SEA GOAT ATTACK!

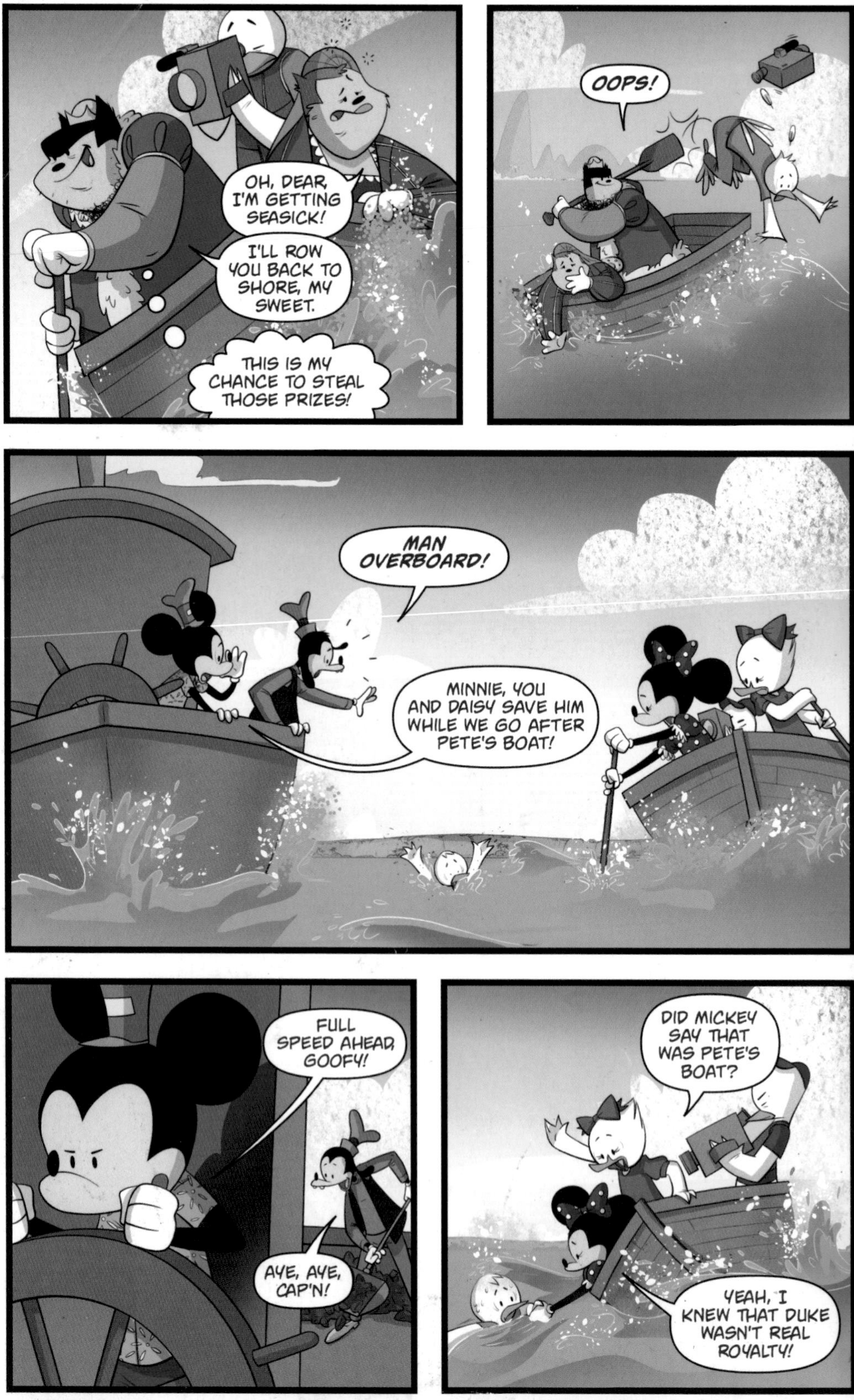
OH, DEAR, I'M GETTING SEASICK!
I'LL ROW YOU BACK TO SHORE, MY SWEET.
THIS IS MY CHANCE TO STEAL THOSE PRIZES!
OOPS!
MAN OVERBOARD!
MINNIE, YOU AND DAISY SAVE HIM WHILE WE GO AFTER PETE'S BOAT!
FULL SPEED AHEAD, GOOFY!
AYE, AYE, CAP'N!
DID MICKEY SAY THAT WAS PETE'S BOAT?
YEAH, I KNEW THAT DUKE WASN'T REAL ROYALTY!

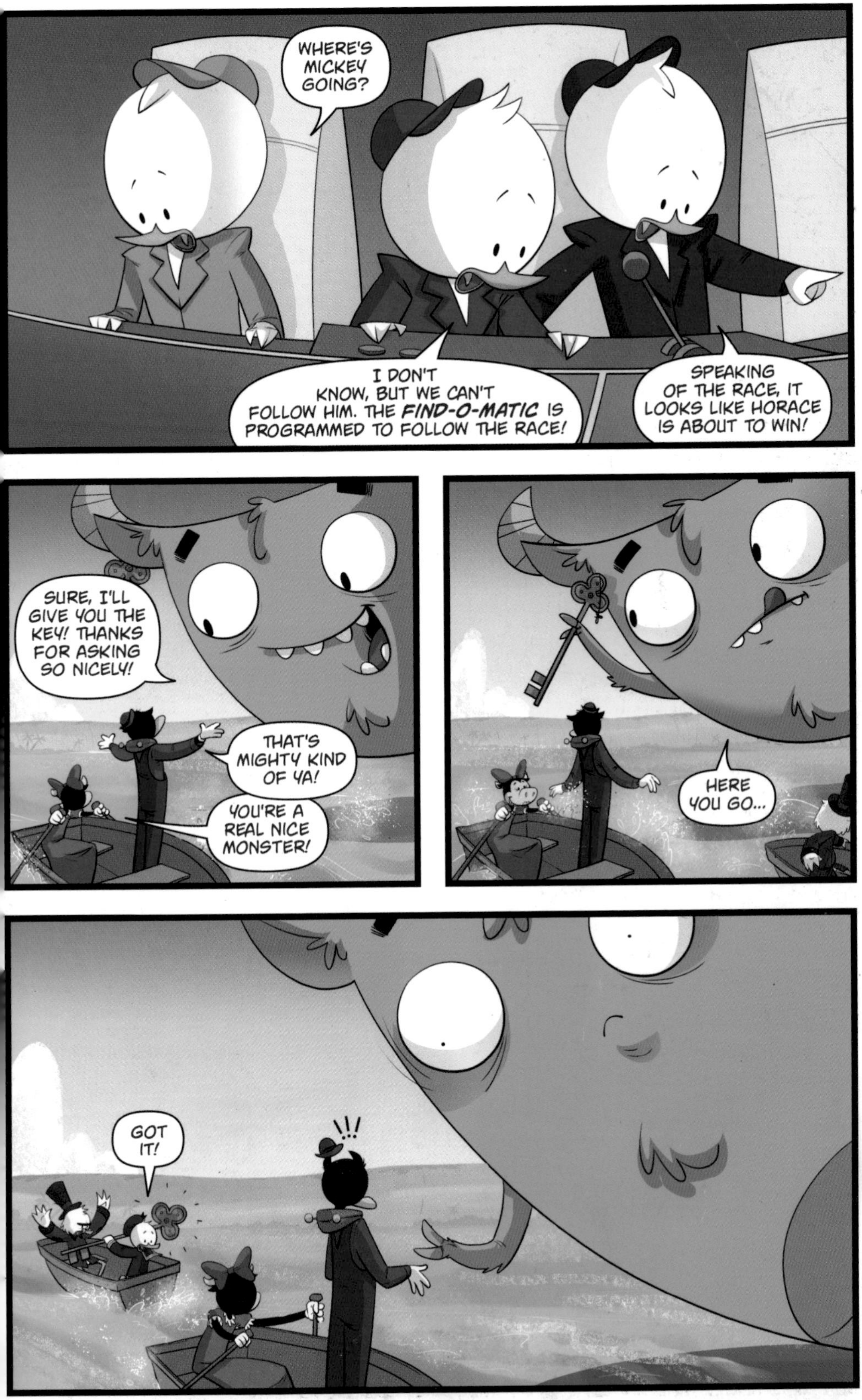
WHERE'S MICKEY GOING?
I DON'T KNOW, BUT WE CAN'T FOLLOW HIM. THE FIND-O-MATIC IS PROGRAMMED TO FOLLOW THE RACE!
SPEAKING OF THE RACE, IT LOOKS LIKE HORACE IS ABOUT TO WIN!
SURE, I'LL GIVE YOU THE KEY! THANKS FOR ASKING SO NICELY!
THAT'S MIGHTY KIND OF YA!
YOU'RE A REAL NICE MONSTER!
HERE YOU GO...
GOT IT!
!!!

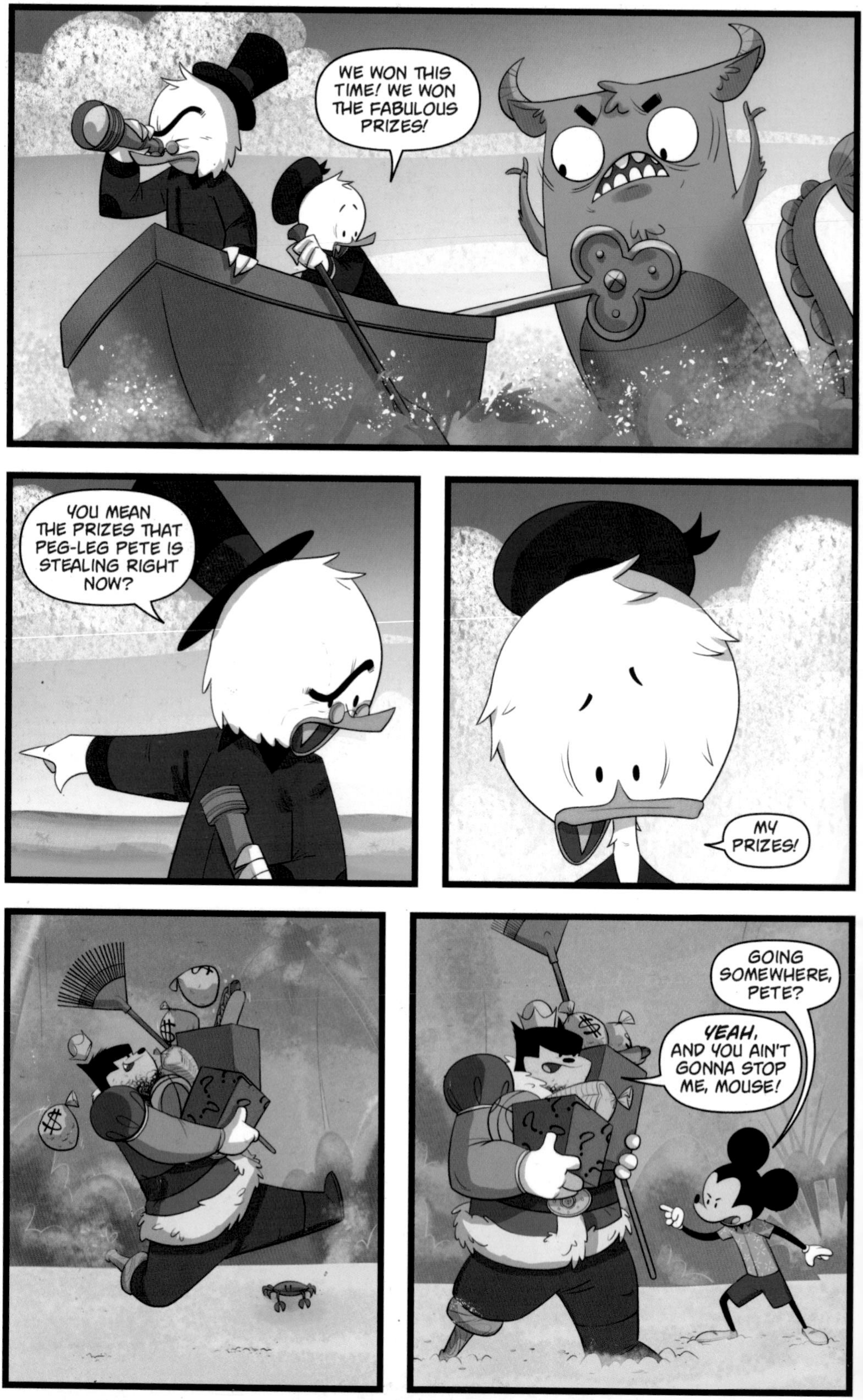
WE WON THIS TIME! WE WON THE FABULOUS PRIZES!
YOU MEAN THE PRIZES THAT PEG-LEG PETE IS STEALING RIGHT NOW?
MY PRIZES!
GOING SOMEWHERE, PETE?
YEAH, AND YOU AIN'T GONNA STOP ME, MOUSE!

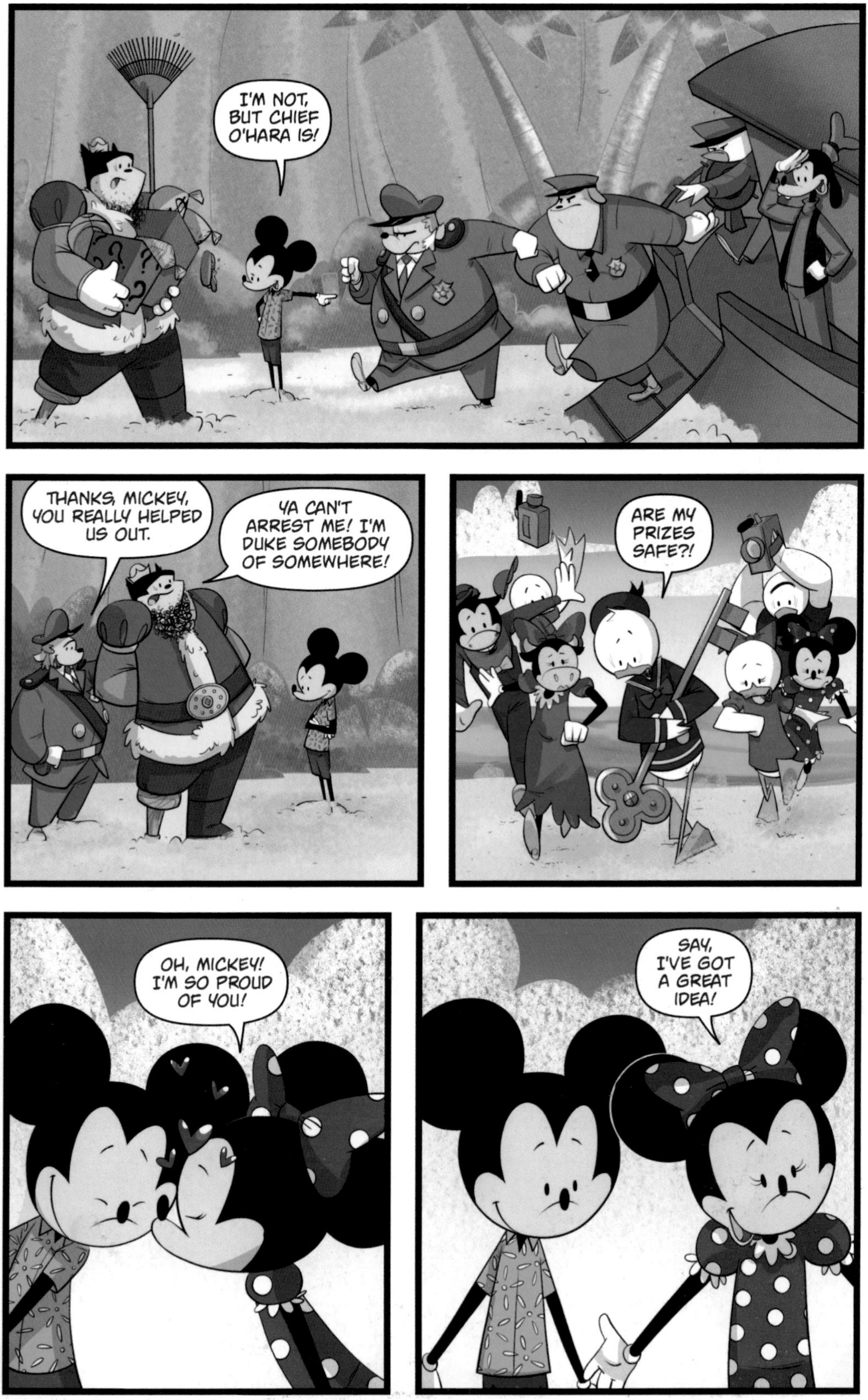
I'M NOT, BUT CHIEF O'HARA IS!
THANKS, MICKEY, YOU REALLY HELPED US OUT.
YA CAN'T ARREST ME! I'M DUKE SOMEBODY OF SOMEWHERE!
ARE MY PRIZES SAFE?!
OH, MICKEY! I'M SO PROUD OF YOU!
SAY, I'VE GOT A GREAT IDEA!

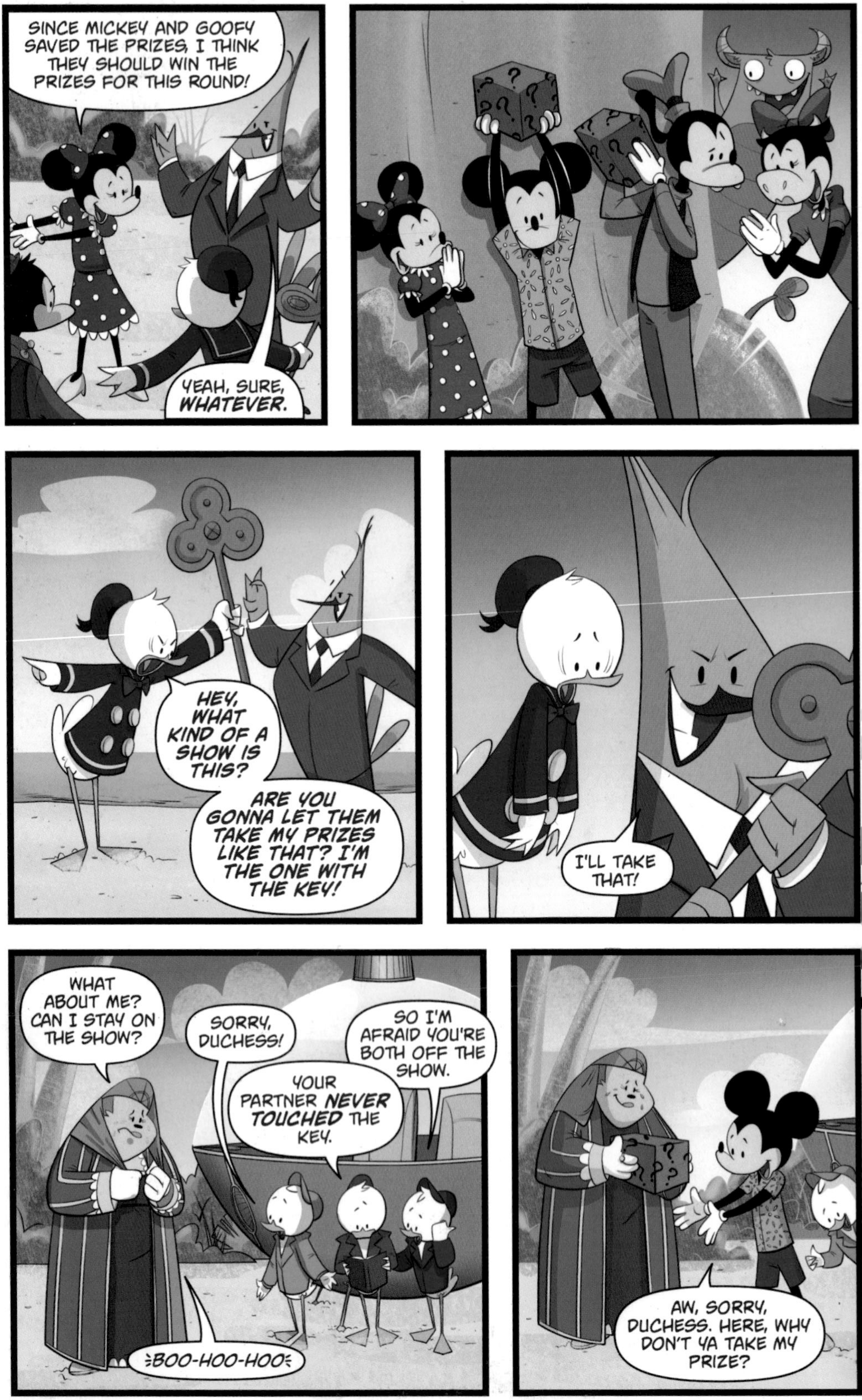
SINCE MICKEY AND GOOFY SAVED THE PRIZES, I THINK THEY SHOULD WIN THE PRIZES FOR THIS ROUND!
YEAH, SURE, WHATEVER.
HEY, WHAT KIND OF A SHOW IS THIS?
ARE YOU GONNA LET THEM TAKE MY PRIZES LIKE THAT? I'M THE ONE WITH THE KEY!
I'LL TAKE THAT!
WHAT ABOUT ME? CAN I STAY ON THE SHOW?
SORRY, DUCHESS!
YOUR PARTNER NEVER TOUCHED THE KEY.
SO I'M AFRAID YOU'RE BOTH OFF THE SHOW.
BOO-HOO-HOO
AW, SORRY, DUCHESS. HERE, WHY DON'T YA TAKE MY PRIZE?

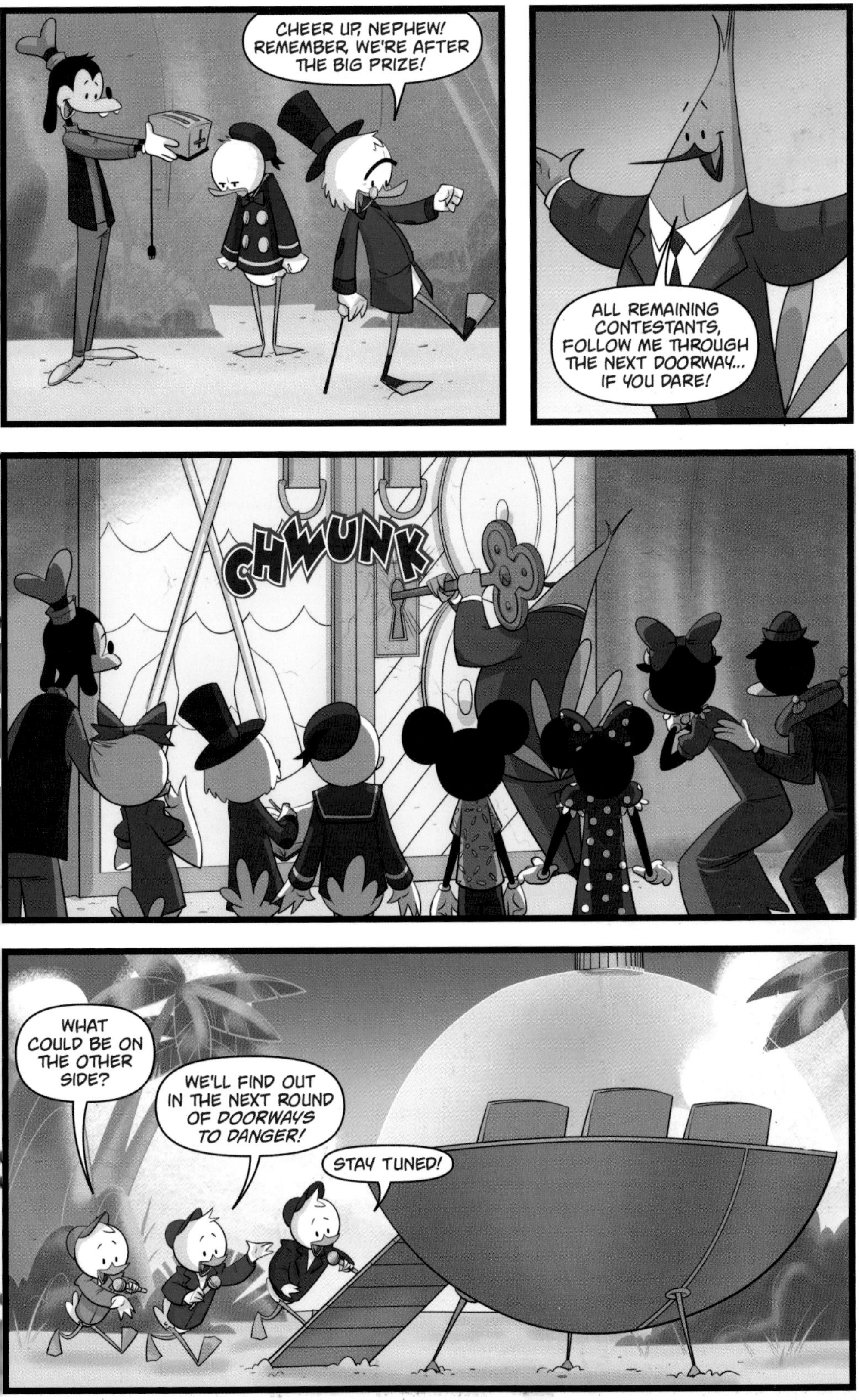
CHEER UP, NEPHEW! REMEMBER, WE'RE AFTER THE BIG PRIZE!
ALL REMAINING CONTESTANTS, FOLLOW ME THROUGH THE NEXT DOORWAY... IF YOU DARE!
CHWUNK
WHAT COULD BE ON THE OTHER SIDE?
WE'LL FIND OUT IN THE NEXT ROUND OF DOORWAYS TO DANGER!
STAY TUNED!

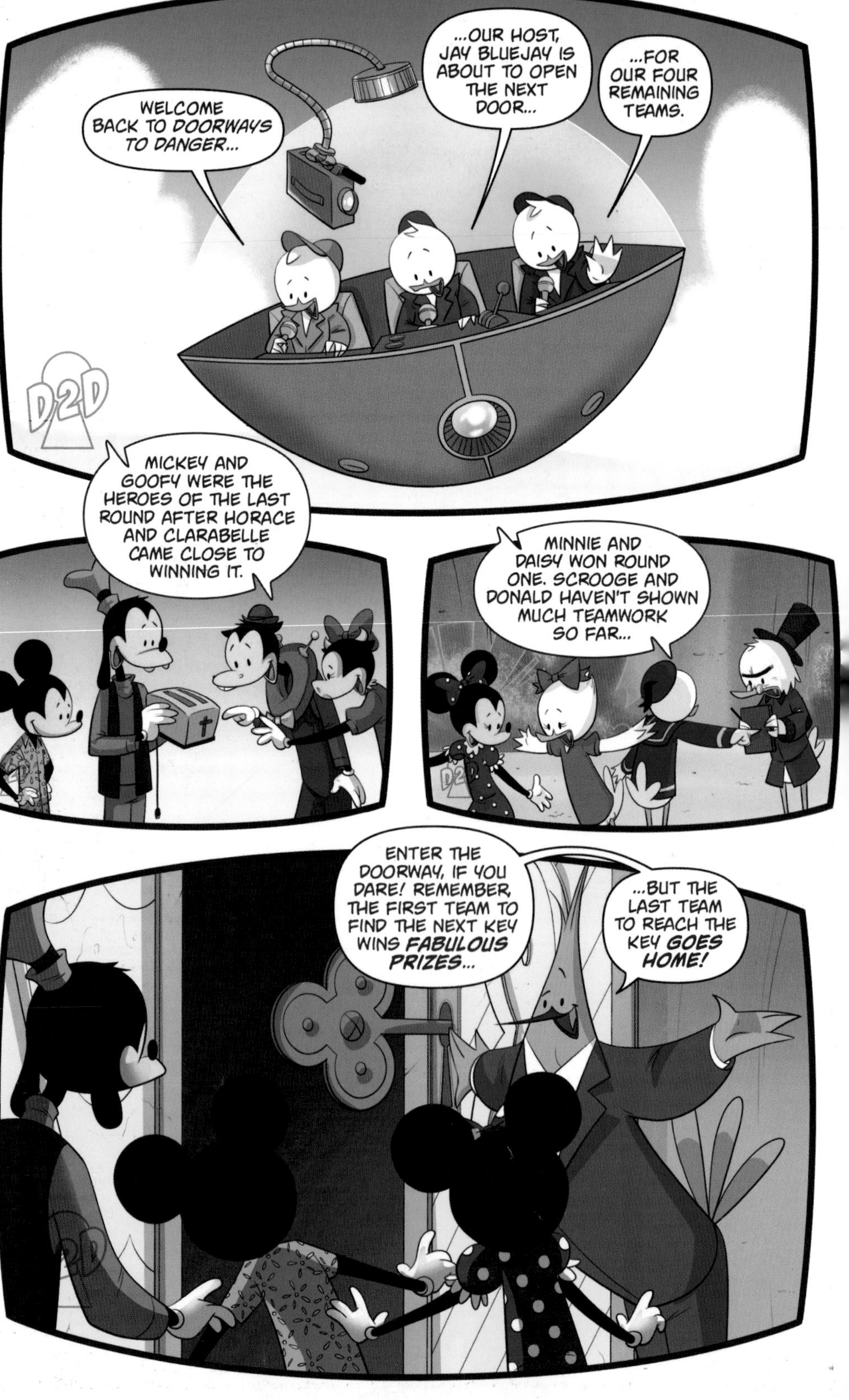
WELCOME BACK TO *DOORWAYS TO DANGER*...
...OUR HOST, JAY BLUEJAY IS ABOUT TO OPEN THE NEXT DOOR...
...FOR OUR FOUR REMAINING TEAMS.
D2D
MICKEY AND GOOFY WERE THE HEROES OF THE LAST ROUND AFTER HORACE AND CLARABELLE CAME CLOSE TO WINNING IT.
MINNIE AND DAISY WON ROUND ONE. SCROOGE AND DONALD HAVEN'T SHOWN MUCH TEAMWORK SO FAR...
ENTER THE DOORWAY, IF YOU DARE! REMEMBER, THE FIRST TEAM TO FIND THE NEXT KEY WINS ***FABULOUS PRIZES***...
...BUT THE LAST TEAM TO REACH THE KEY ***GOES HOME!***

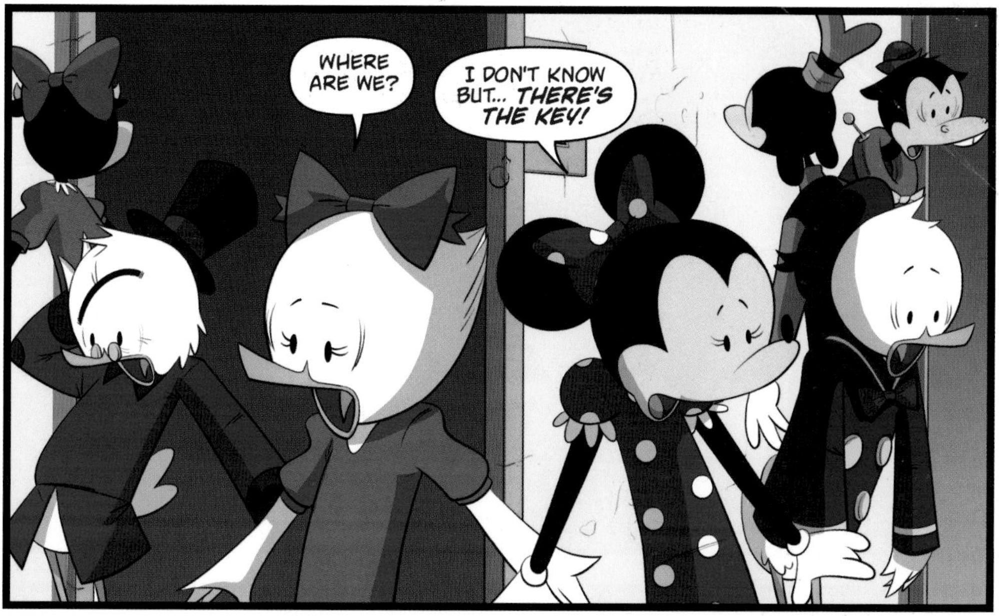
WHERE ARE WE?
I DON'T KNOW BUT... *THERE'S THE KEY!*

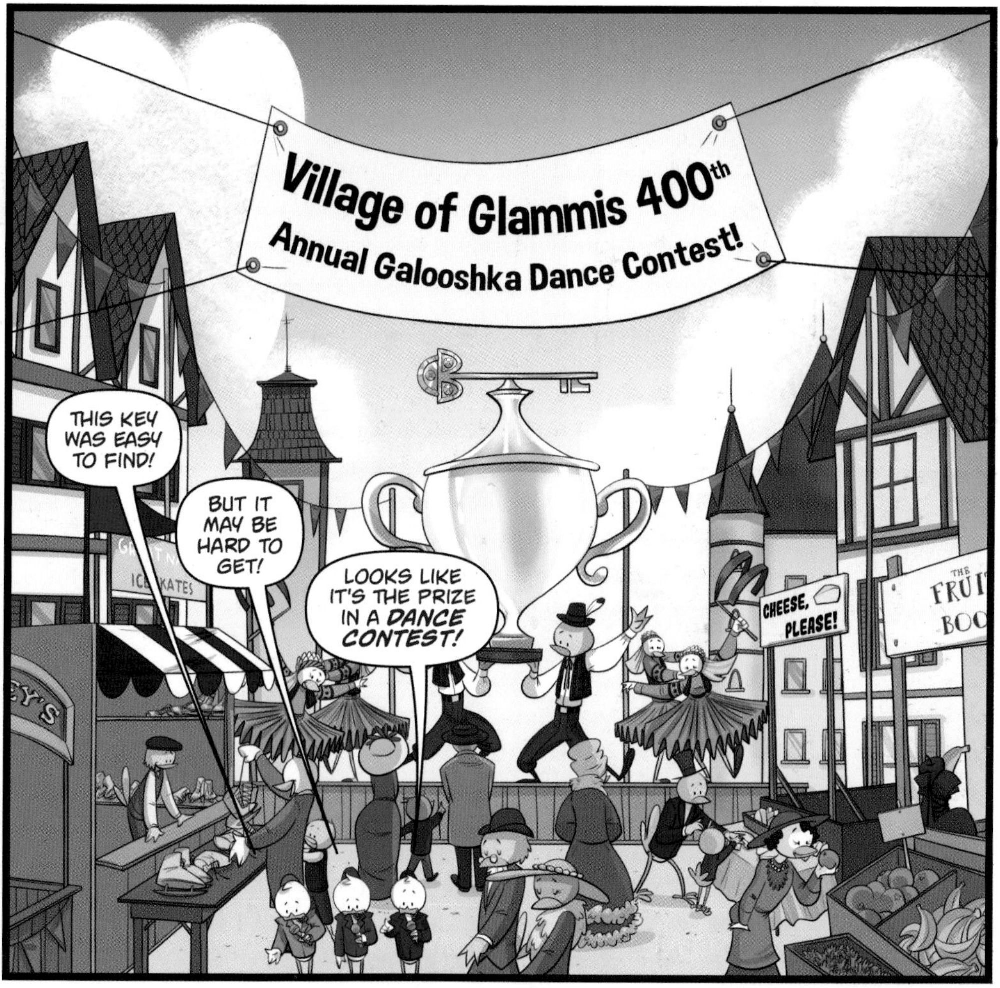
Village of Glammis 400th Annual Galooshka Dance Contest!
THIS KEY WAS EASY TO FIND!
BUT IT MAY BE HARD TO GET!
LOOKS LIKE IT'S THE PRIZE IN A *DANCE CONTEST!*
CHEESE, PLEASE!

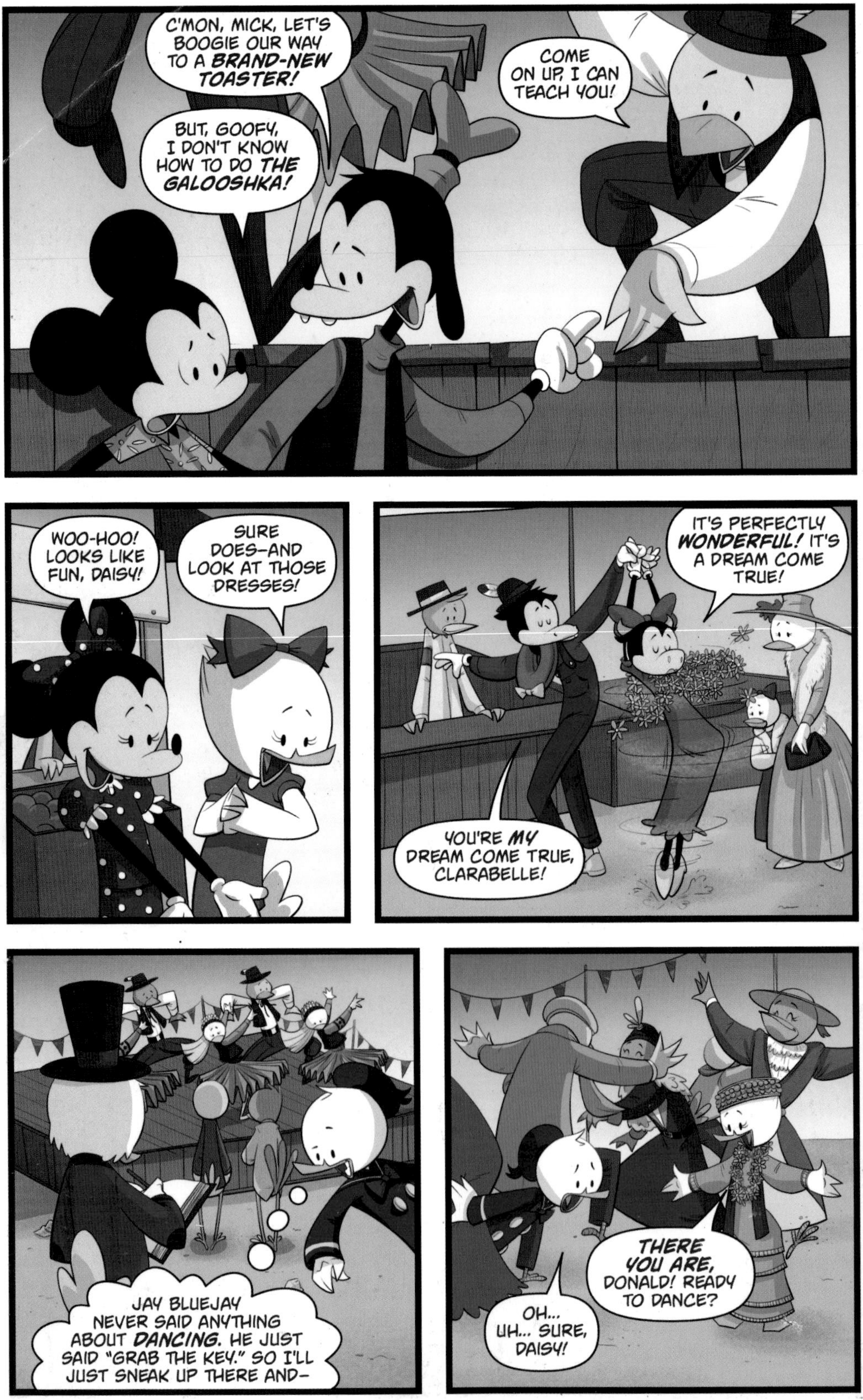
C'MON, MICK, LET'S BOOGIE OUR WAY TO A BRAND-NEW TOASTER!
BUT, GOOFY, I DON'T KNOW HOW TO DO THE GALOOSHKA!
COME ON UP, I CAN TEACH YOU!
WOO-HOO! LOOKS LIKE FUN, DAISY!
SURE DOES—AND LOOK AT THOSE DRESSES!
IT'S PERFECTLY WONDERFUL! IT'S A DREAM COME TRUE!
YOU'RE MY DREAM COME TRUE, CLARABELLE!
JAY BLUEJAY NEVER SAID ANYTHING ABOUT DANCING. HE JUST SAID "GRAB THE KEY." SO I'LL JUST SNEAK UP THERE AND—
THERE YOU ARE, DONALD! READY TO DANCE?
OH... UH... SURE, DAISY!

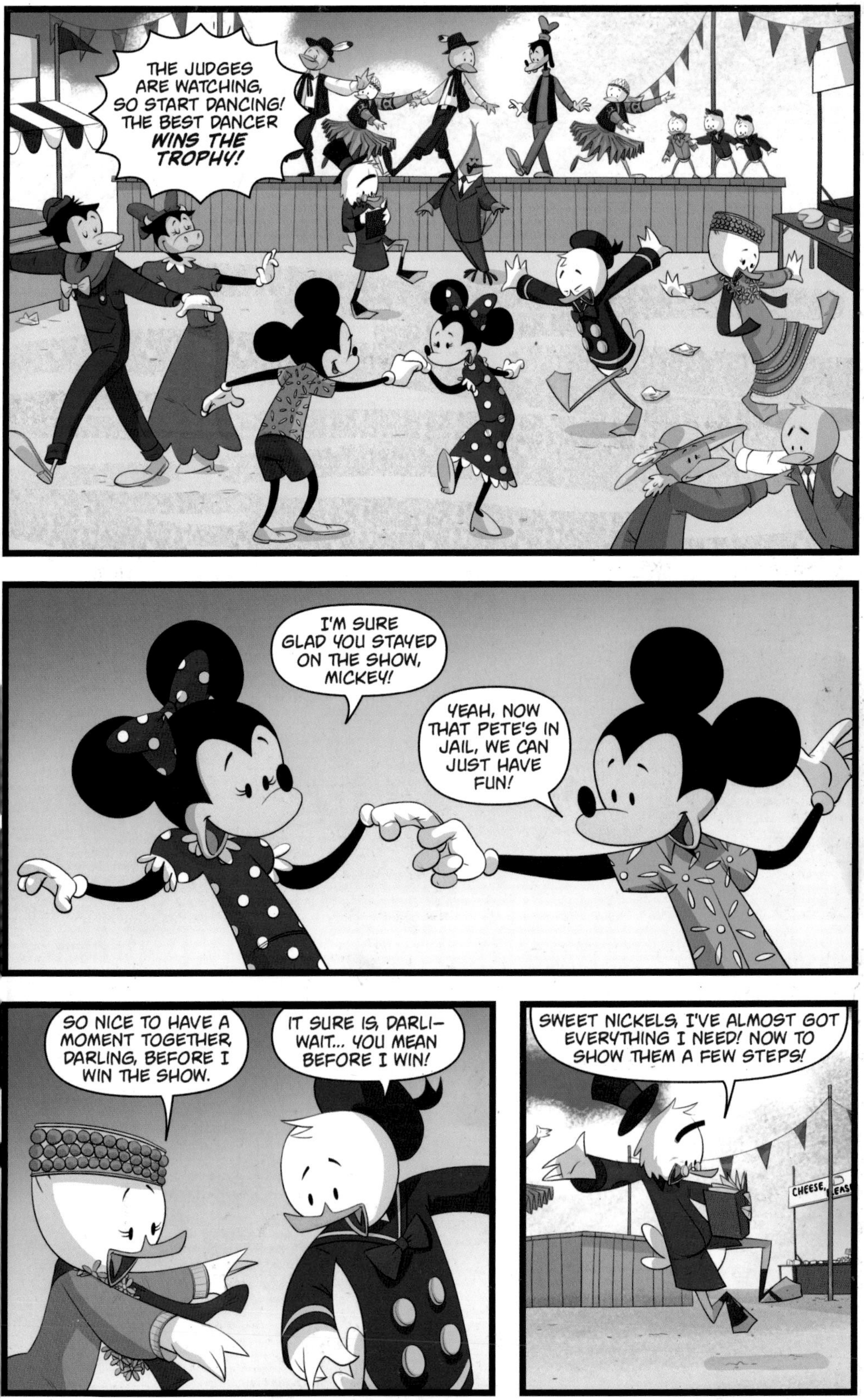
THE JUDGES ARE WATCHING, SO START DANCING! THE BEST DANCER WINS THE TROPHY!
I'M SURE GLAD YOU STAYED ON THE SHOW, MICKEY!
YEAH, NOW THAT PETE'S IN JAIL, WE CAN JUST HAVE FUN!
SO NICE TO HAVE A MOMENT TOGETHER, DARLING, BEFORE I WIN THE SHOW.
IT SURE IS, DARLI— WAIT... YOU MEAN BEFORE I WIN!
SWEET NICKELS, I'VE ALMOST GOT EVERYTHING I NEED! NOW TO SHOW THEM A FEW STEPS!
CHEESE,

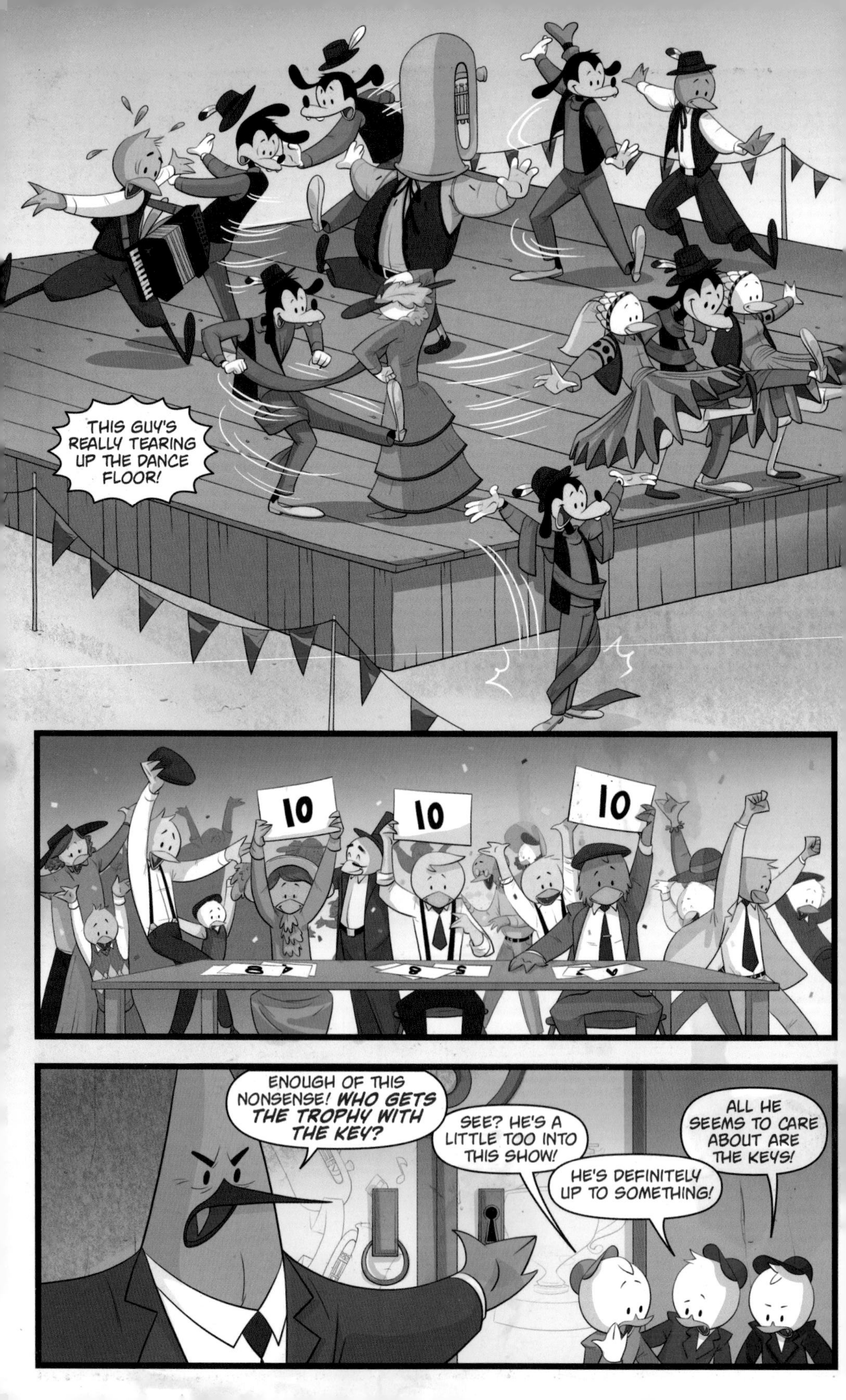
THIS GUY'S REALLY TEARING UP THE DANCE FLOOR!
10
10
10
ENOUGH OF THIS NONSENSE! WHO GETS THE TROPHY WITH THE KEY?
SEE? HE'S A LITTLE TOO INTO THIS SHOW!
HE'S DEFINITELY UP TO SOMETHING!
ALL HE SEEMS TO CARE ABOUT ARE THE KEYS!

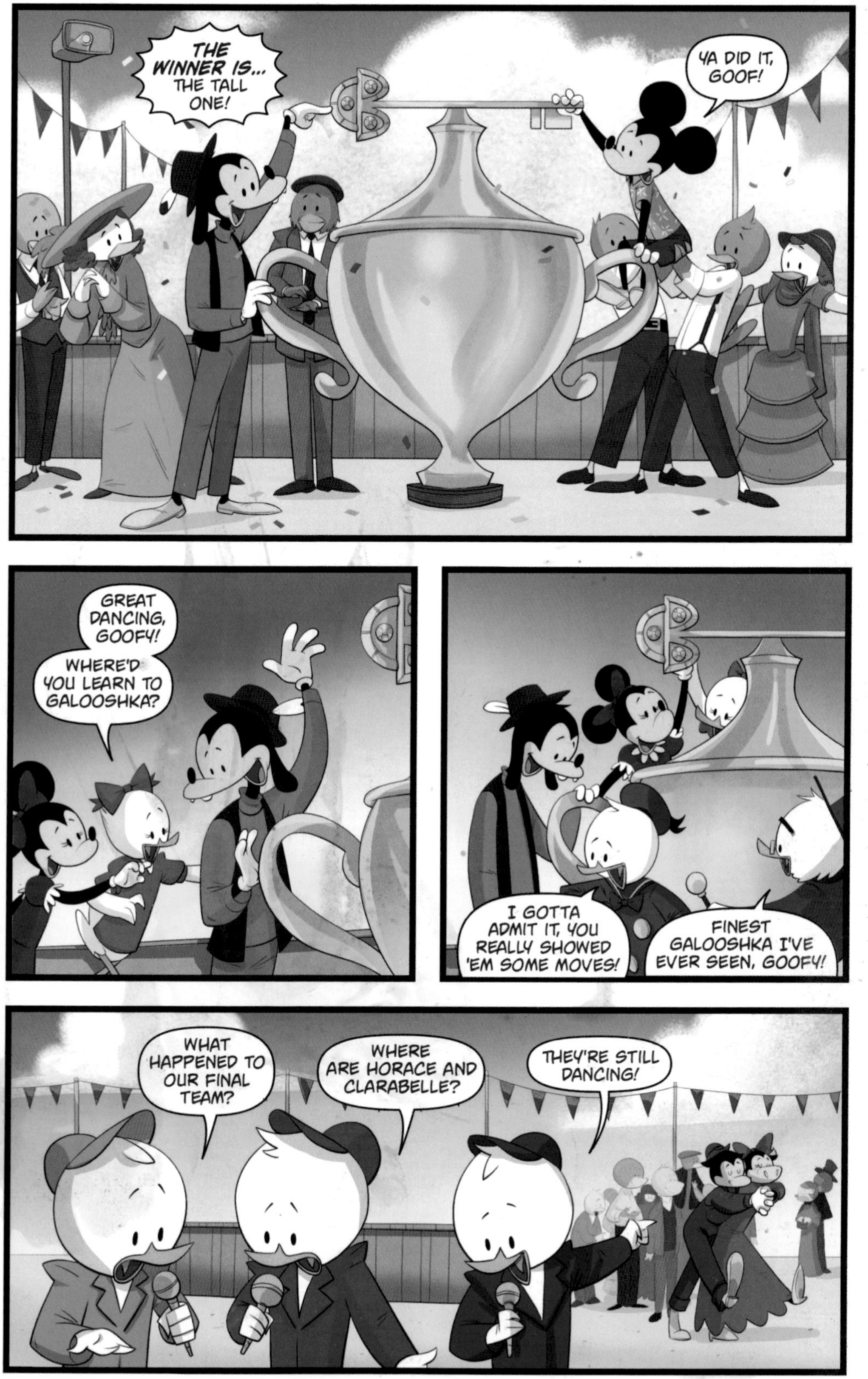
THE WINNER IS... THE TALL ONE!
YA DID IT, GOOF!
GREAT DANCING, GOOFY!
WHERE'D YOU LEARN TO GALOOSHKA?
I GOTTA ADMIT IT, YOU REALLY SHOWED 'EM SOME MOVES!
FINEST GALOOSHKA I'VE EVER SEEN, GOOFY!
WHAT HAPPENED TO OUR FINAL TEAM?
WHERE ARE HORACE AND CLARABELLE?
THEY'RE STILL DANCING!

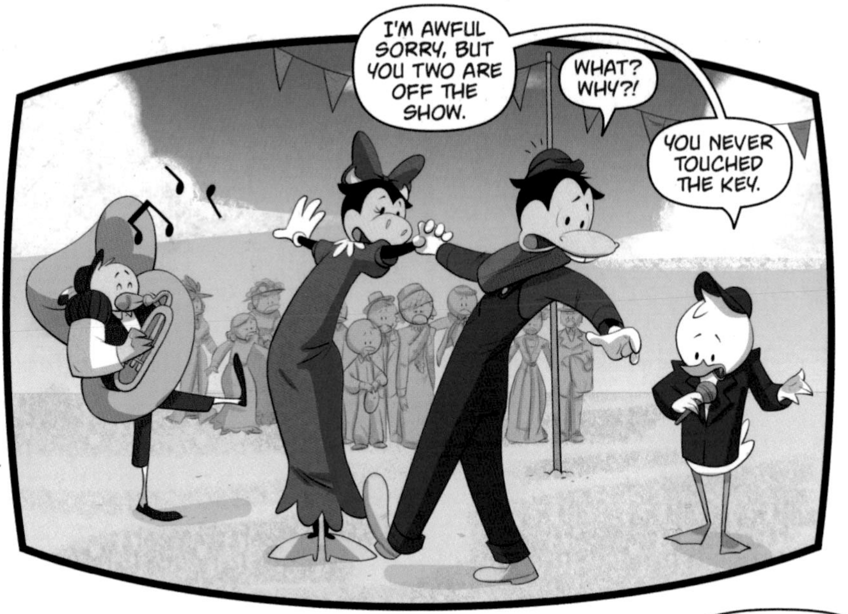
I'M AWFUL SORRY, BUT YOU TWO ARE OFF THE SHOW.
WHAT? WHY?!
YOU NEVER TOUCHED THE KEY.

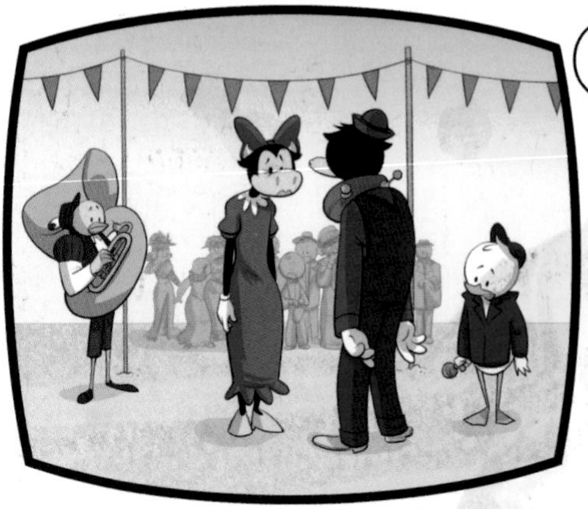

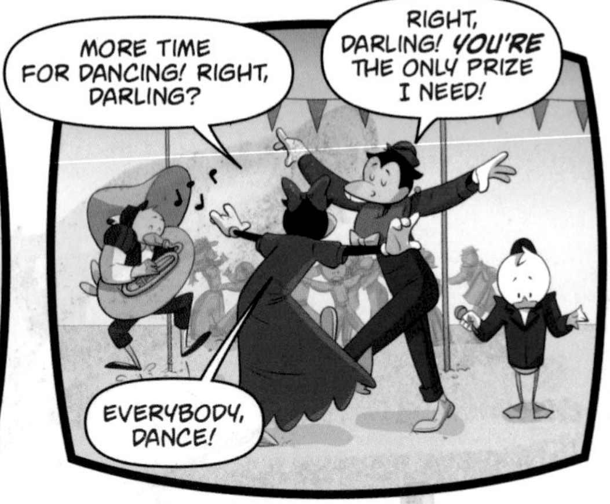
MORE TIME FOR DANCING! RIGHT, DARLING?
RIGHT, DARLING! YOU'RE THE ONLY PRIZE I NEED!
EVERYBODY, DANCE!

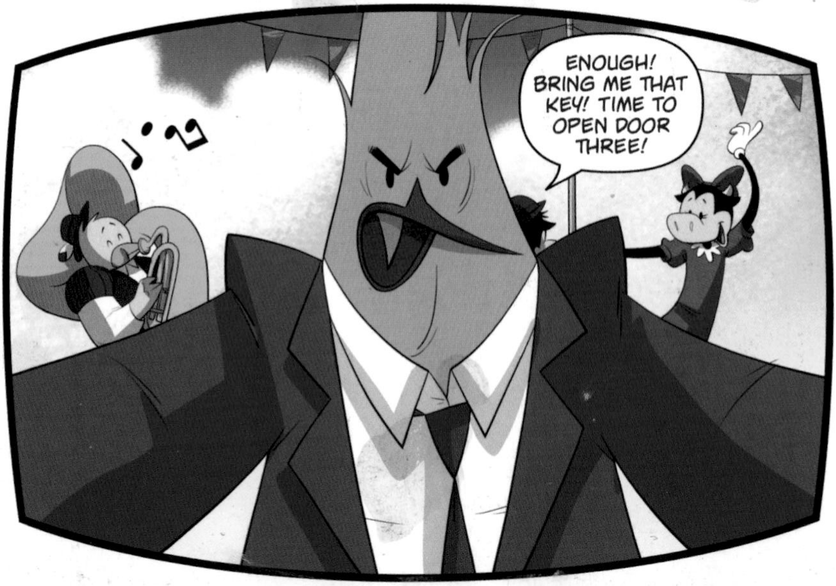
ENOUGH! BRING ME THAT KEY! TIME TO OPEN DOOR THREE!

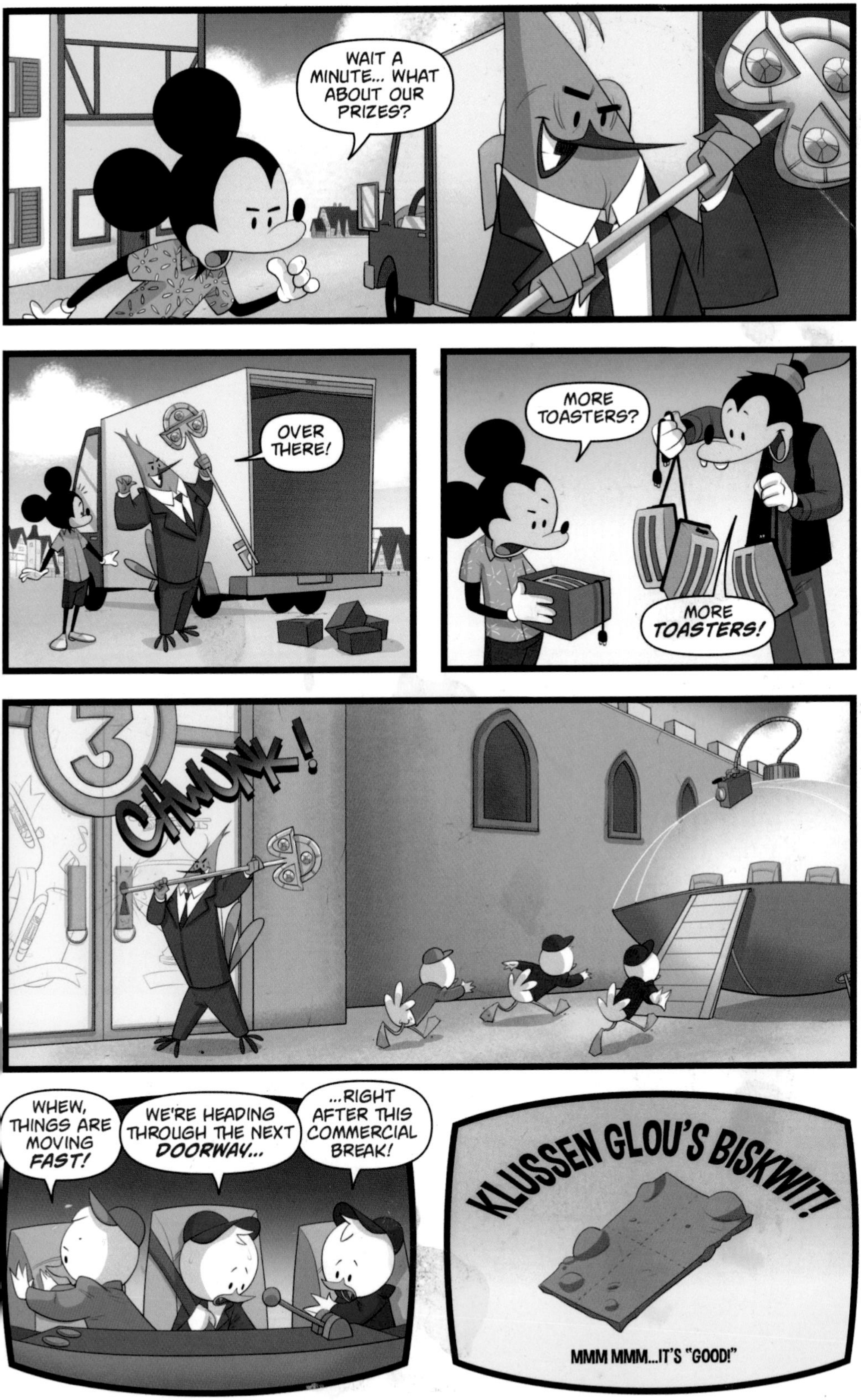

WAIT A MINUTE... WHAT ABOUT OUR PRIZES?
OVER THERE!
MORE TOASTERS?
MORE TOASTERS!
CHUNK!
WHEW, THINGS ARE MOVING FAST!
WE'RE HEADING THROUGH THE NEXT DOORWAY...
...RIGHT AFTER THIS COMMERCIAL BREAK!
KLUSSEN GLOU'S BISKWIT!
MMM MMM...IT'S "GOOD!"

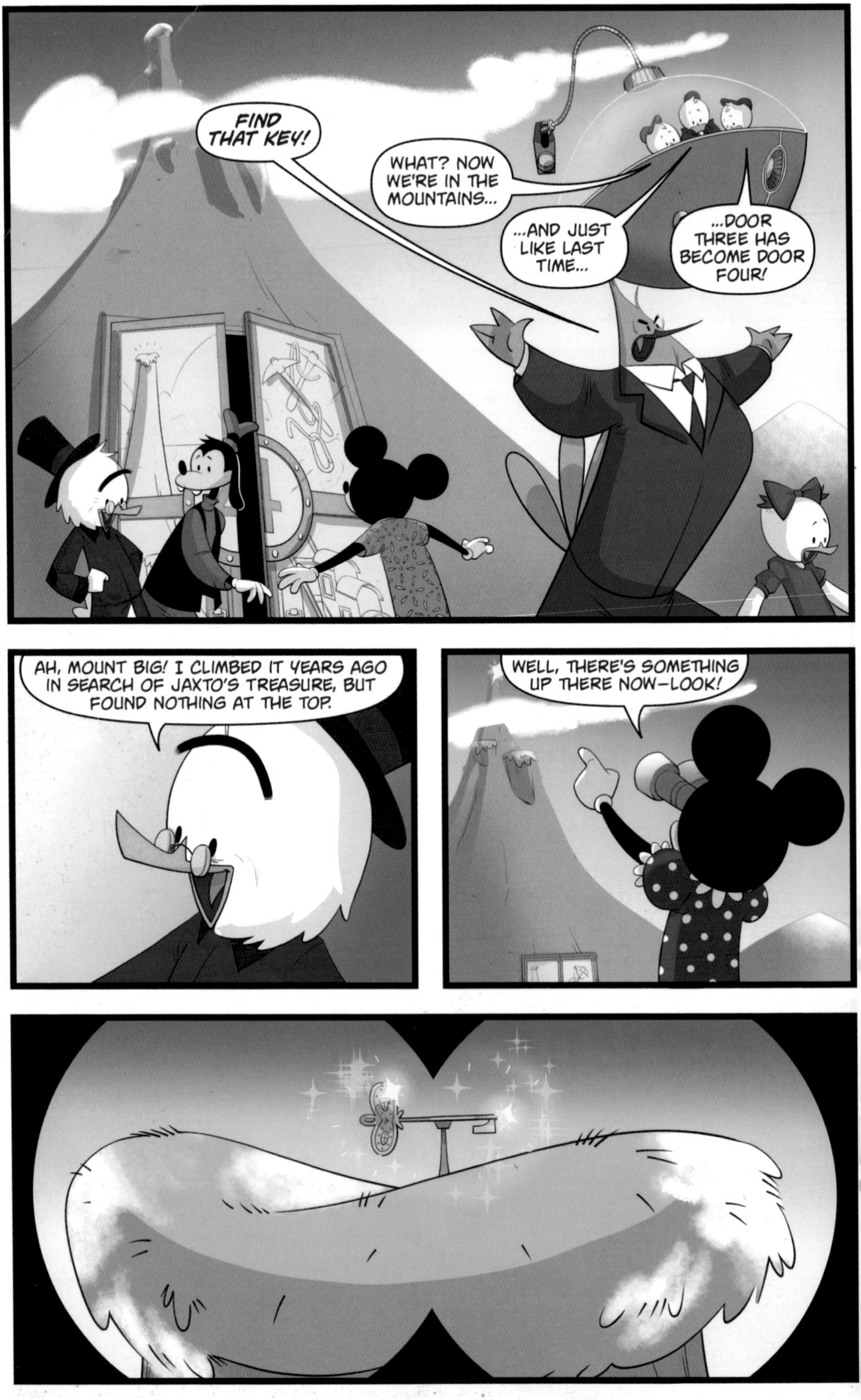
FIND THAT KEY!
WHAT? NOW WE'RE IN THE MOUNTAINS...
...AND JUST LIKE LAST TIME...
...DOOR THREE HAS BECOME DOOR FOUR!
AH, MOUNT BIG! I CLIMBED IT YEARS AGO IN SEARCH OF JAXTO'S TREASURE, BUT FOUND NOTHING AT THE TOP.
WELL, THERE'S SOMETHING UP THERE NOW—LOOK!

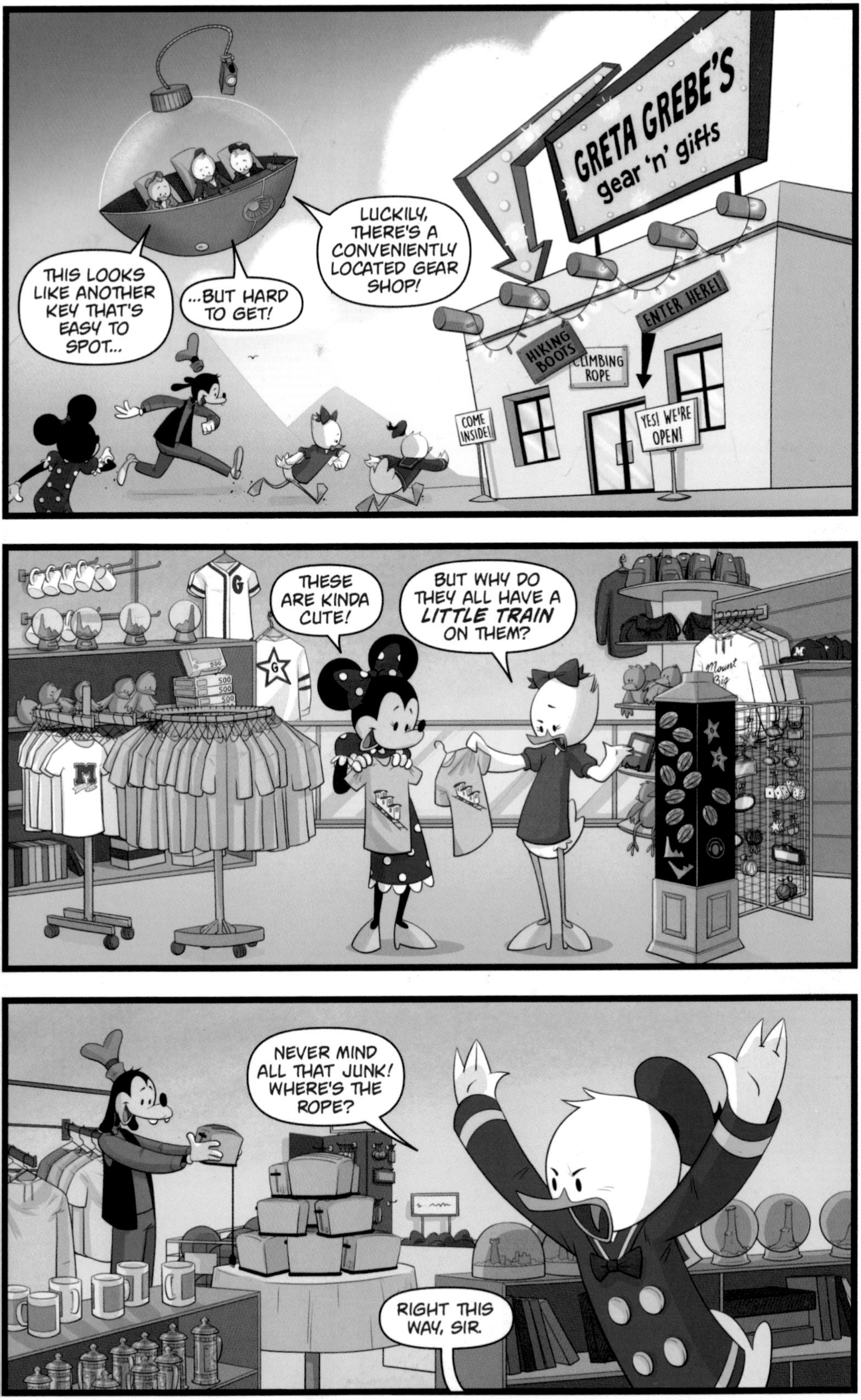
GRETA GREBE'S
gear 'n' gifts
THIS LOOKS LIKE ANOTHER KEY THAT'S EASY TO SPOT...
...BUT HARD TO GET!
LUCKILY, THERE'S A CONVENIENTLY LOCATED GEAR SHOP!
ENTER HERE!
HIKING BOOTS
CLIMBING ROPE
COME INSIDE!
YES! WE'RE OPEN!
THESE ARE KINDA CUTE!
BUT WHY DO THEY ALL HAVE A *LITTLE TRAIN* ON THEM?
NEVER MIND ALL THAT JUNK! WHERE'S THE ROPE?
RIGHT THIS WAY, SIR.

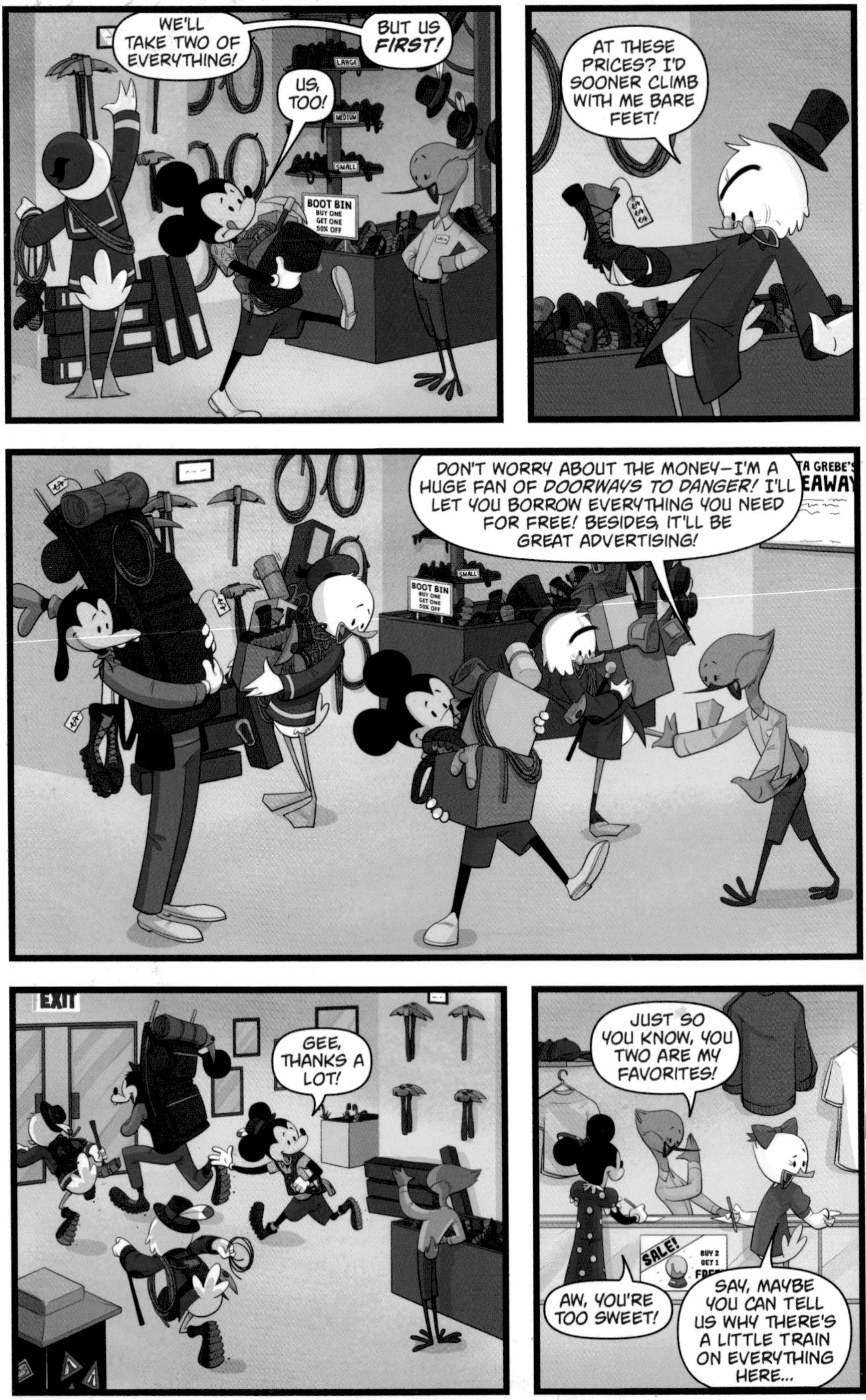
WE'LL TAKE TWO OF EVERYTHING!
BUT US *FIRST!*
US, TOO!
LARGE
MEDIUM
SMALL
BOOT BIN BUY ONE GET ONE 50% OFF
AT THESE PRICES? I'D SOONER CLIMB WITH ME BARE FEET!
DON'T WORRY ABOUT THE MONEY—I'M A HUGE FAN OF *DOORWAYS TO DANGER!* I'LL LET YOU BORROW EVERYTHING YOU NEED FOR FREE! BESIDES, IT'LL BE GREAT ADVERTISING!
BOOT BIN BUY ONE GET ONE 50% OFF
SMALL
EXIT
GEE, THANKS A LOT!
JUST SO YOU KNOW, YOU TWO ARE MY FAVORITES!
SALE!
BUY 2 GET 1
AW, YOU'RE TOO SWEET!
SAY, MAYBE YOU CAN TELL US WHY THERE'S A LITTLE TRAIN ON EVERYTHING HERE...

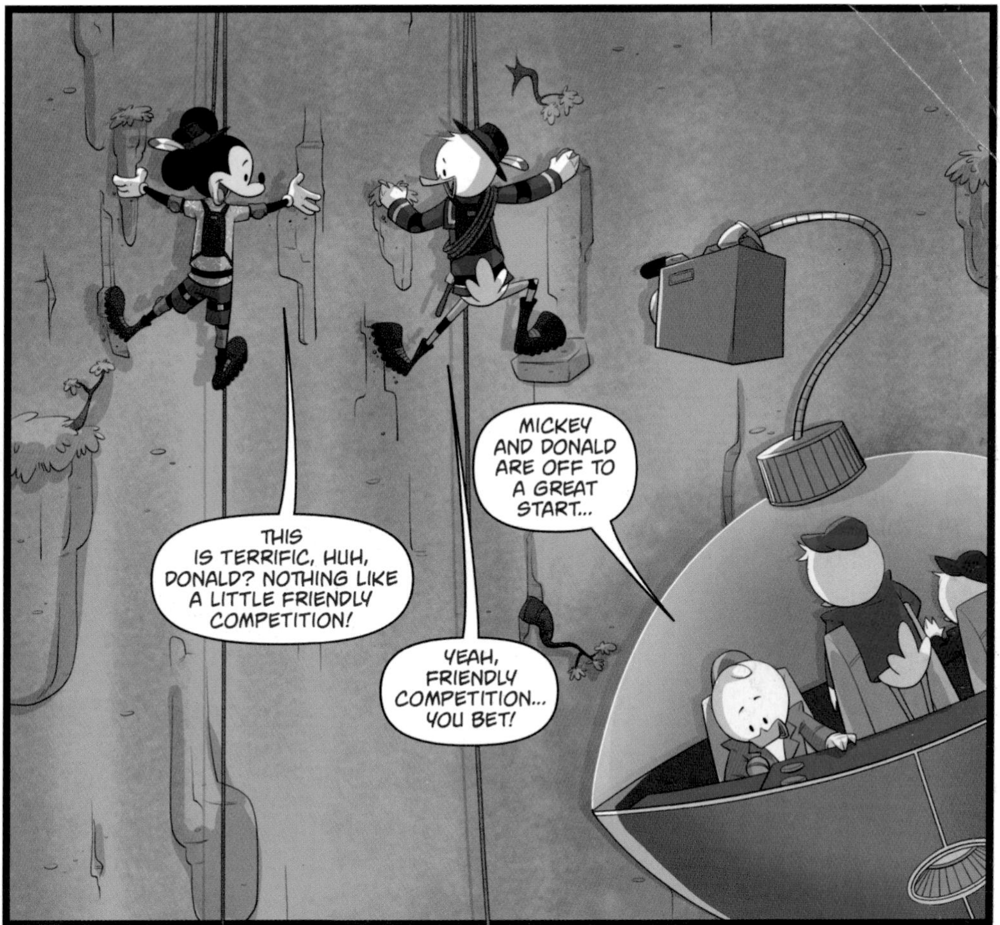
THIS IS TERRIFIC, HUH, DONALD? NOTHING LIKE A LITTLE FRIENDLY COMPETITION!
YEAH, FRIENDLY COMPETITION... YOU BET!
MICKEY AND DONALD ARE OFF TO A GREAT START...

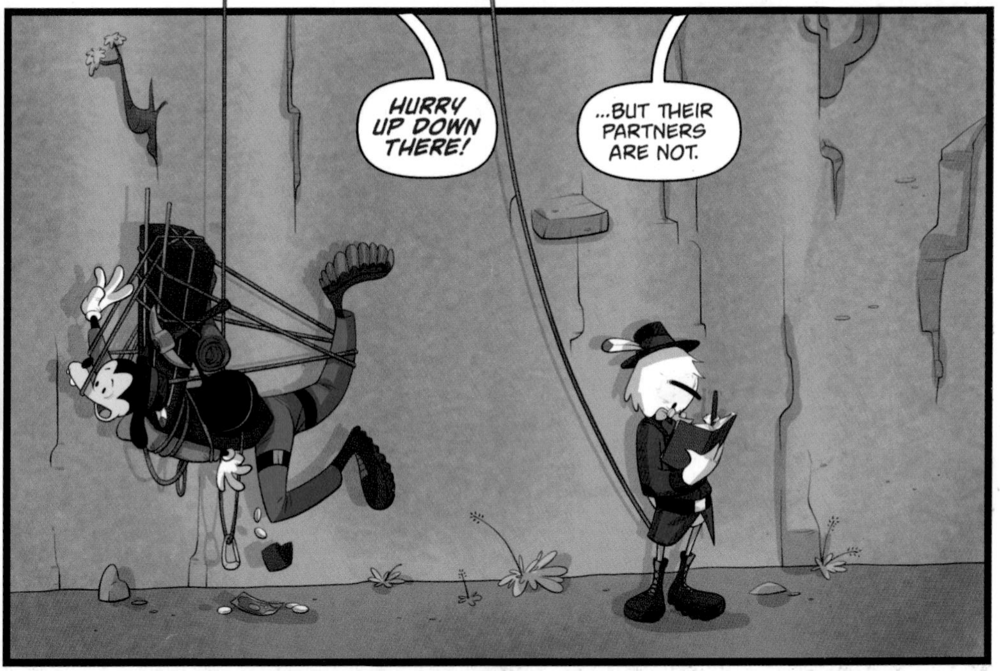
HURRY UP DOWN THERE!
...BUT THEIR PARTNERS ARE NOT.

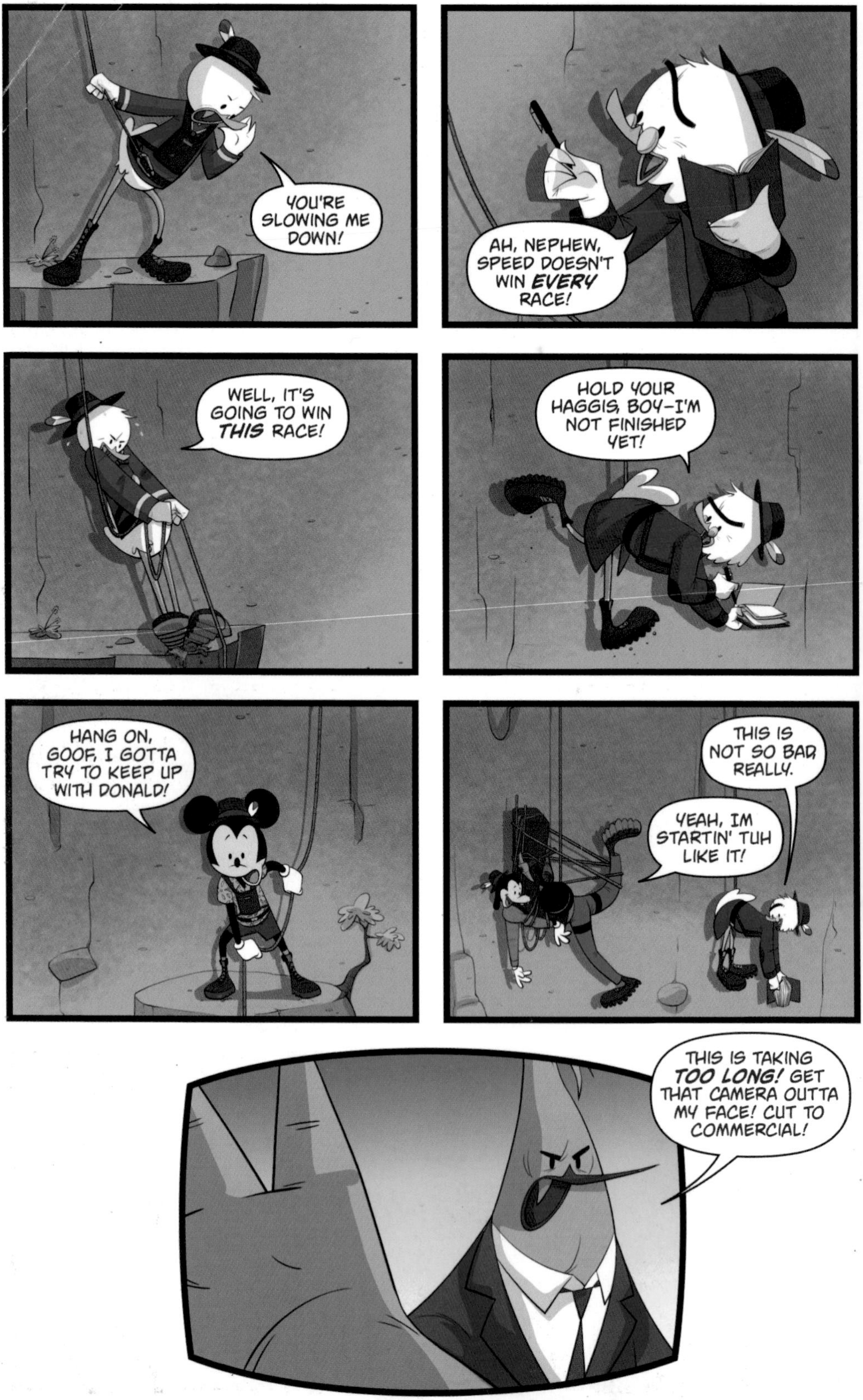
YOU'RE SLOWING ME DOWN!
AH, NEPHEW, SPEED DOESN'T WIN EVERY RACE!
WELL, IT'S GOING TO WIN THIS RACE!
HOLD YOUR HAGGIS, BOY—I'M NOT FINISHED YET!
HANG ON, GOOF, I GOTTA TRY TO KEEP UP WITH DONALD!
THIS IS NOT SO BAD REALLY.
YEAH, IM STARTIN' TUH LIKE IT!
THIS IS TAKING TOO LONG! GET THAT CAMERA OUTTA MY FACE! CUT TO COMMERCIAL!

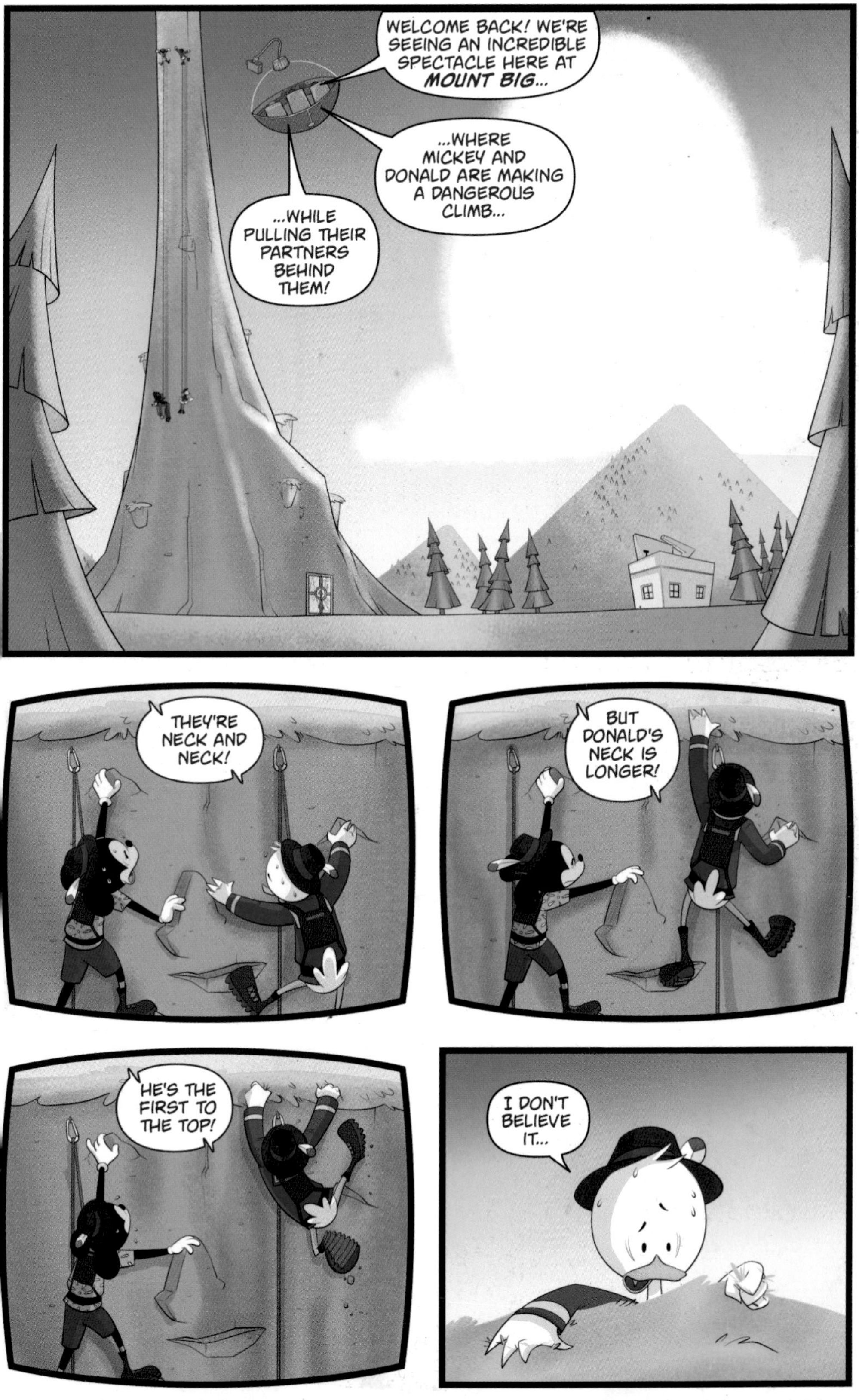
WELCOME BACK! WE'RE SEEING AN INCREDIBLE SPECTACLE HERE AT MOUNT BIG...
...WHERE MICKEY AND DONALD ARE MAKING A DANGEROUS CLIMB...
...WHILE PULLING THEIR PARTNERS BEHIND THEM!
THEY'RE NECK AND NECK!
BUT DONALD'S NECK IS LONGER!
HE'S THE FIRST TO THE TOP!
I DON'T BELIEVE IT...

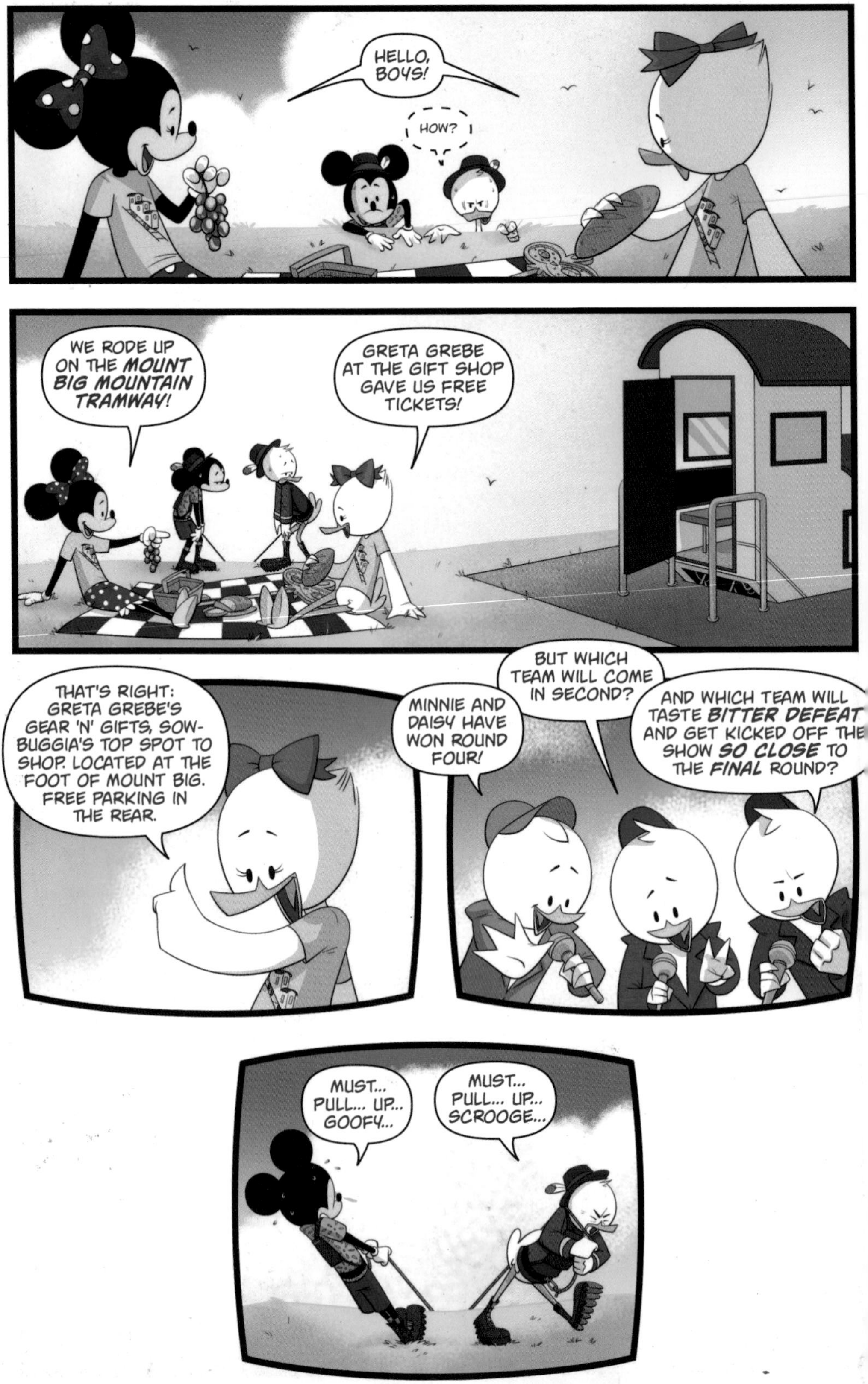
HELLO, BOYS!
HOW?
WE RODE UP ON THE MOUNT BIG MOUNTAIN TRAMWAY!
GRETA GREBE AT THE GIFT SHOP GAVE US FREE TICKETS!
THAT'S RIGHT: GRETA GREBE'S GEAR 'N' GIFTS, SOW-BUGGIA'S TOP SPOT TO SHOP. LOCATED AT THE FOOT OF MOUNT BIG. FREE PARKING IN THE REAR.
MINNIE AND DAISY HAVE WON ROUND FOUR!
BUT WHICH TEAM WILL COME IN SECOND?
AND WHICH TEAM WILL TASTE BITTER DEFEAT AND GET KICKED OFF THE SHOW SO CLOSE TO THE FINAL ROUND?
MUST... PULL... UP... GOOFY...
MUST... PULL... UP... SCROOGE...

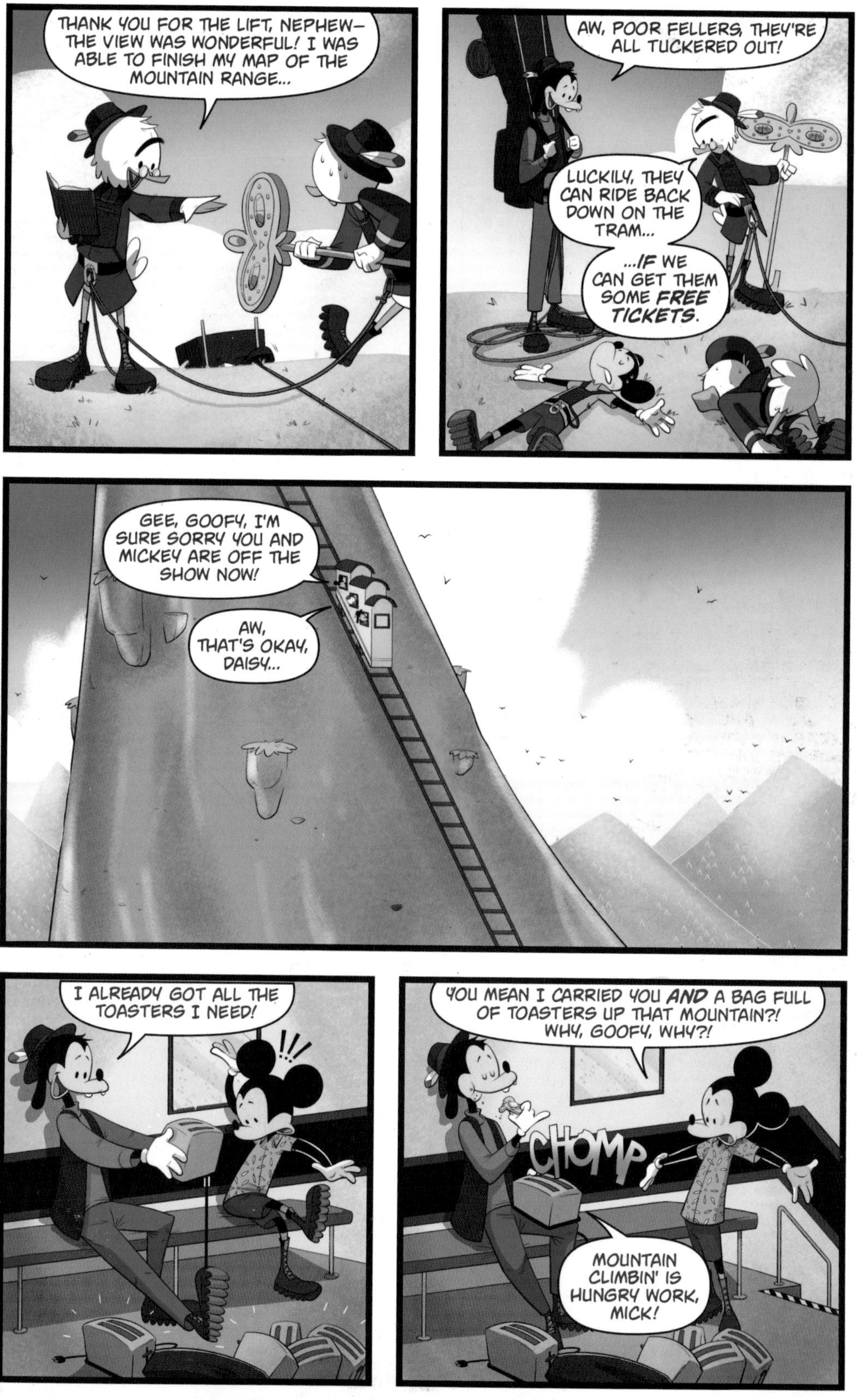
THANK YOU FOR THE LIFT, NEPHEW— THE VIEW WAS WONDERFUL! I WAS ABLE TO FINISH MY MAP OF THE MOUNTAIN RANGE...
AW, POOR FELLERS, THEY'RE ALL TUCKERED OUT!
LUCKILY, THEY CAN RIDE BACK DOWN ON THE TRAM...
...IF WE CAN GET THEM SOME FREE TICKETS.
GEE, GOOFY, I'M SURE SORRY YOU AND MICKEY ARE OFF THE SHOW NOW!
AW, THAT'S OKAY, DAISY...
I ALREADY GOT ALL THE TOASTERS I NEED!
!!!
YOU MEAN I CARRIED YOU AND A BAG FULL OF TOASTERS UP THAT MOUNTAIN?! WHY, GOOFY, WHY?!
CHOMP
MOUNTAIN CLIMBIN' IS HUNGRY WORK, MICK!

YEP, MORE TOASTERS...

DON'T WORRY... THE *BIG* PRIZE IS JUST AHEAD IN THE FINAL ROUND! COMING UP RIGHT AFTER THIS COMMERCIAL!

IT BETTER BE, BUB!

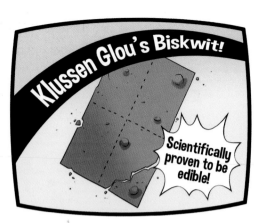

Klussen Glou's Biskwit!

Scientifically proven to be edible!

UNCA DONALD, WE GOTTA TALK TO YOU DURING THIS COMMERCIAL! JAY BLUEJAY IS *DEFINITELY* UP TO SOMETHING!

WE'VE BEEN WATCHING HIM... HE DOESN'T EVEN CARE ABOUT THE SHOW, HE JUST WANTS THOSE *KEYS*!

HE'S TRICKING ALL OF YOU! WE THINK YOU SHOULD DROP OUT!

DROP OUT? DIDN'T YOU HEAR HIM? THE *BIG* PRIZE IS JUST AHEAD!

YEAH, WE HEARD HIM, BUT WE DON'T *BELIEVE* HIM!

COMMERCIAL'S ALMOST OVER, I GOTTA GO!

I GUESS THAT MEANS WE GOTTA GO, TOO...

...AND BE READY TO HELP UNCA DONALD...

...WHEN JAY BLUEJAY MAKES HIS MOVE!

PLUS, WE'VE STILL GOT A JOB TO DO!

WE'RE BACK ON THE AIR IN...

...FIVE... FOUR... THREE... TWO... ONE...

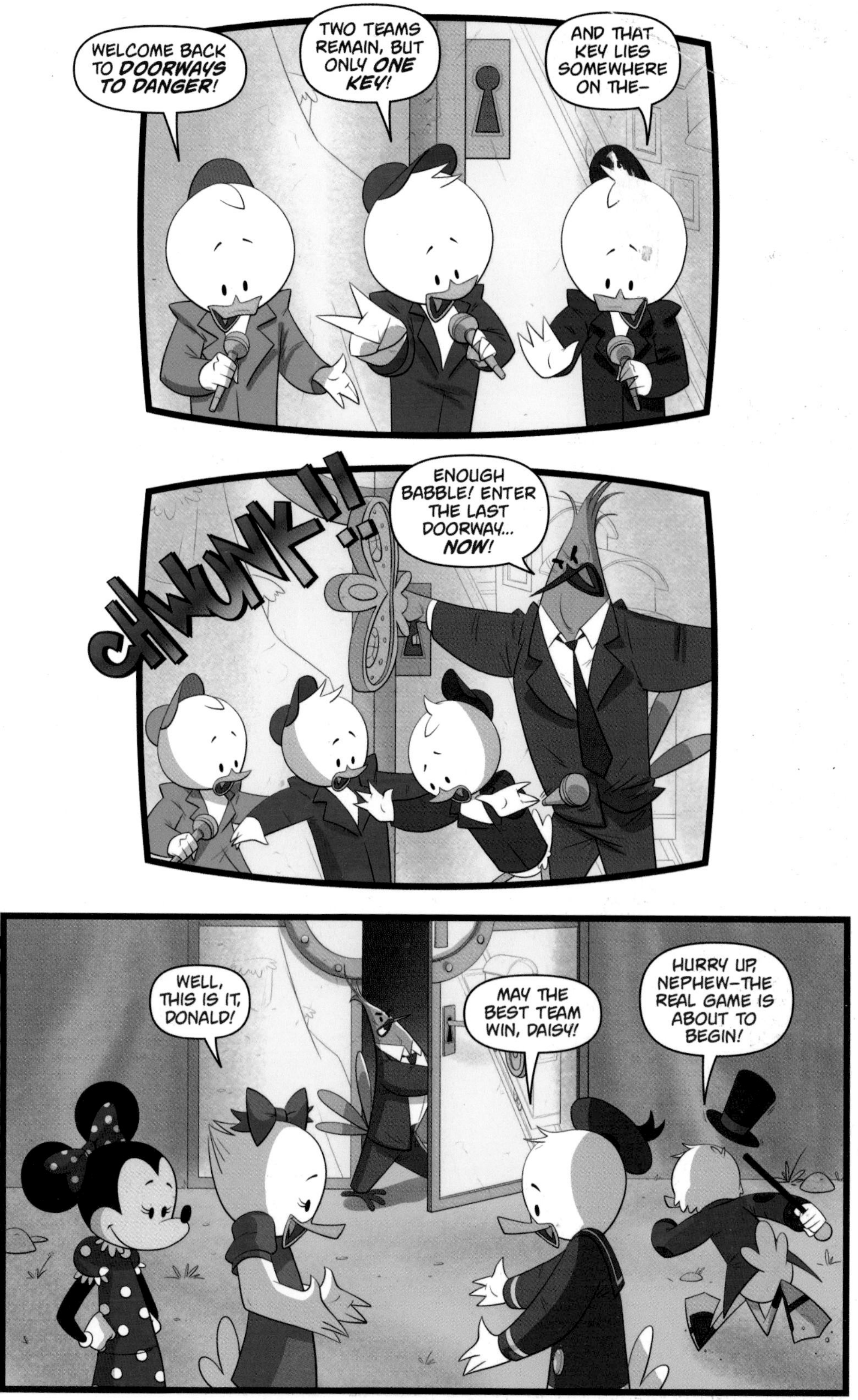
WELCOME BACK TO *DOORWAYS TO DANGER*!
TWO TEAMS REMAIN, BUT ONLY *ONE KEY*!
AND THAT KEY LIES SOMEWHERE ON THE–
CHUNK!!
ENOUGH BABBLE! ENTER THE LAST DOORWAY... *NOW*!
WELL, THIS IS IT, DONALD!
MAY THE BEST TEAM WIN, DAISY!
HURRY UP, NEPHEW–THE REAL GAME IS ABOUT TO BEGIN!

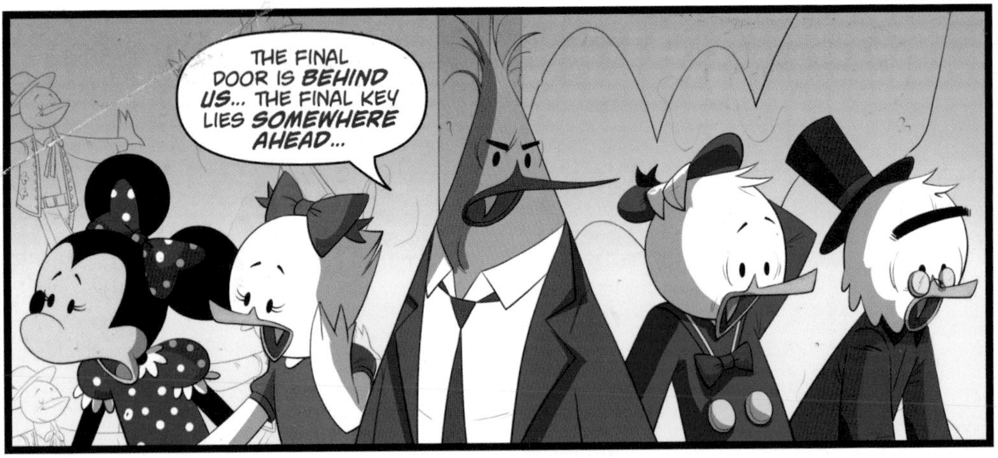
THE FINAL DOOR IS BEHIND US... THE FINAL KEY LIES SOMEWHERE AHEAD...

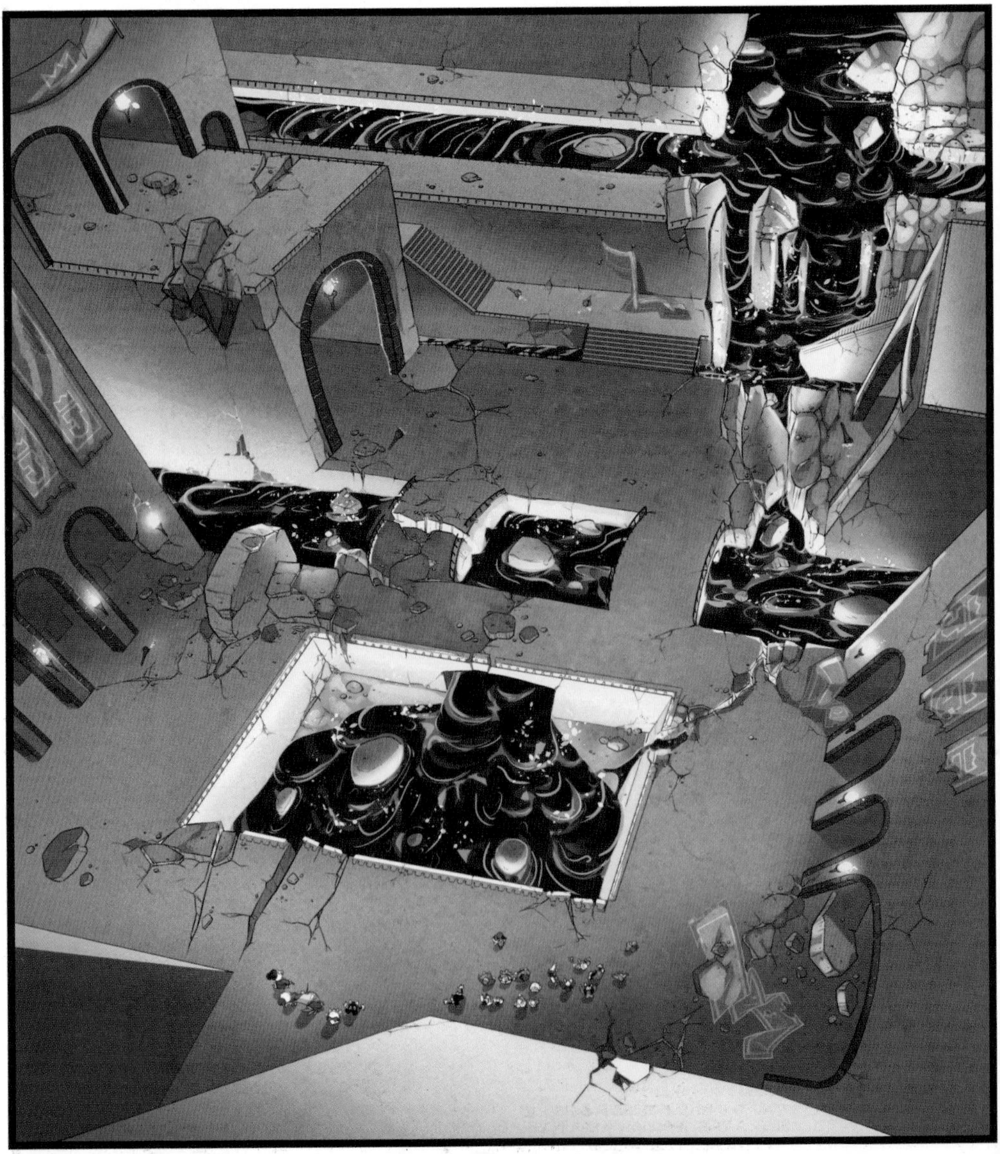

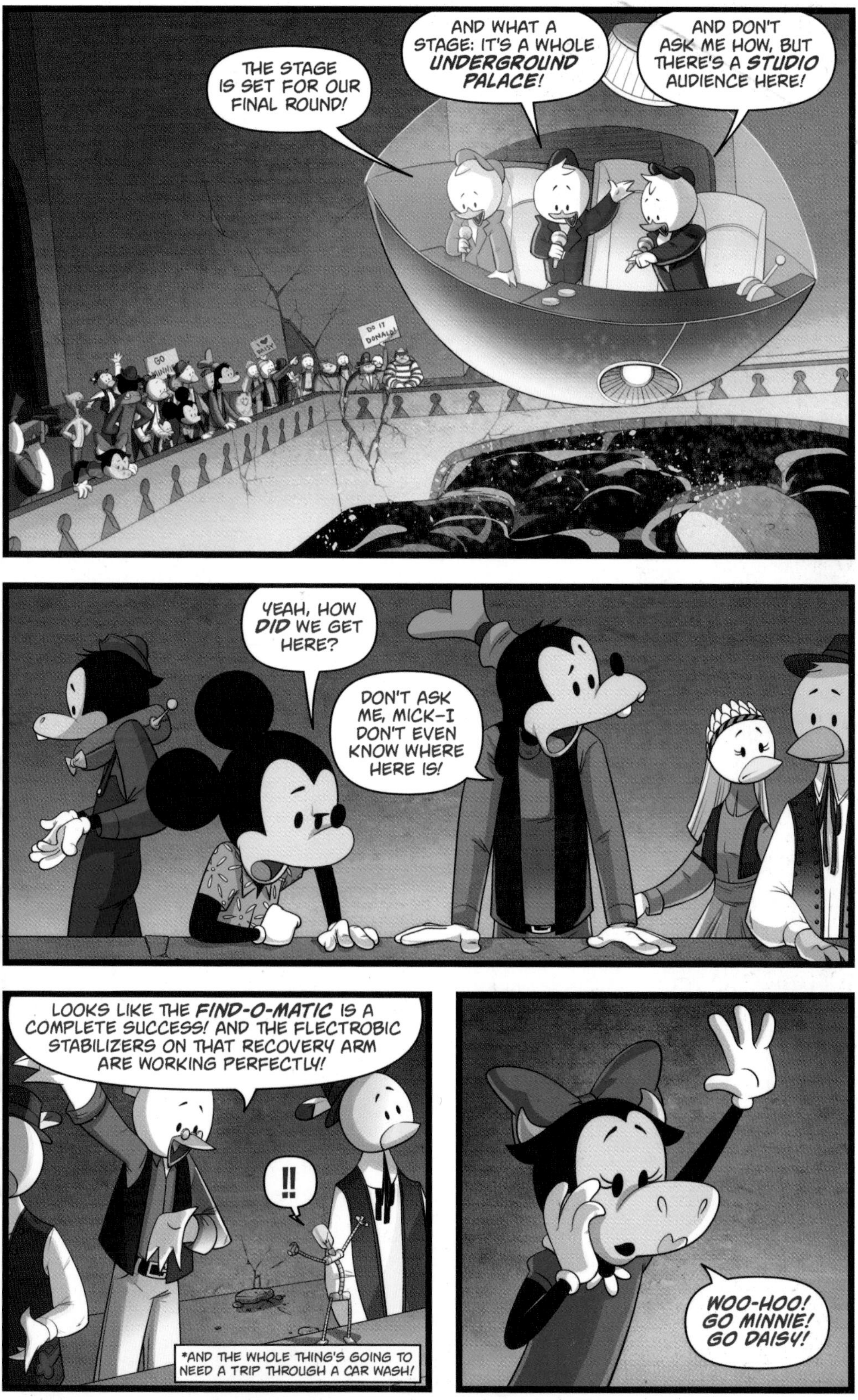
THE STAGE IS SET FOR OUR FINAL ROUND!
AND WHAT A STAGE: IT'S A WHOLE *UNDERGROUND PALACE*!
AND DON'T ASK ME HOW, BUT THERE'S A *STUDIO* AUDIENCE HERE!
YEAH, HOW *DID* WE GET HERE?
DON'T ASK ME, MICK–I DON'T EVEN KNOW WHERE HERE IS!
LOOKS LIKE THE *FIND-O-MATIC* IS A COMPLETE SUCCESS! AND THE FLECTROBIC STABILIZERS ON THAT RECOVERY ARM ARE WORKING PERFECTLY!
!!
*AND THE WHOLE THING'S GOING TO NEED A TRIP THROUGH A CAR WASH!
WOO-HOO! GO MINNIE! GO DAISY!

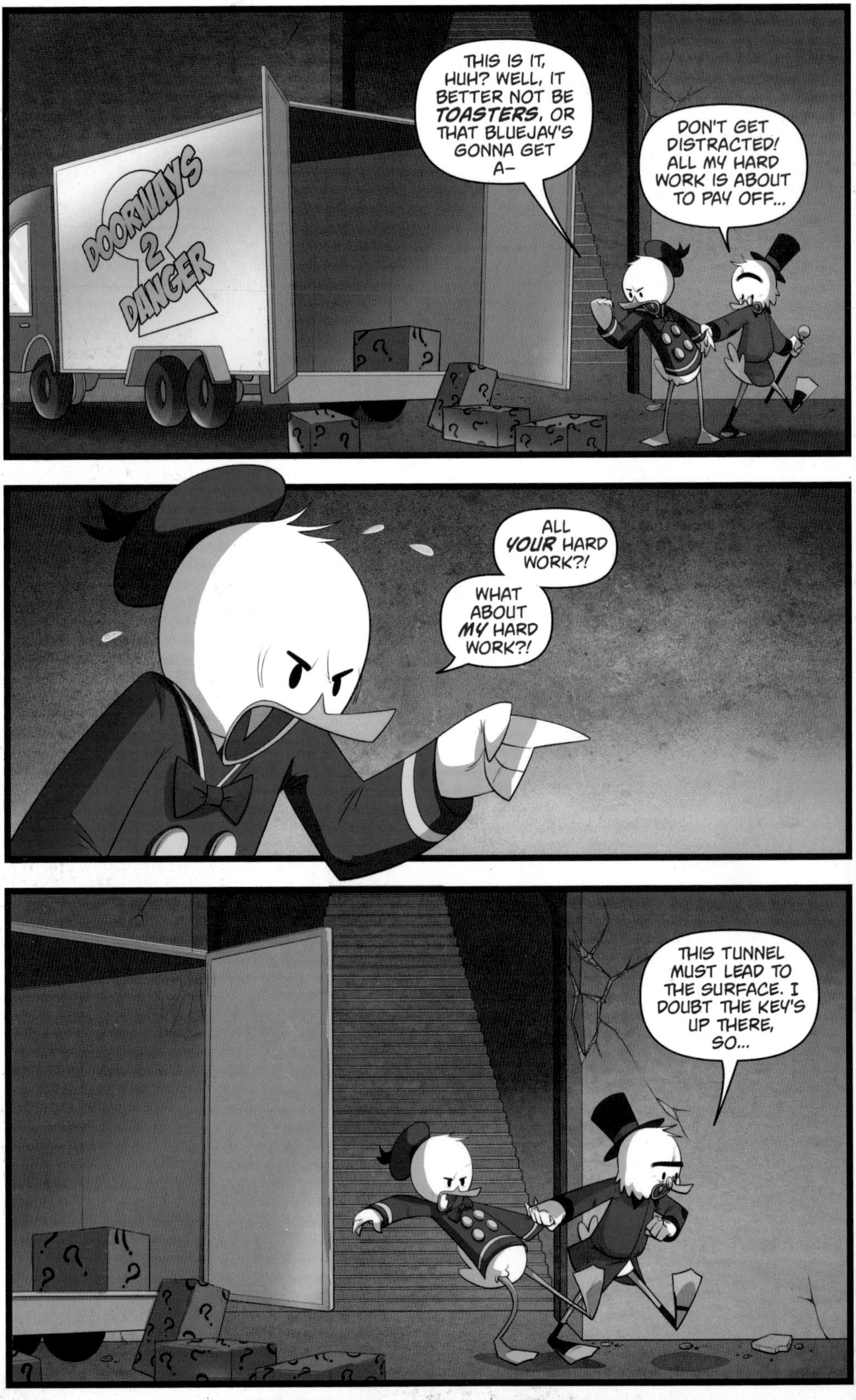
THIS IS IT, HUH? WELL, IT BETTER NOT BE TOASTERS, OR THAT BLUEJAY'S GONNA GET A–
DON'T GET DISTRACTED! ALL MY HARD WORK IS ABOUT TO PAY OFF...
DOORWAYS 2 DANGER
ALL YOUR HARD WORK?!
WHAT ABOUT MY HARD WORK?!
THIS TUNNEL MUST LEAD TO THE SURFACE. I DOUBT THE KEY'S UP THERE, SO...

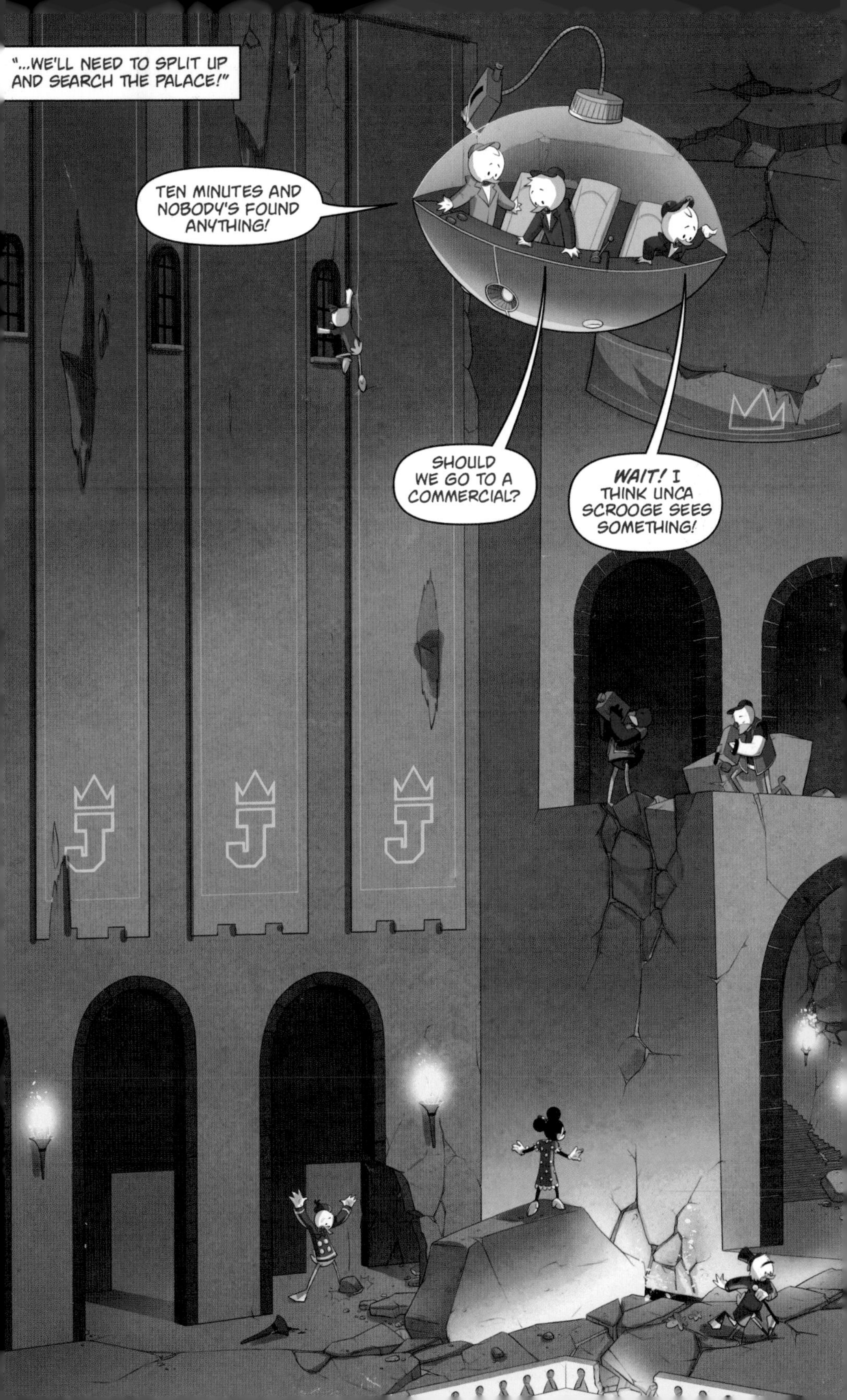
"...WE'LL NEED TO SPLIT UP AND SEARCH THE PALACE!"
TEN MINUTES AND NOBODY'S FOUND ANYTHING!
SHOULD WE GO TO A COMMERCIAL?
WAIT! I THINK UNCA SCROOGE SEES SOMETHING!

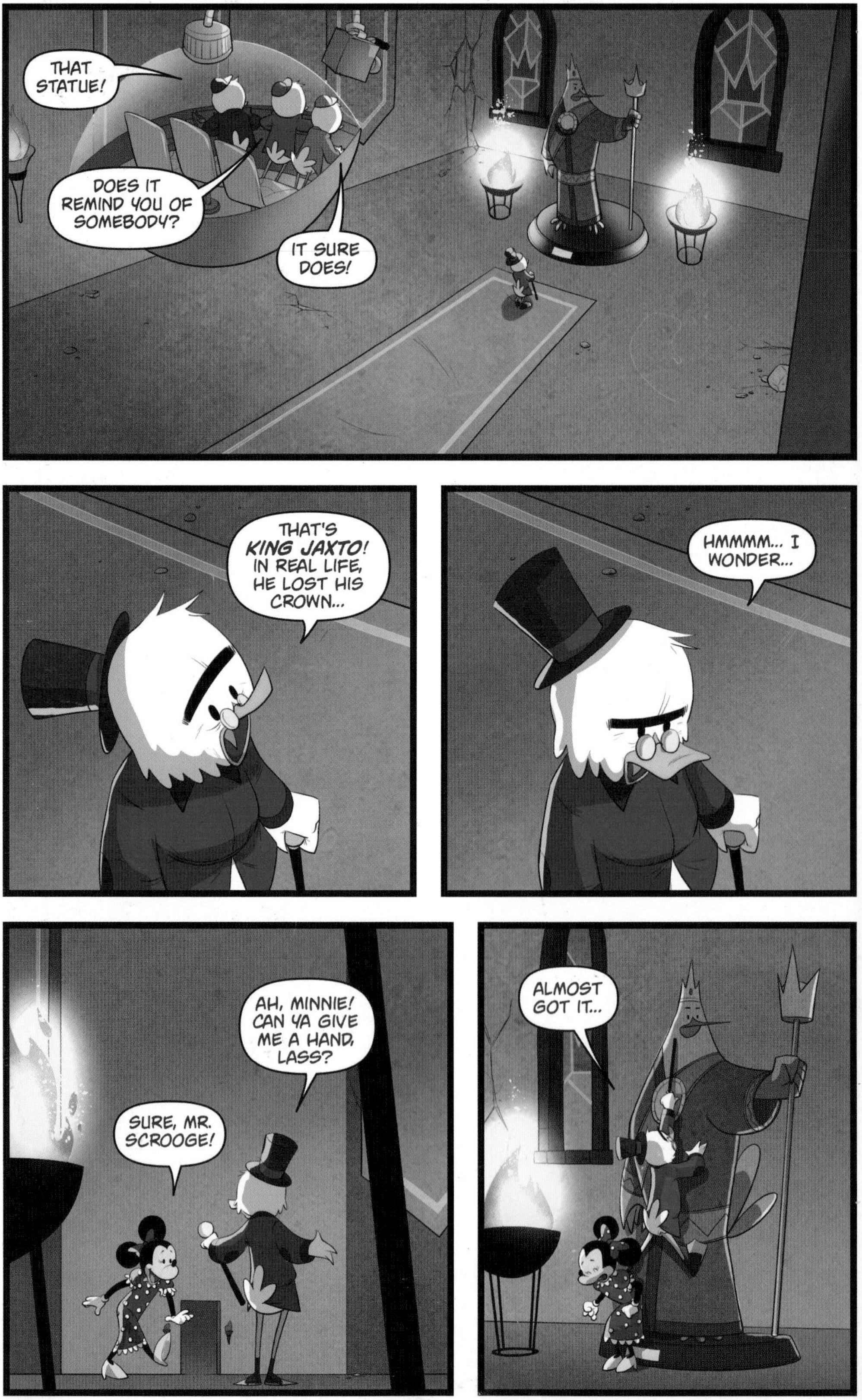
THAT STATUE!
DOES IT REMIND YOU OF SOMEBODY?
IT SURE DOES!
THAT'S *KING JAXTO*! IN REAL LIFE, HE LOST HIS CROWN...
HMMMM... I WONDER...
AH, MINNIE! CAN YA GIVE ME A HAND, LASS?
SURE, MR. SCROOGE!
ALMOST GOT IT...

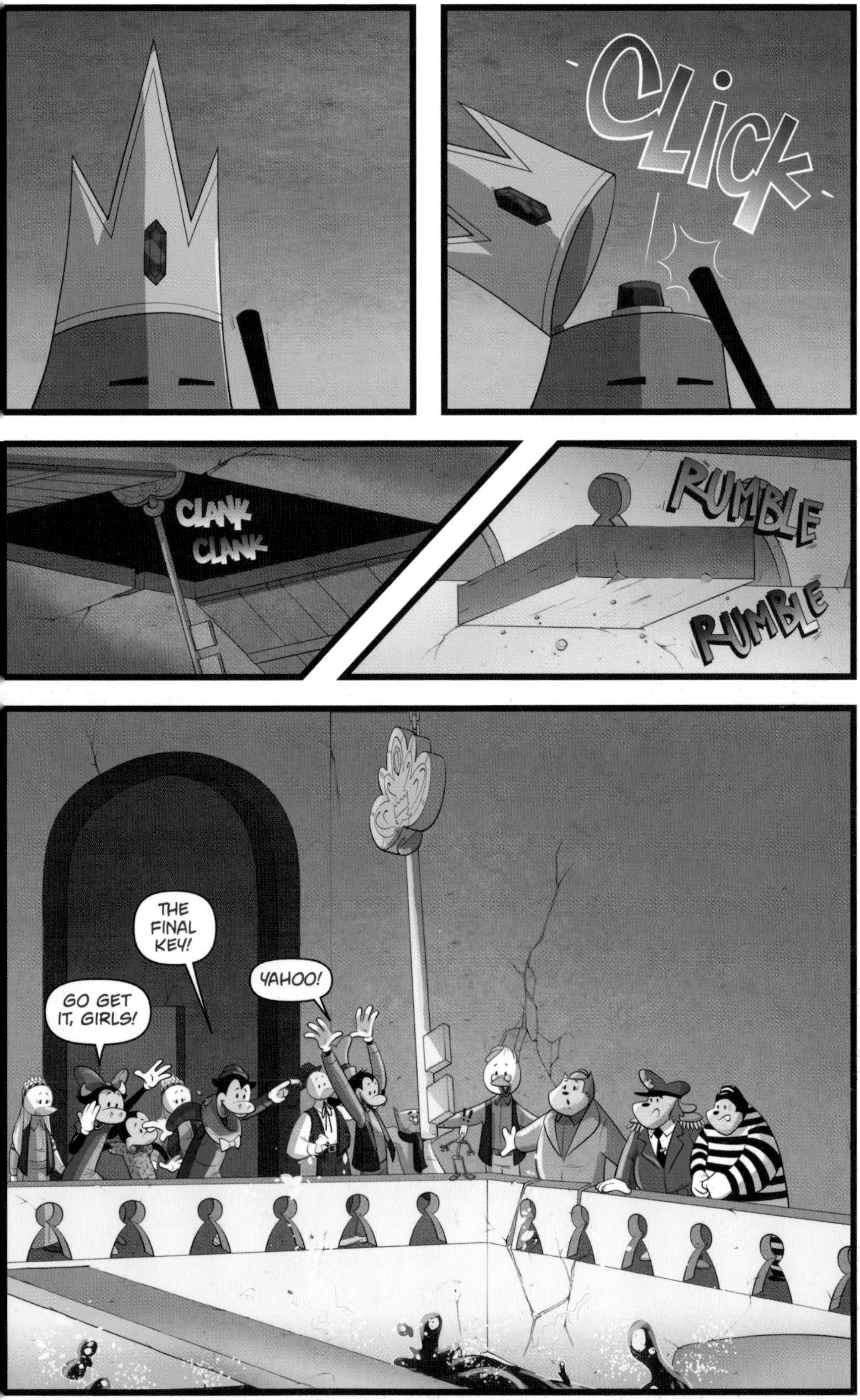
CLICK
CLANK
CLANK
RUMBLE
RUMBLE
THE FINAL KEY!
GO GET IT, GIRLS!
YAHOO!

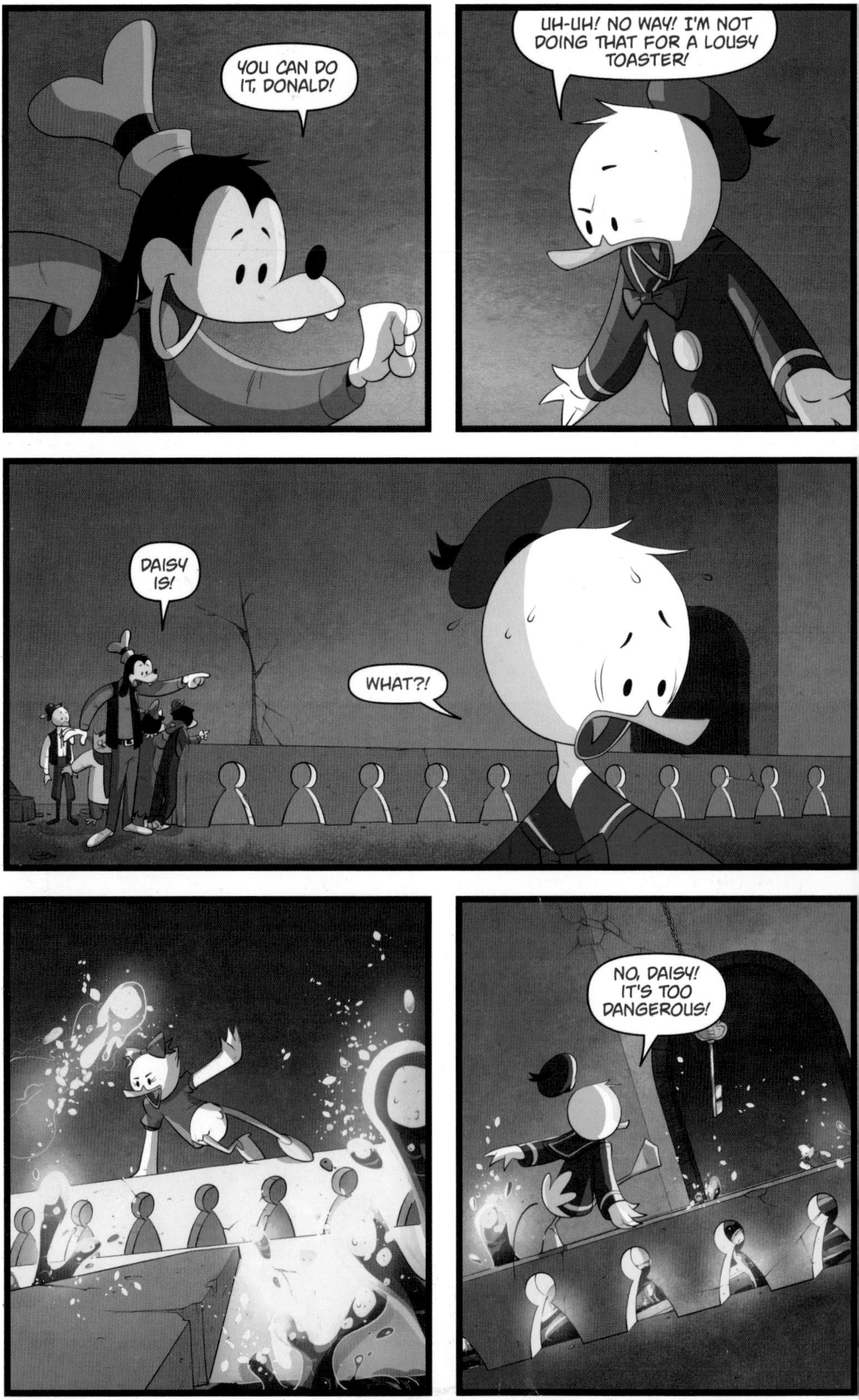
YOU CAN DO IT, DONALD!
UH-UH! NO WAY! I'M NOT DOING THAT FOR A LOUSY TOASTER!
DAISY IS!
WHAT?!
NO, DAISY! IT'S TOO DANGEROUS!

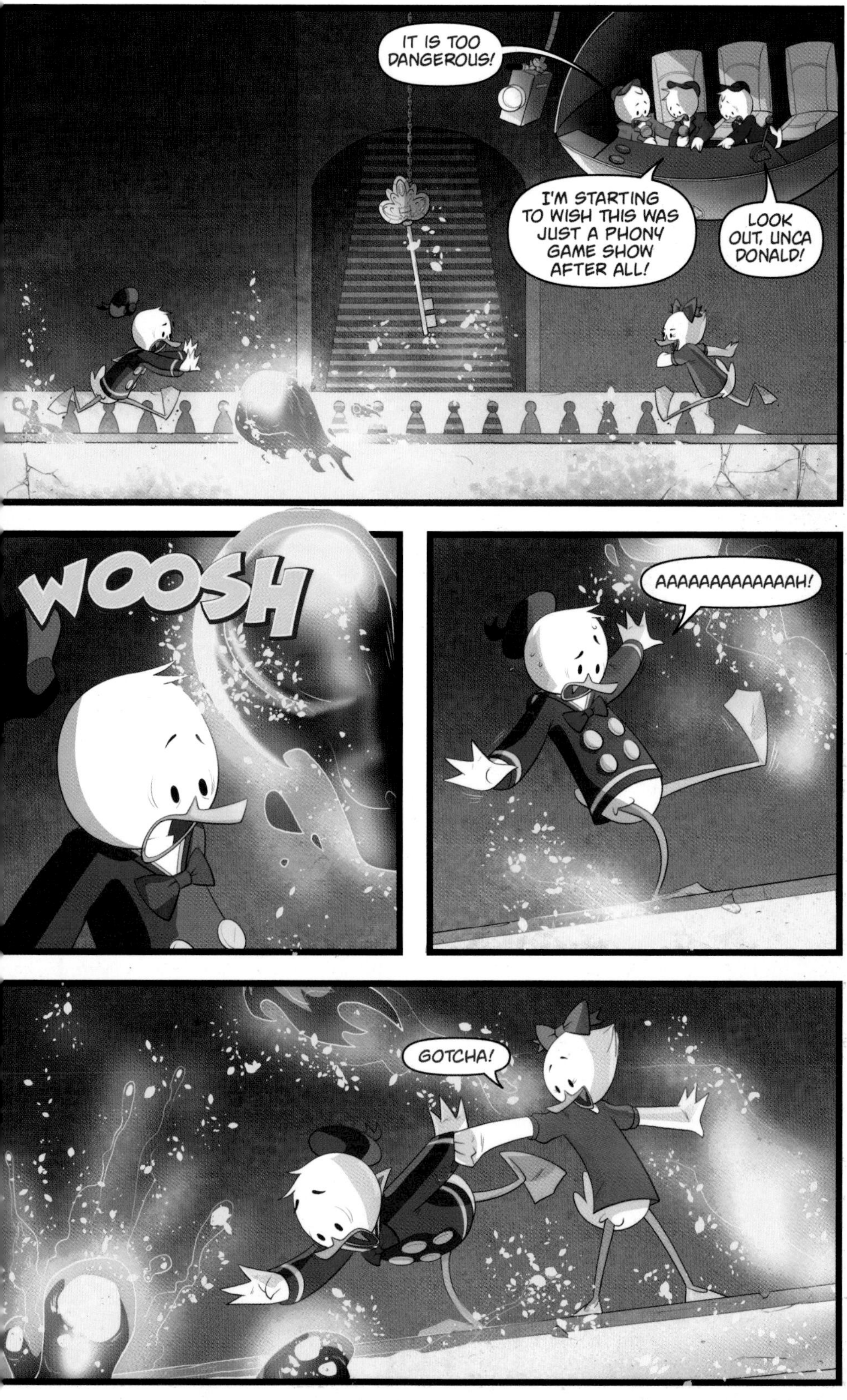
IT IS TOO DANGEROUS!
I'M STARTING TO WISH THIS WAS JUST A PHONY GAME SHOW AFTER ALL!
LOOK OUT, UNCA DONALD!
WOOSH
AAAAAAAAAAAAAH!
GOTCHA!

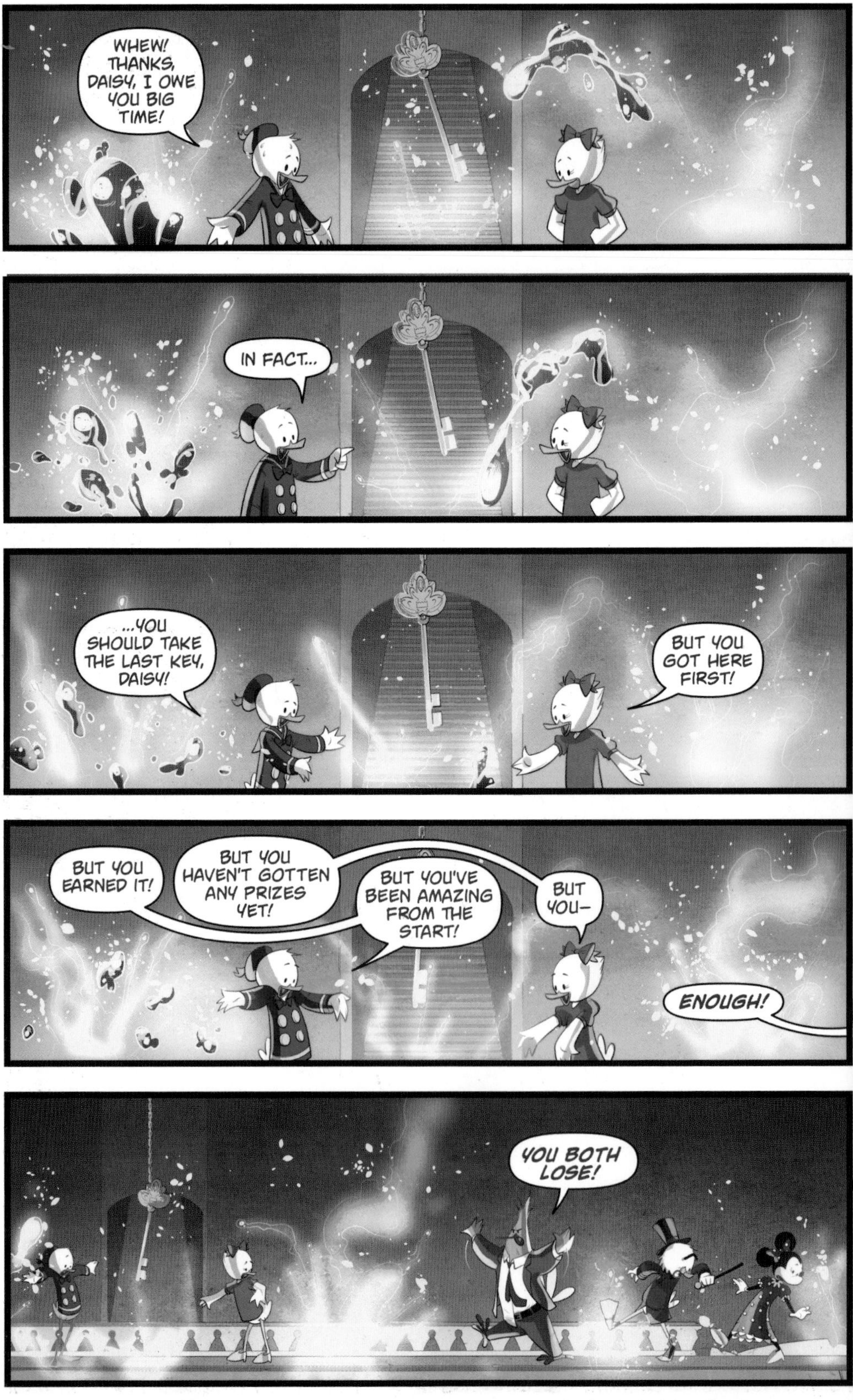

WHEW! THANKS, DAISY, I OWE YOU BIG TIME!
IN FACT...
...YOU SHOULD TAKE THE LAST KEY, DAISY!
BUT YOU GOT HERE FIRST!
BUT YOU EARNED IT!
BUT YOU HAVEN'T GOTTEN ANY PRIZES YET!
BUT YOU'VE BEEN AMAZING FROM THE START!
BUT YOU–
ENOUGH!
YOU BOTH LOSE!

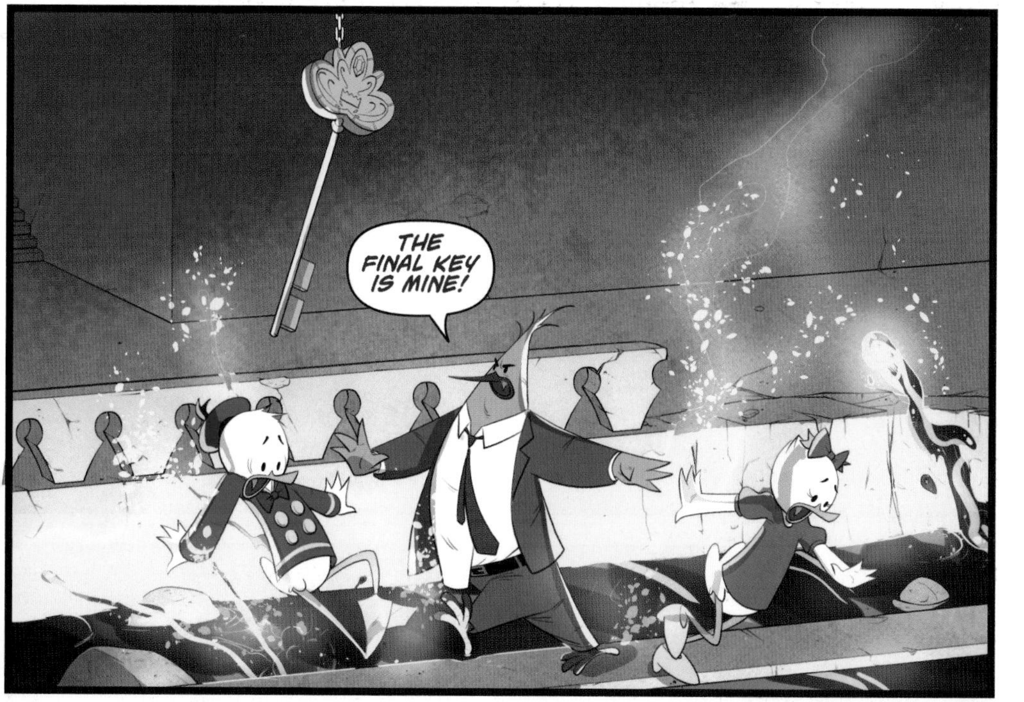
THE FINAL KEY IS MINE!

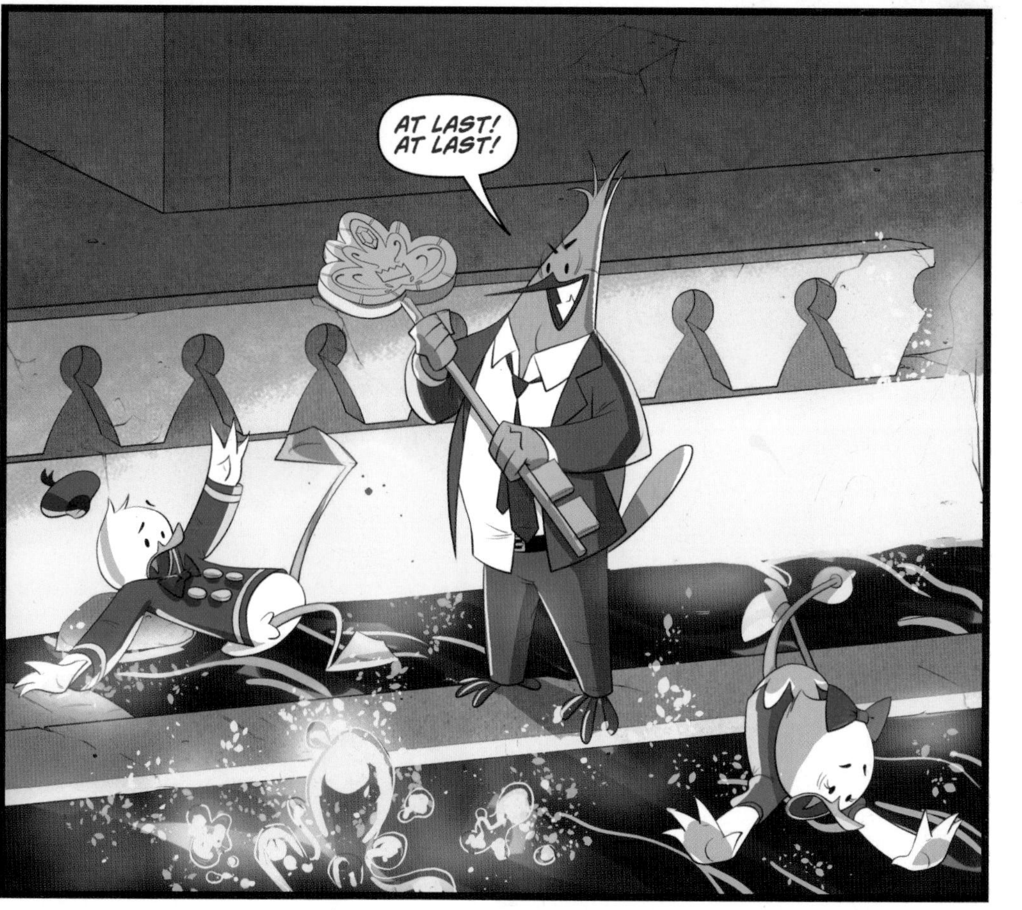
AT LAST! AT LAST!

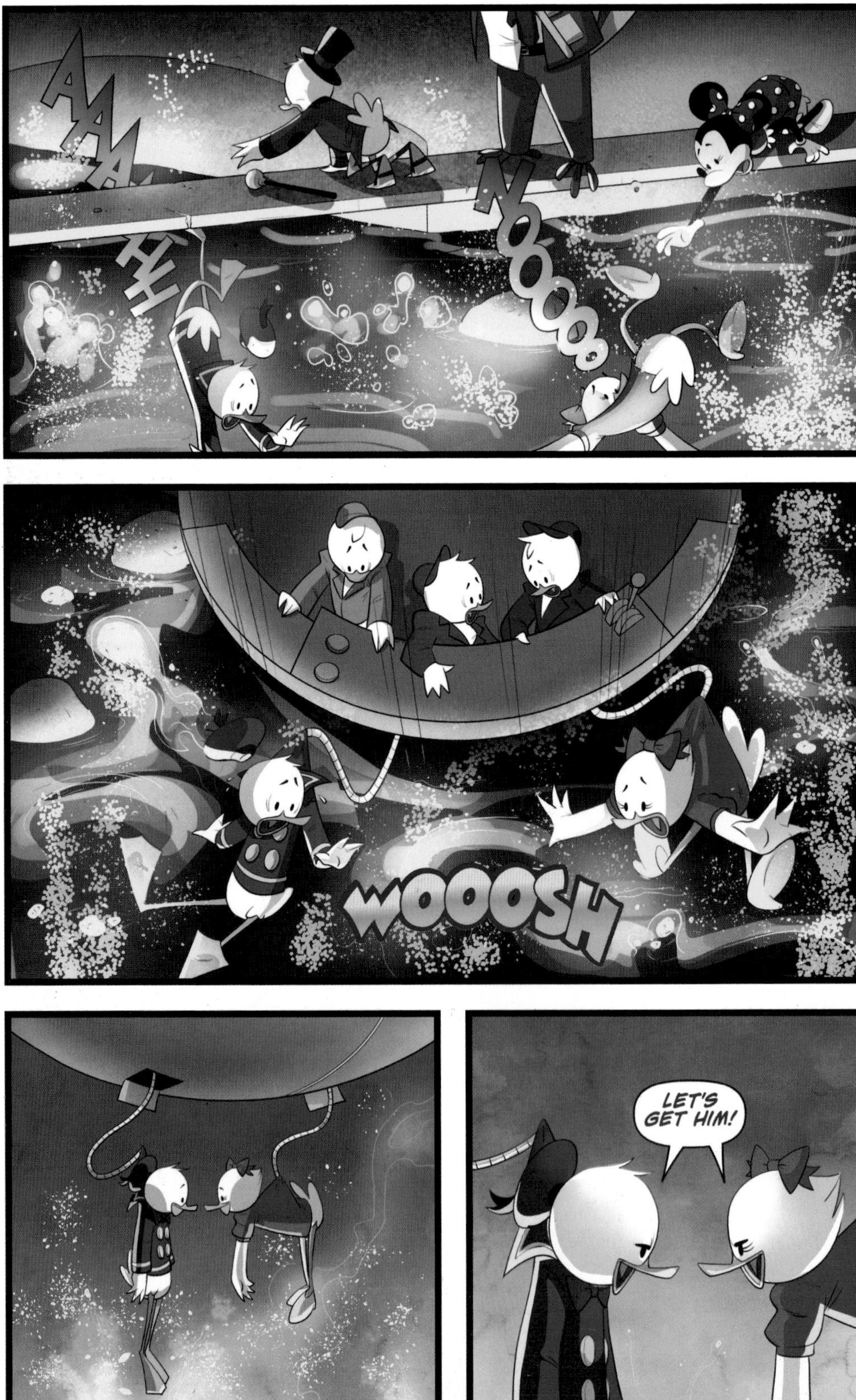
AAAA
EEEE
NOOOOO
WOOOSH
LET'S GET HIM!

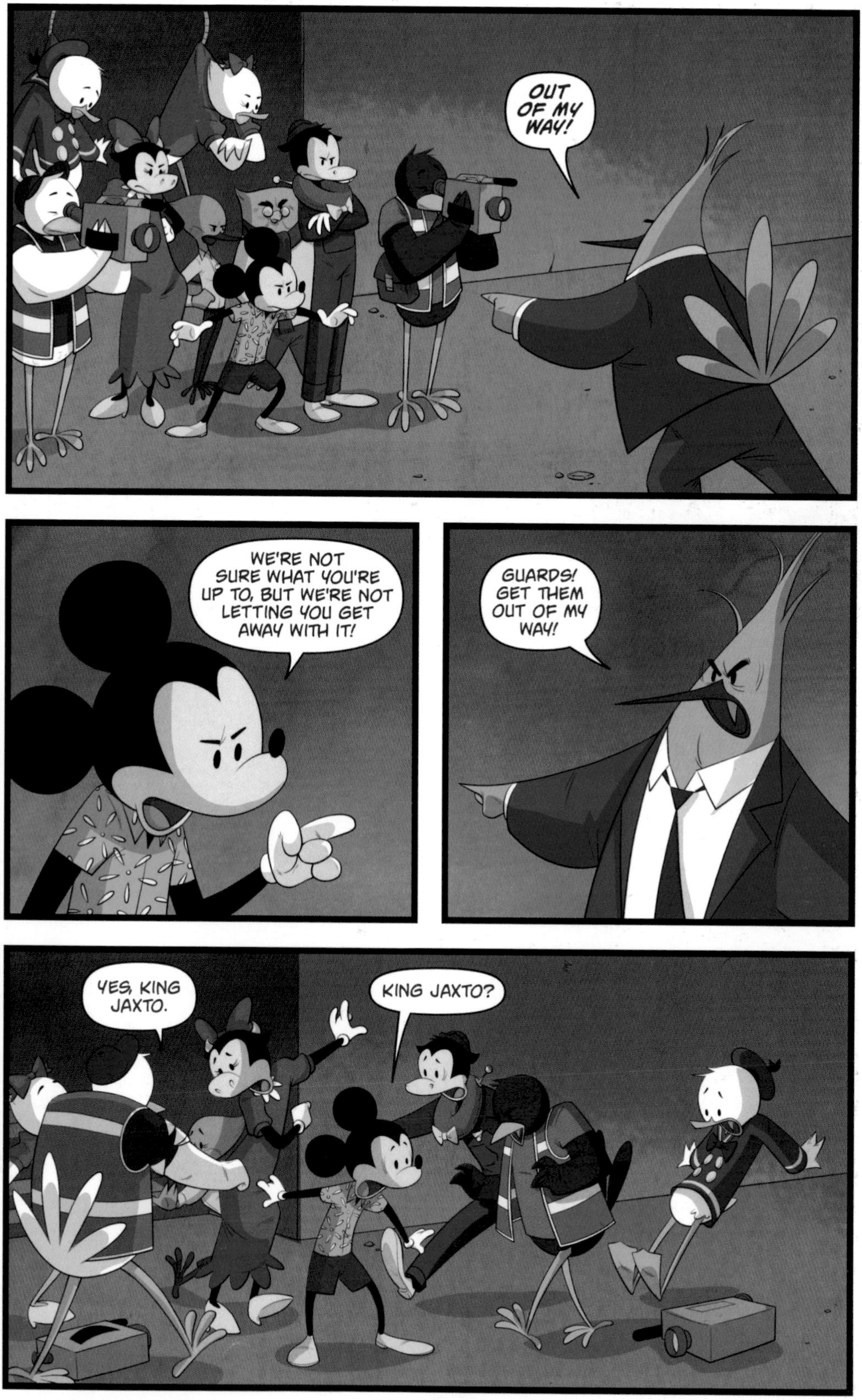
OUT OF MY WAY!
WE'RE NOT SURE WHAT YOU'RE UP TO, BUT WE'RE NOT LETTING YOU GET AWAY WITH IT!
GUARDS! GET THEM OUT OF MY WAY!
YES, KING JAXTO.
KING JAXTO?

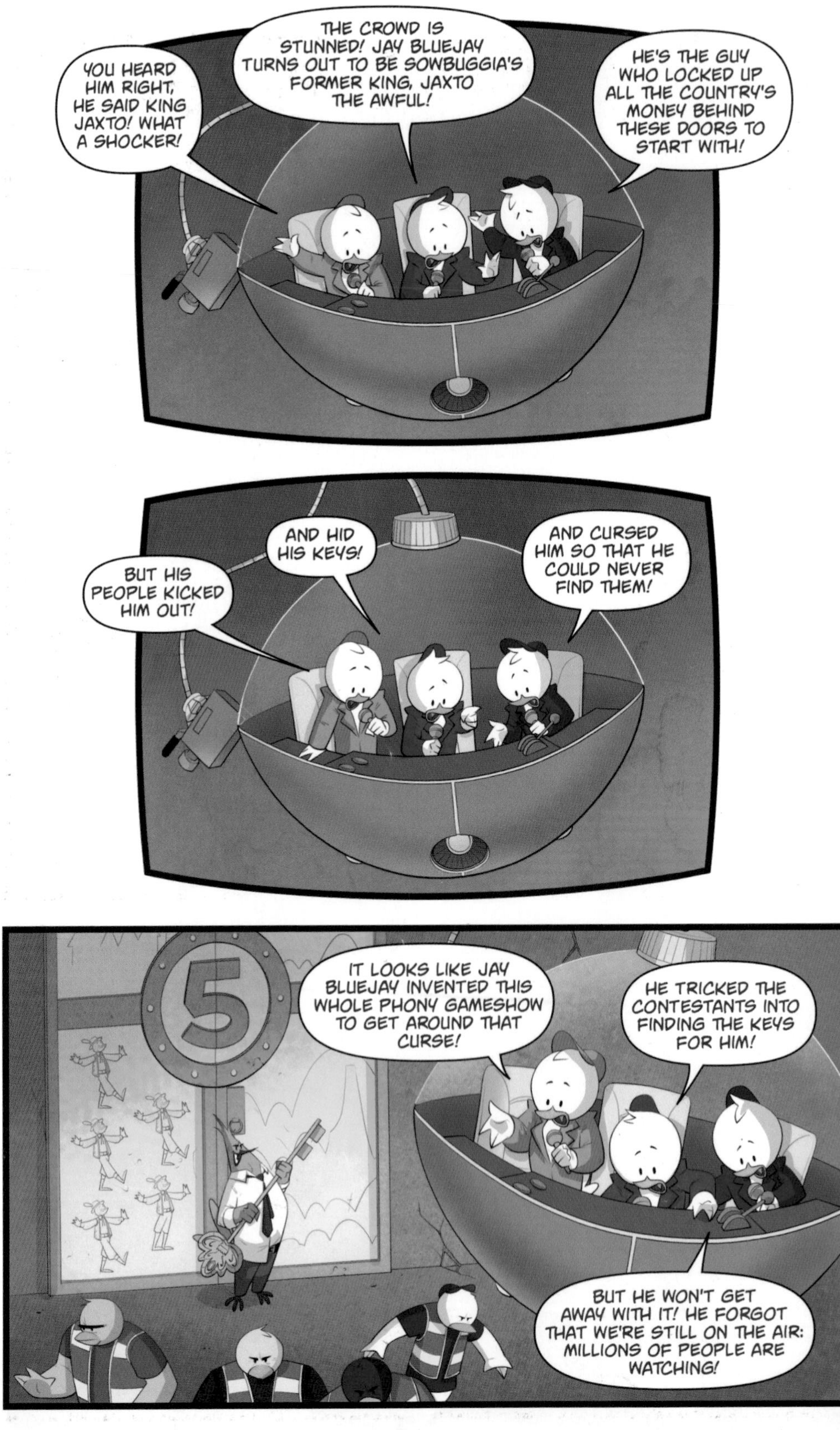
YOU HEARD HIM RIGHT, HE SAID KING JAXTO! WHAT A SHOCKER!
THE CROWD IS STUNNED! JAY BLUEJAY TURNS OUT TO BE SOWBUGGIA'S FORMER KING, JAXTO THE AWFUL!
HE'S THE GUY WHO LOCKED UP ALL THE COUNTRY'S MONEY BEHIND THESE DOORS TO START WITH!
BUT HIS PEOPLE KICKED HIM OUT!
AND HID HIS KEYS!
AND CURSED HIM SO THAT HE COULD NEVER FIND THEM!
5
IT LOOKS LIKE JAY BLUEJAY INVENTED THIS WHOLE PHONY GAMESHOW TO GET AROUND THAT CURSE!
HE TRICKED THE CONTESTANTS INTO FINDING THE KEYS FOR HIM!
BUT HE WON'T GET AWAY WITH IT! HE FORGOT THAT WE'RE STILL ON THE AIR: MILLIONS OF PEOPLE ARE WATCHING!

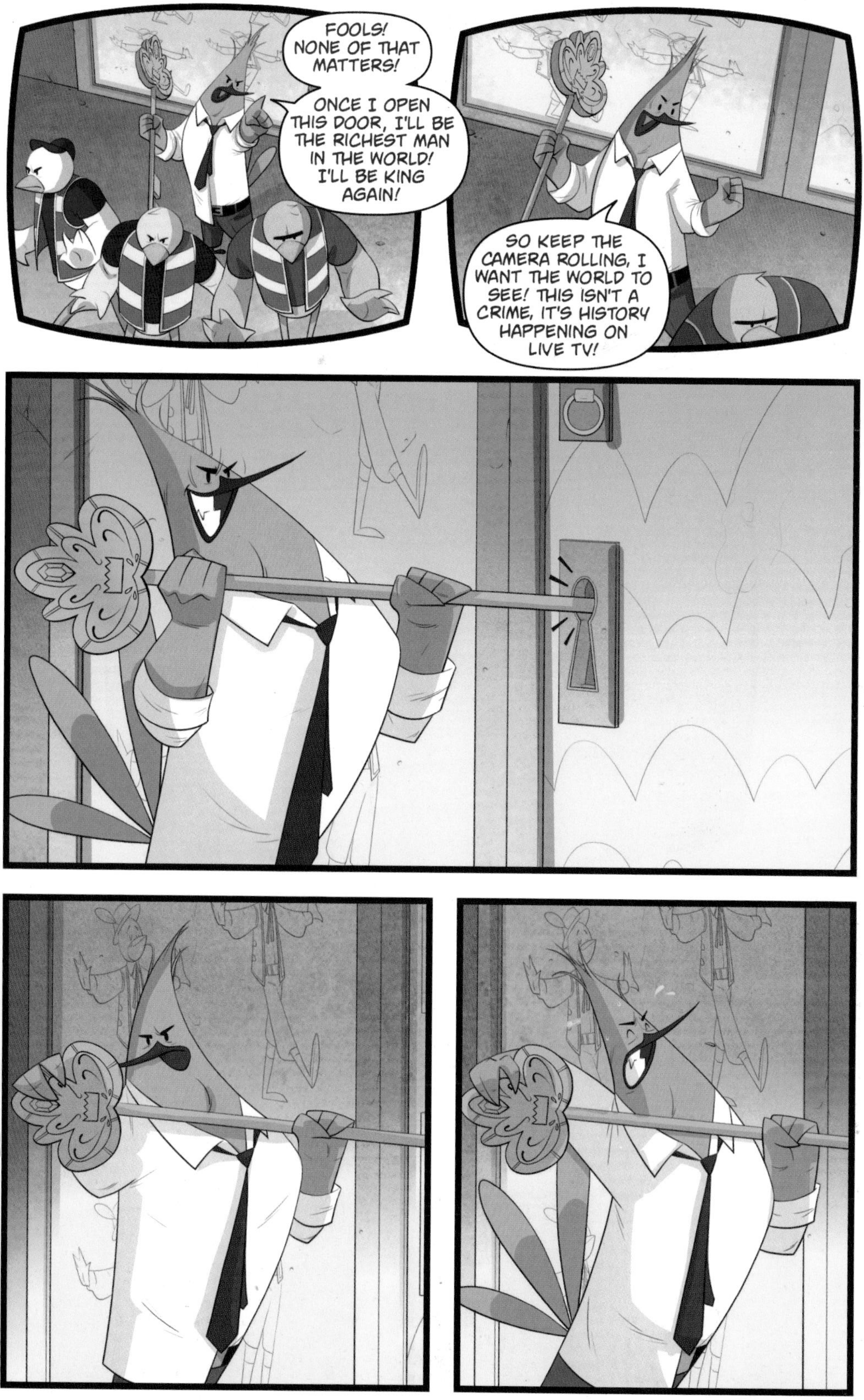
FOOLS! NONE OF THAT MATTERS!
ONCE I OPEN THIS DOOR, I'LL BE THE RICHEST MAN IN THE WORLD! I'LL BE KING AGAIN!
SO KEEP THE CAMERA ROLLING, I WANT THE WORLD TO SEE! THIS ISN'T A CRIME, IT'S HISTORY HAPPENING ON LIVE TV!

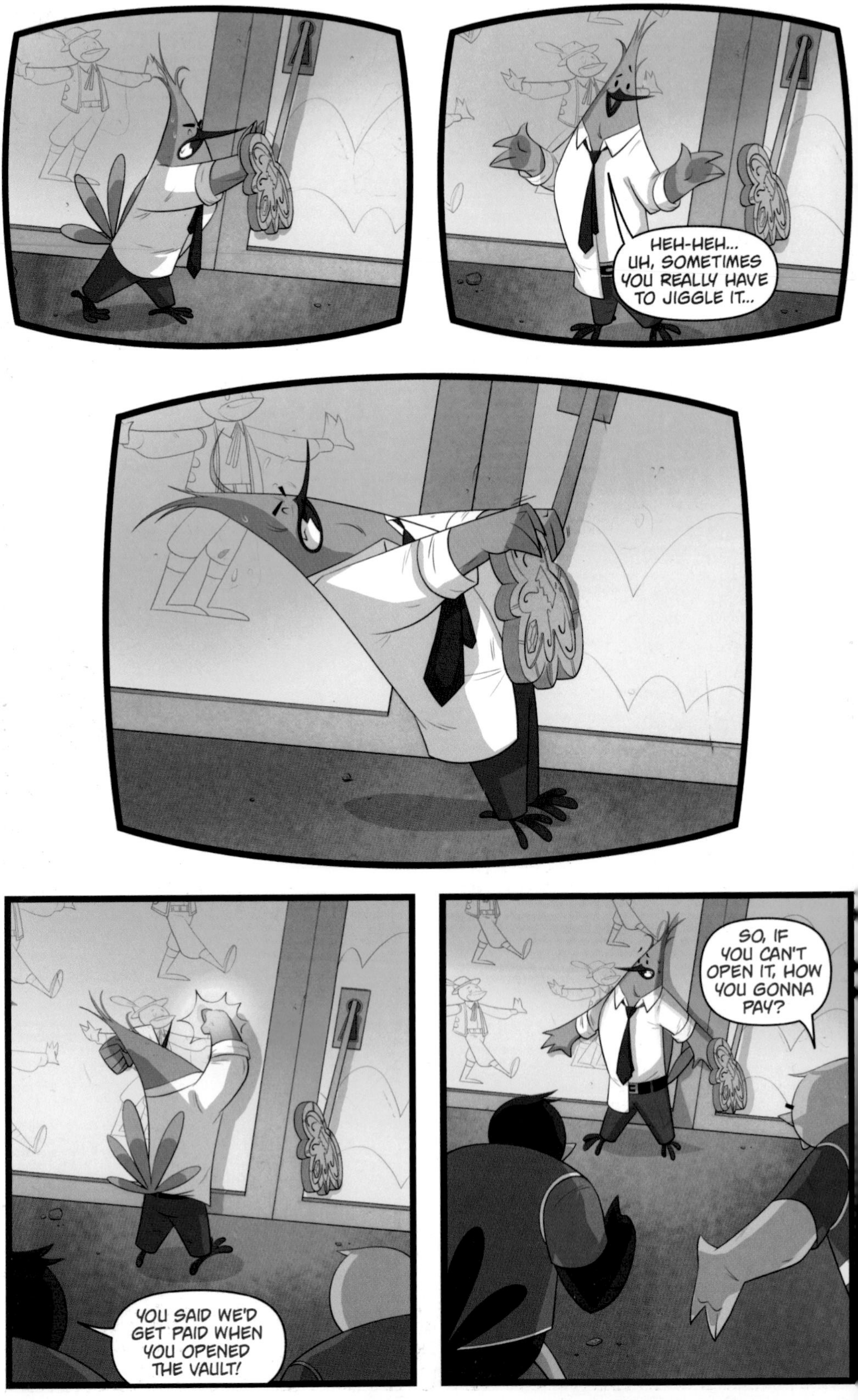
HEH-HEH... UH, SOMETIMES YOU REALLY HAVE TO JIGGLE IT...
YOU SAID WE'D GET PAID WHEN YOU OPENED THE VAULT!
SO, IF YOU CAN'T OPEN IT, HOW YOU GONNA PAY?

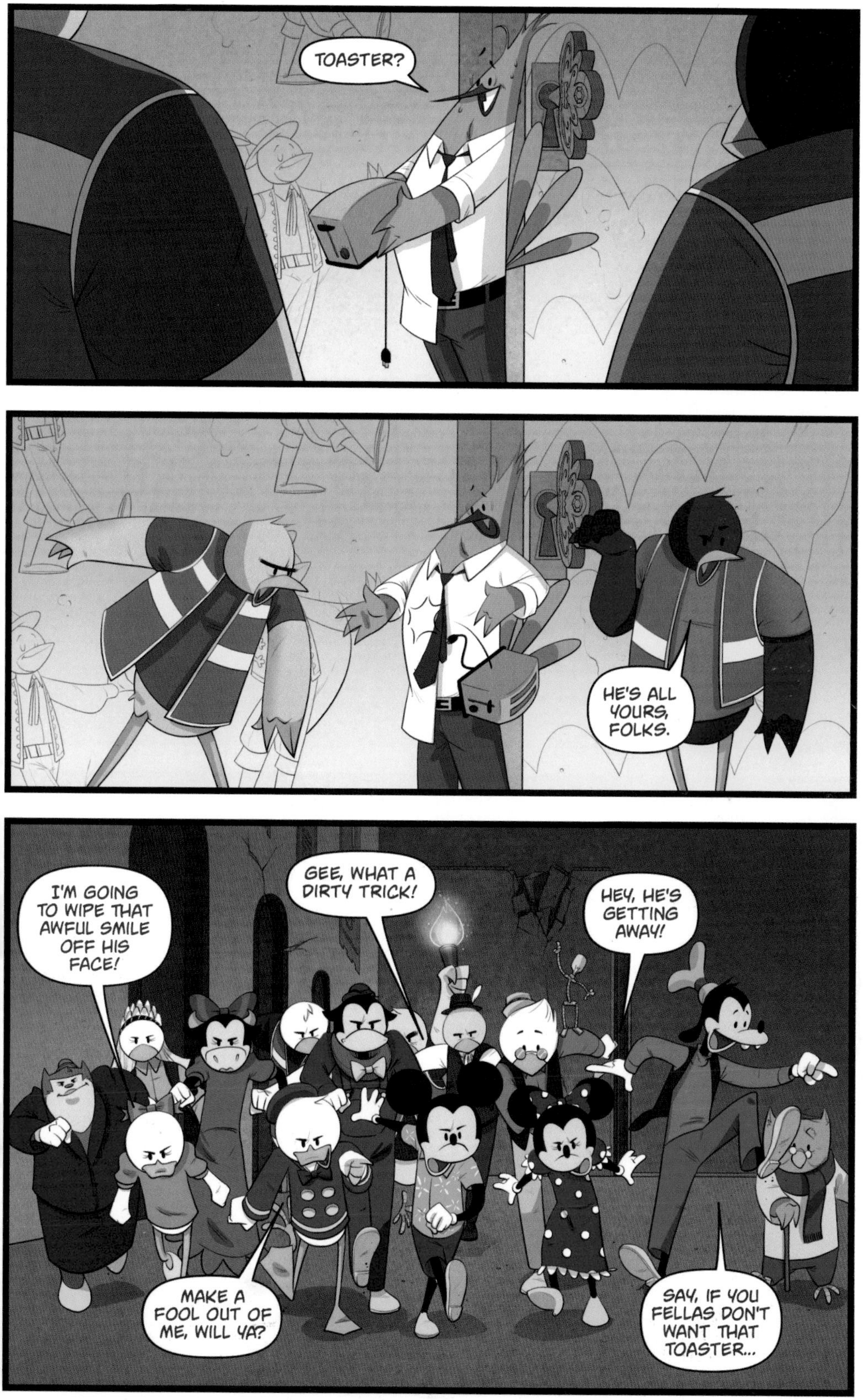
TOASTER?
HE'S ALL YOURS, FOLKS.
I'M GOING TO WIPE THAT AWFUL SMILE OFF HIS FACE!
GEE, WHAT A DIRTY TRICK!
HEY, HE'S GETTING AWAY!
MAKE A FOOL OUT OF ME, WILL YA?
SAY, IF YOU FELLAS DON'T WANT THAT TOASTER...

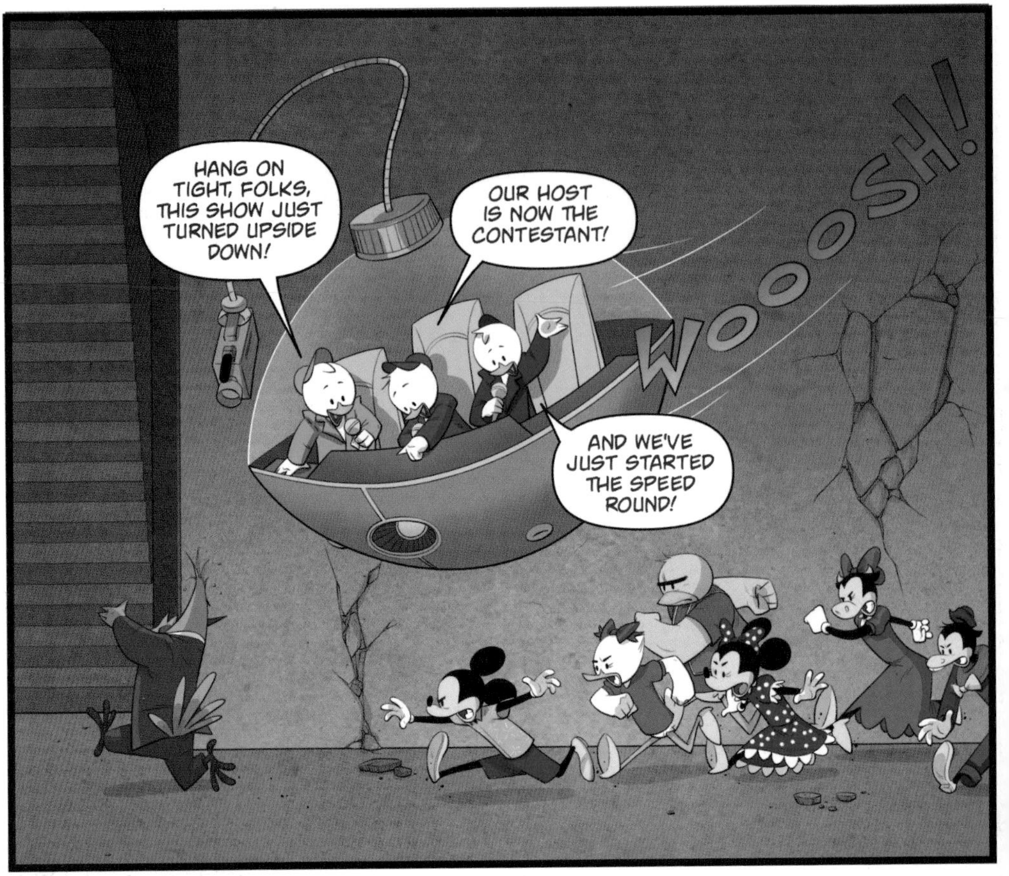
HANG ON TIGHT, FOLKS, THIS SHOW JUST TURNED UPSIDE DOWN!
OUR HOST IS NOW THE CONTESTANT!
AND WE'VE JUST STARTED THE SPEED ROUND!
WOOOOSH!

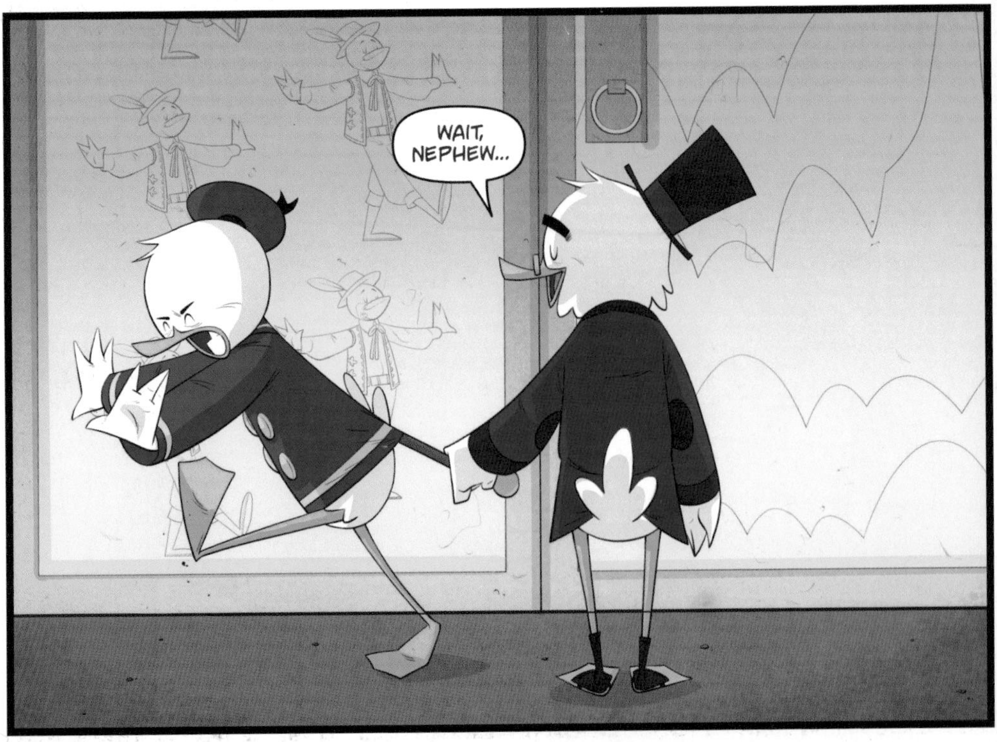
WAIT, NEPHEW...

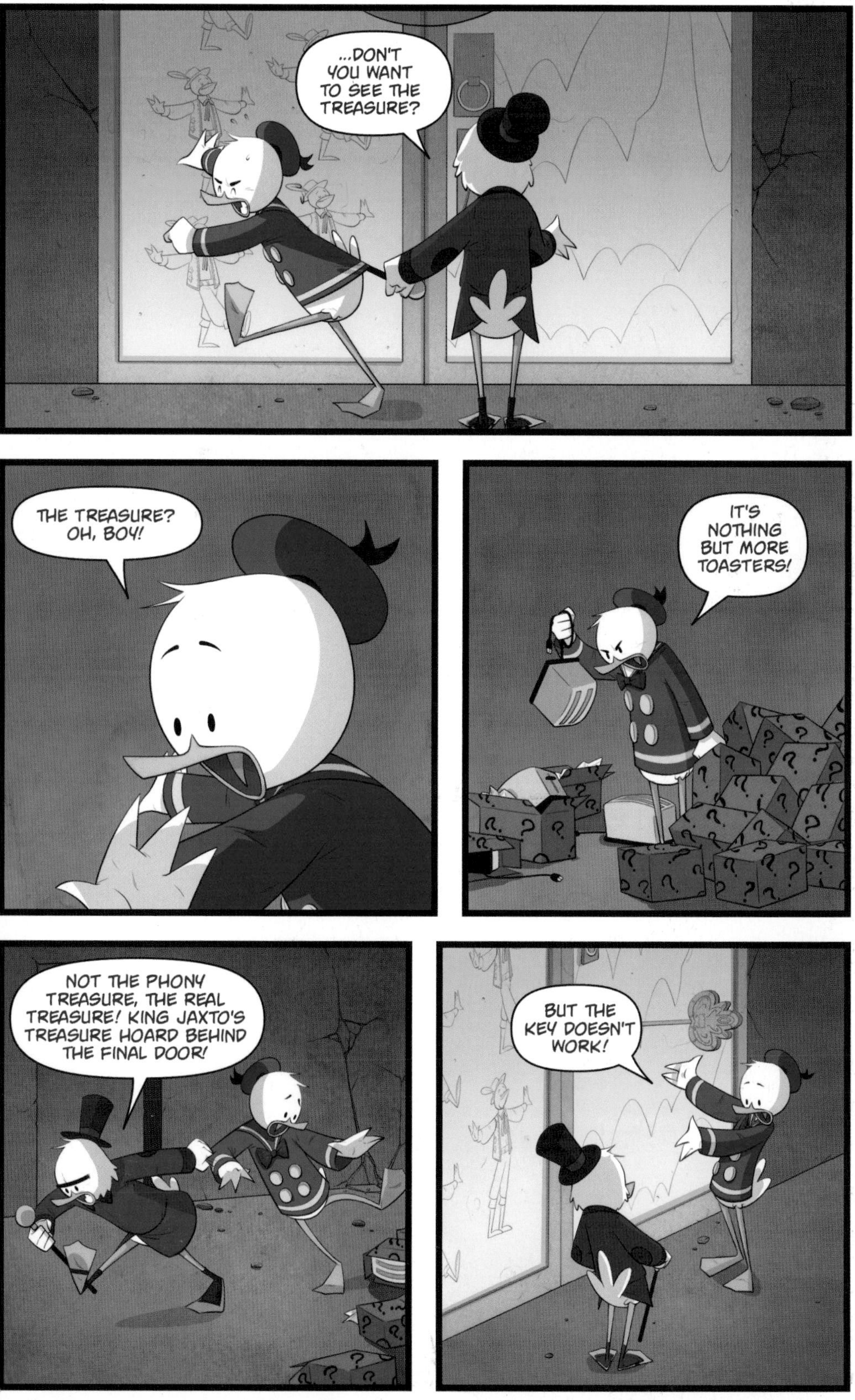
...DON'T YOU WANT TO SEE THE TREASURE?
THE TREASURE? OH, BOY!
IT'S NOTHING BUT MORE TOASTERS!
NOT THE PHONY TREASURE, THE REAL TREASURE! KING JAXTO'S TREASURE HOARD BEHIND THE FINAL DOOR!
BUT THE KEY DOESN'T WORK!

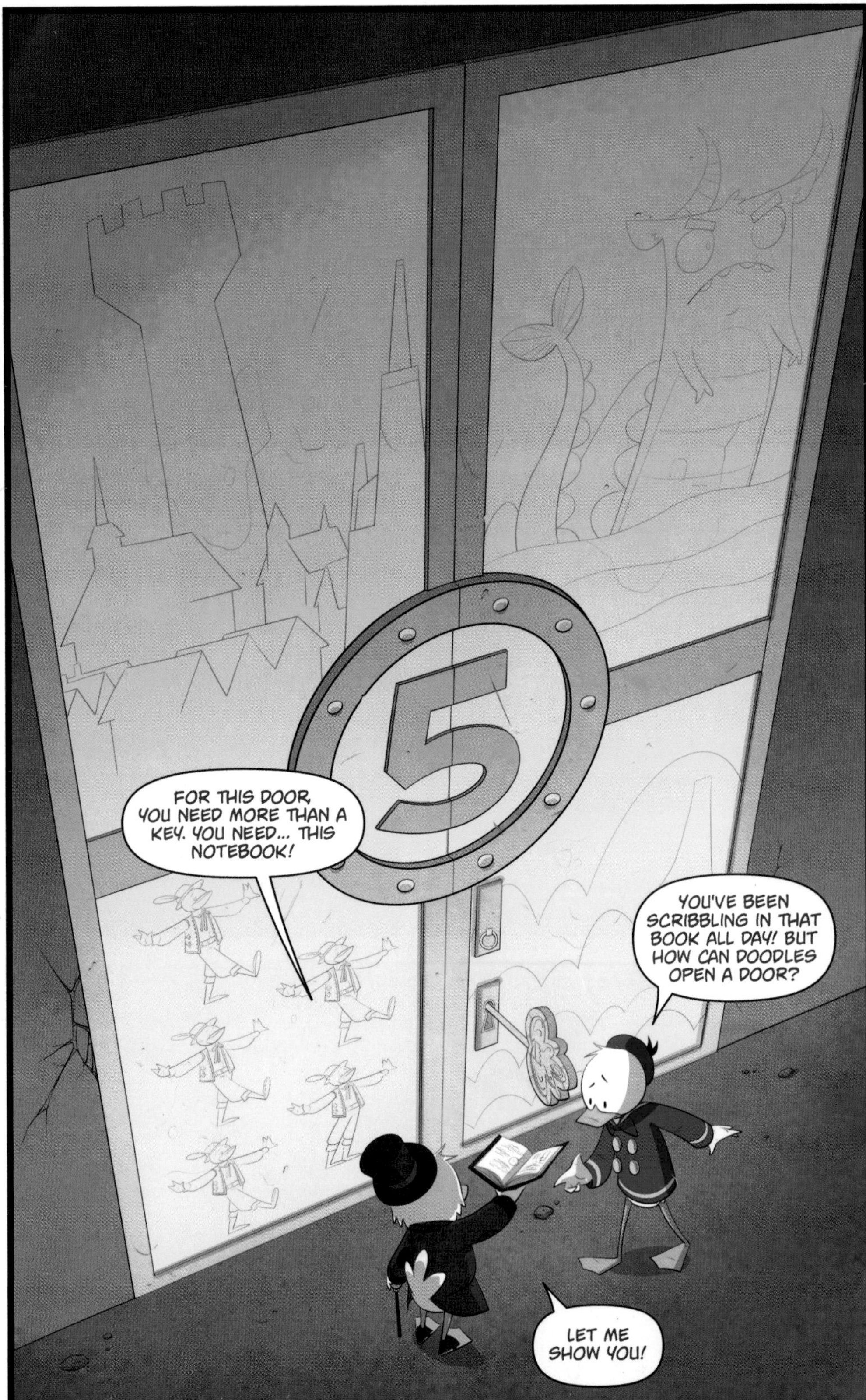
FOR THIS DOOR, YOU NEED MORE THAN A KEY. YOU NEED... THIS NOTEBOOK!
YOU'VE BEEN SCRIBBLING IN THAT BOOK ALL DAY! BUT HOW CAN DOODLES OPEN A DOOR?
LET ME SHOW YOU!

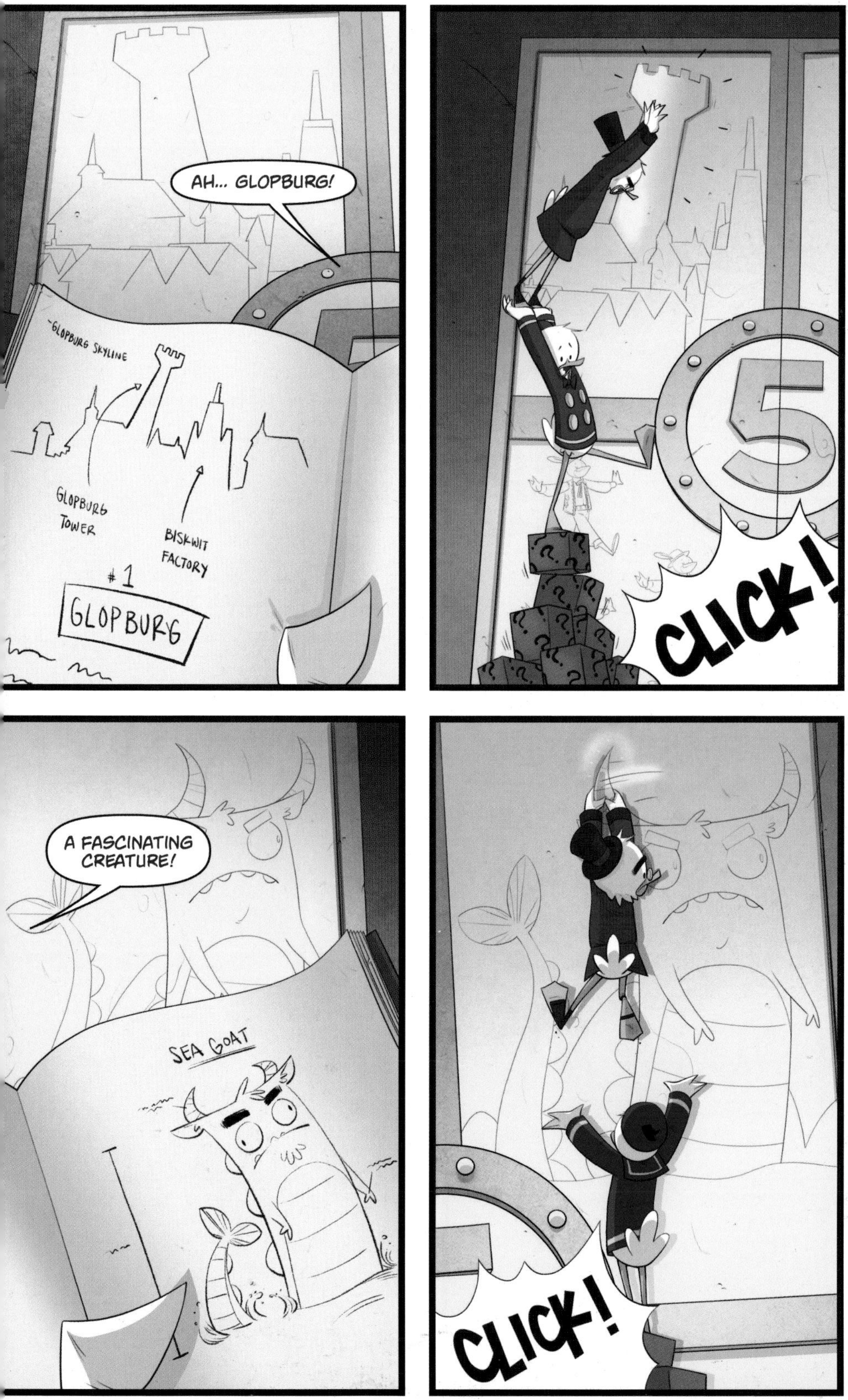
AH... GLOPBURG!
GLOPBURG SKYLINE
GLOPBURG TOWER
BISKWIT FACTORY
#1
GLOPBURG
5
CLICK!
A FASCINATING CREATURE!
SEA GOAT
CLICK!

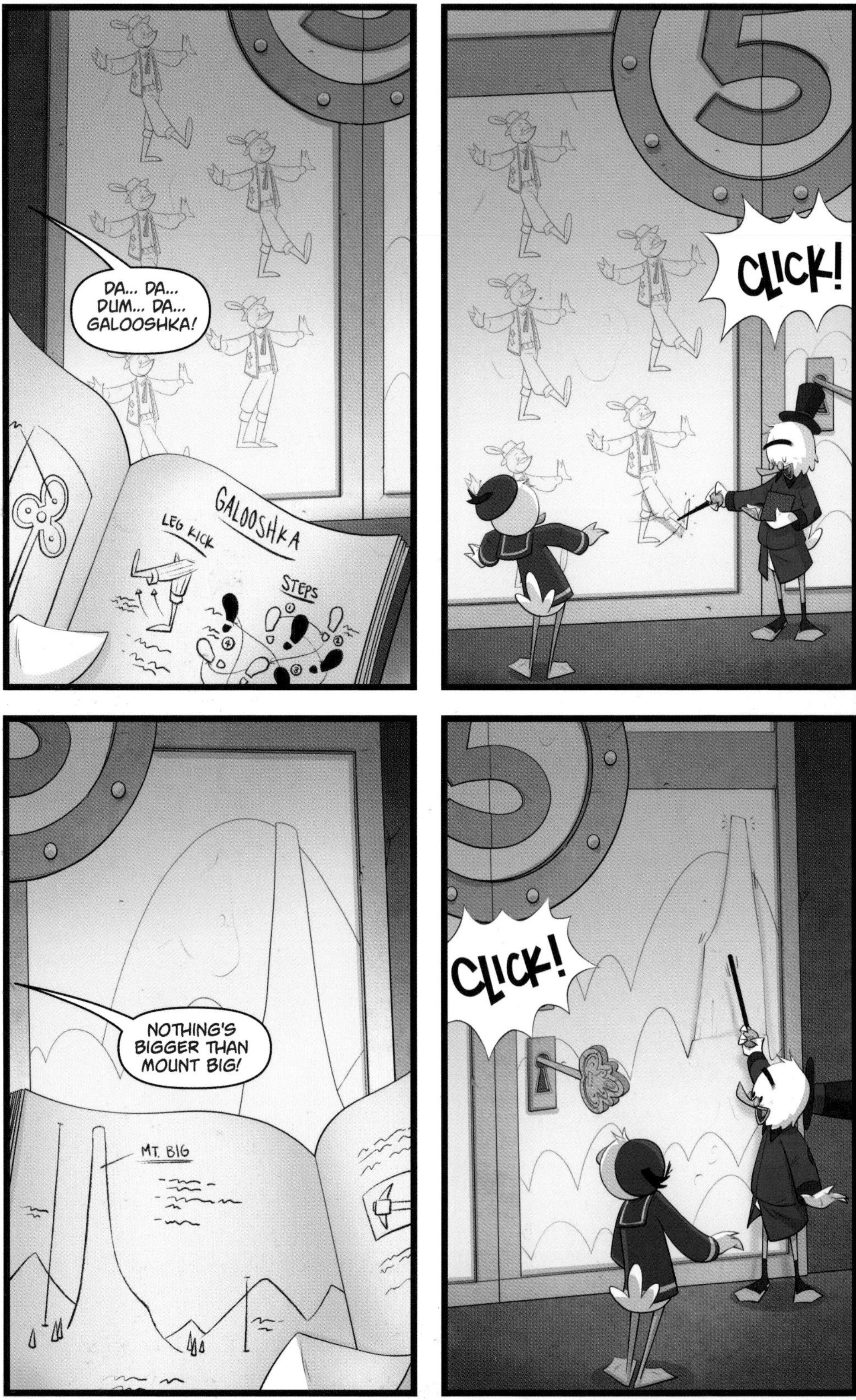
DA... DA...
DUM... DA...
GALOOSHKA!
GALOOSHKA
LEG KICK
STEPS
CLICK!
NOTHING'S
BIGGER THAN
MOUNT BIG!
MT. BIG
CLICK!

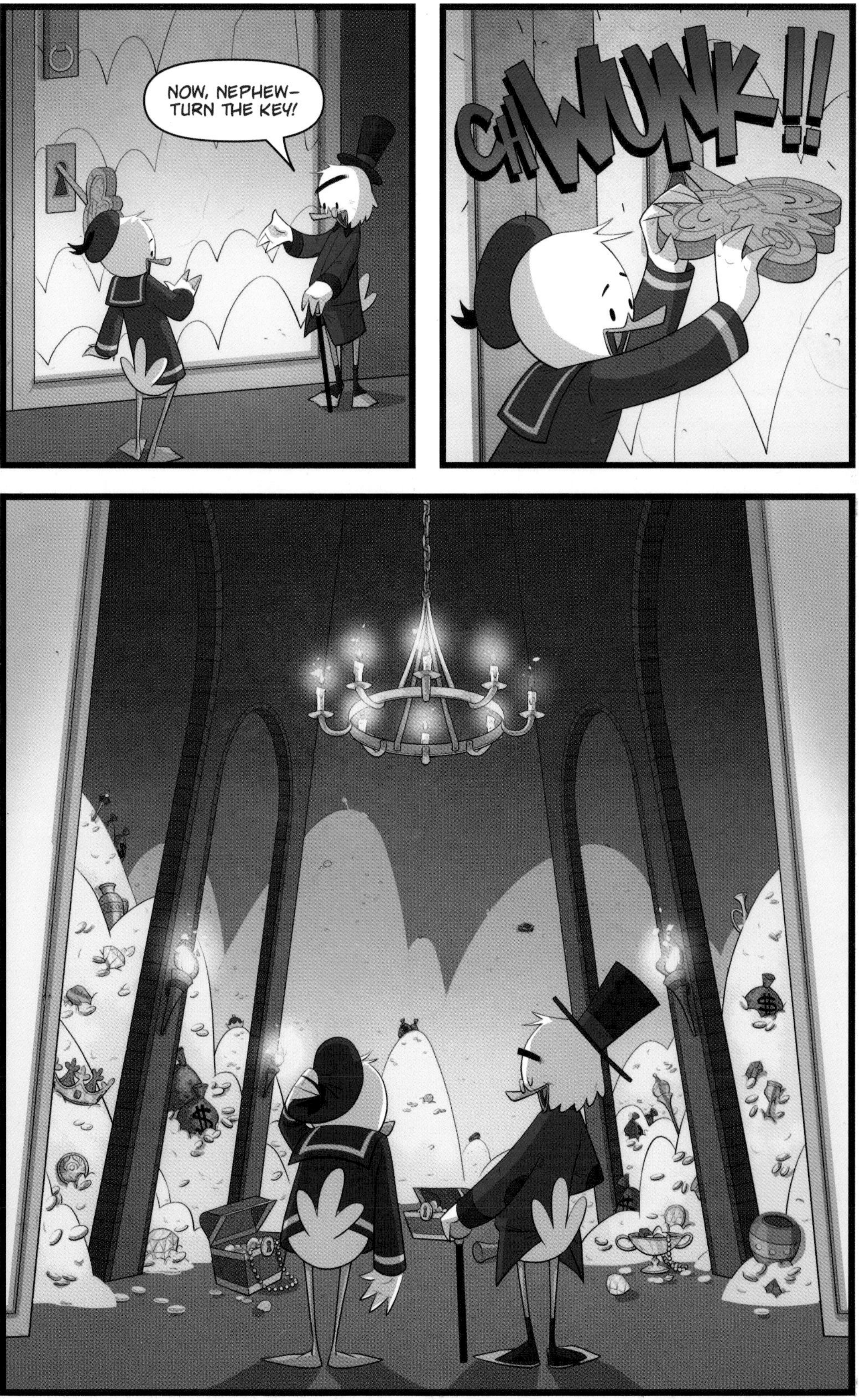
NOW, NEPHEW–
TURN THE KEY!
CHWUNK!!

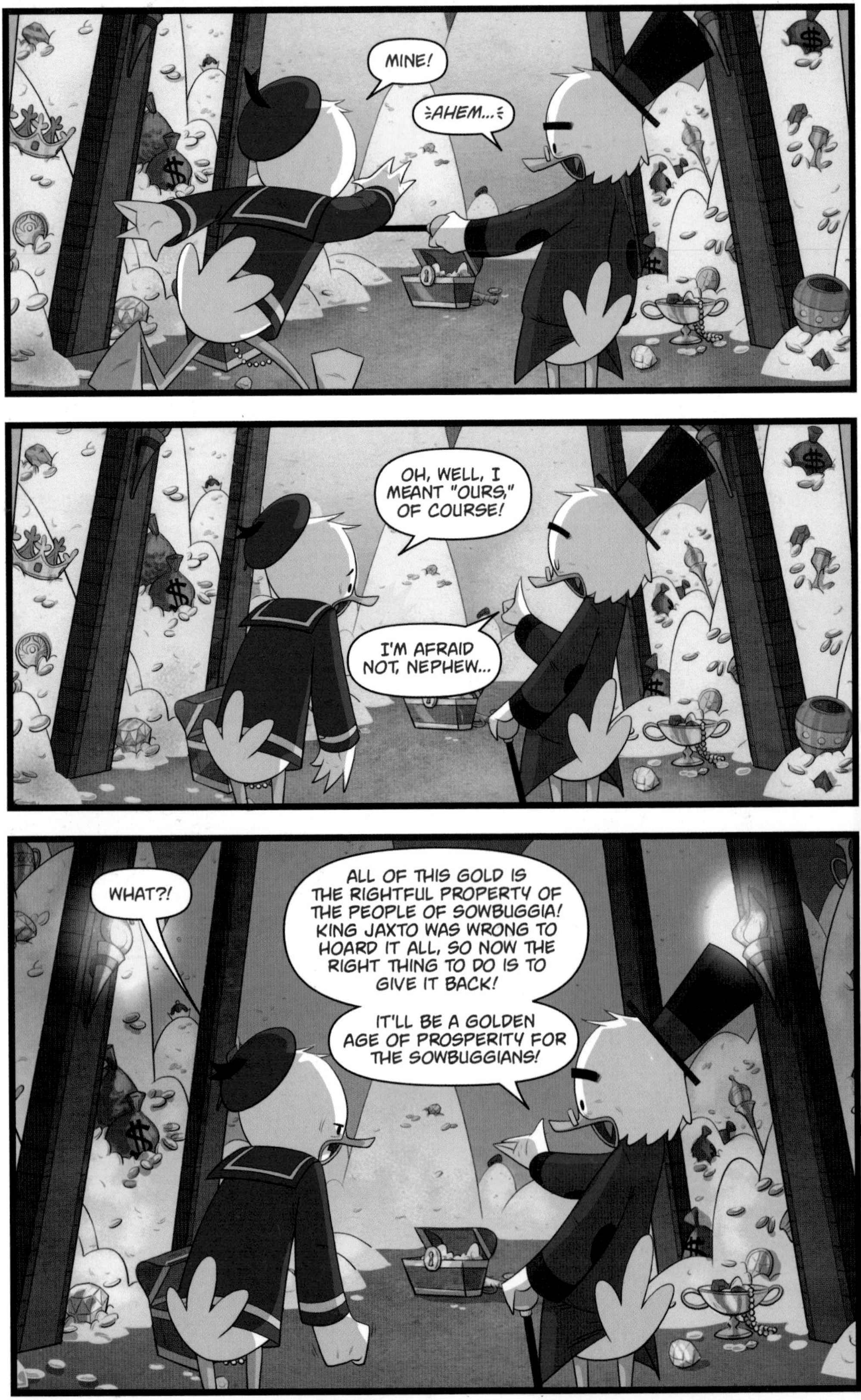
MINE!
AHEM...
OH, WELL, I MEANT "OURS," OF COURSE!
I'M AFRAID NOT, NEPHEW...
WHAT?!
ALL OF THIS GOLD IS THE RIGHTFUL PROPERTY OF THE PEOPLE OF SOWBUGGIA! KING JAXTO WAS WRONG TO HOARD IT ALL, SO NOW THE RIGHT THING TO DO IS TO GIVE IT BACK!
IT'LL BE A GOLDEN AGE OF PROSPERITY FOR THE SOWBUGGIANS!

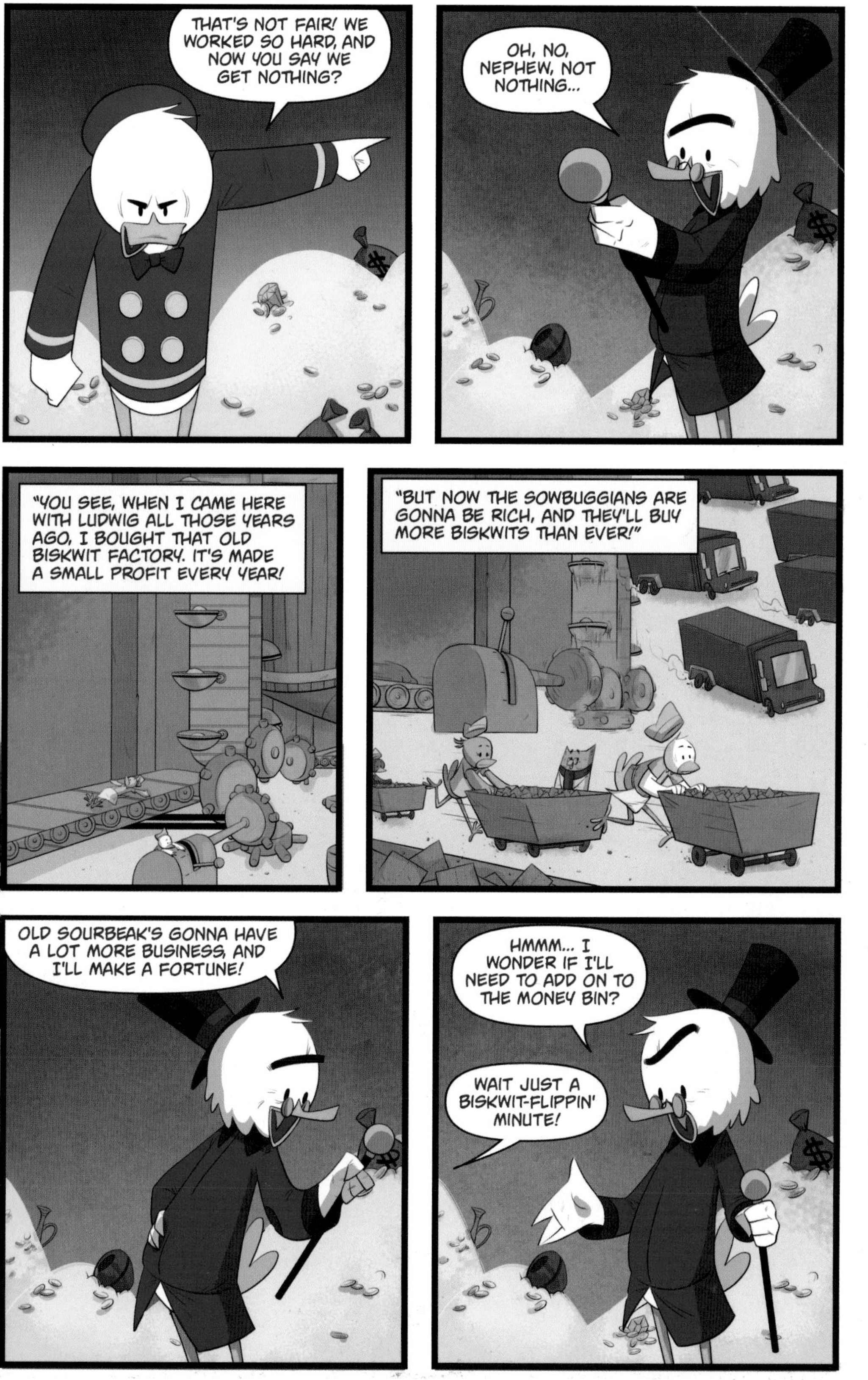
THAT'S NOT FAIR! WE WORKED SO HARD, AND NOW YOU SAY WE GET NOTHING?
OH, NO, NEPHEW, NOT NOTHING...
"YOU SEE, WHEN I CAME HERE WITH LUDWIG ALL THOSE YEARS AGO, I BOUGHT THAT OLD BISKWIT FACTORY. IT'S MADE A SMALL PROFIT EVERY YEAR!
"BUT NOW THE SOWBUGGIANS ARE GONNA BE RICH, AND THEY'LL BUY MORE BISKWITS THAN EVER!"
OLD SOURBEAK'S GONNA HAVE A LOT MORE BUSINESS, AND I'LL MAKE A FORTUNE!
HMMM... I WONDER IF I'LL NEED TO ADD ON TO THE MONEY BIN?
WAIT JUST A BISKWIT-FLIPPIN' MINUTE!

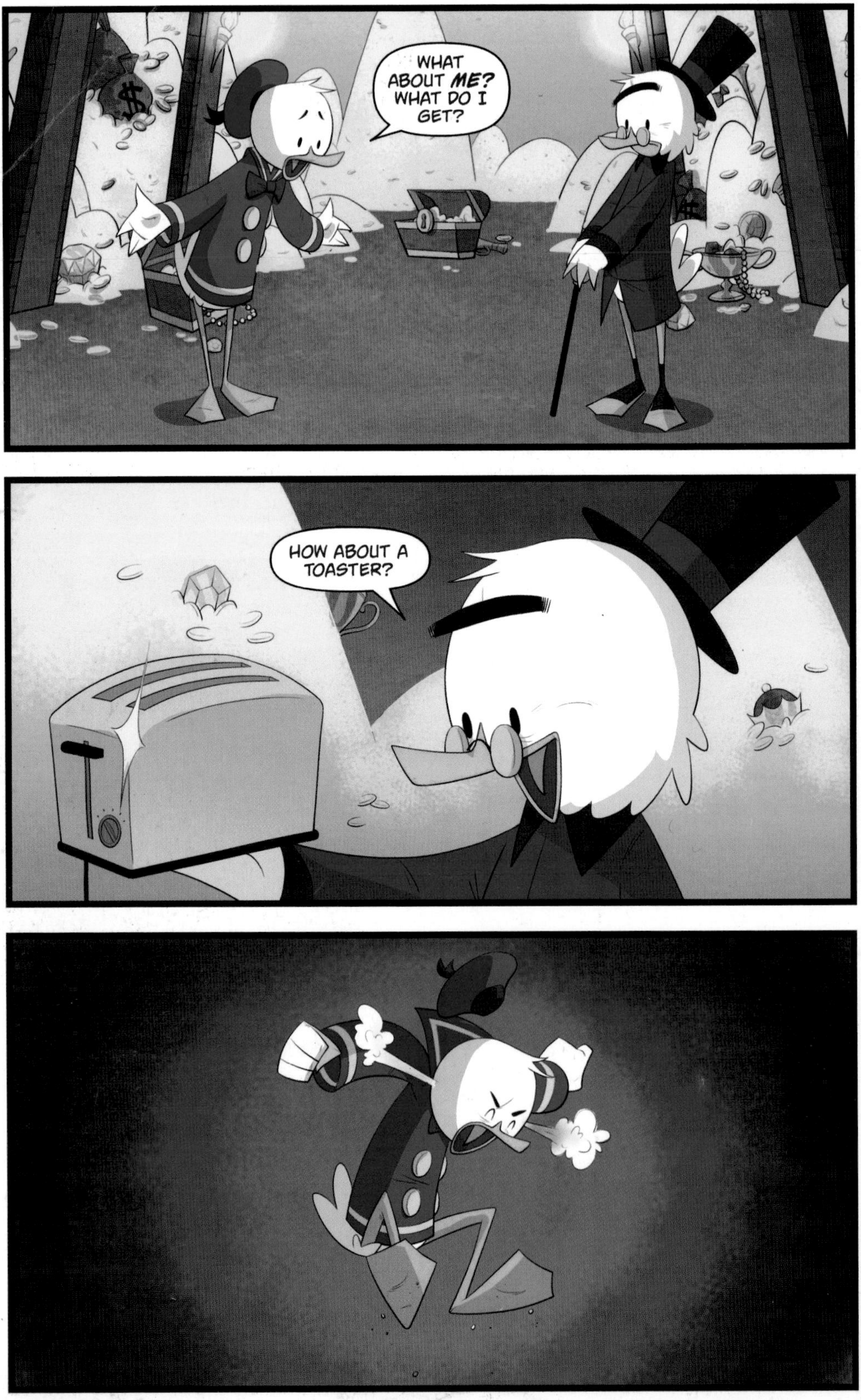
WHAT ABOUT ***ME?*** WHAT DO I GET?
HOW ABOUT A TOASTER?

IT LOOKS LIKE THE WINNER OF THE HIT GAME SHOW *DOORWAYS TO DANGER* IS...

...THE ENTIRE NATION OF SOWBUGGIA!

BREAKING NEWS: GAME SHOW GOTCHA!

CONTESTANTS OPENED A HIDDEN VAULT AND FOUND THE NATION'S LONG-MISSING TREASURY...

...SUDDENLY, SOWBUGGIA IS ONE OF THE RICHEST COUNTRIES ON EARTH!

BREAKING NEWS: GLOPBURG'S NEW GOLDEN AGE!

MEANWHILE, POLICE WERE ABLE TO ARREST THE MAN WHO STOLE THAT MONEY—FORMER KING JAXTO...

...THANKS TO A TIP MADE ON LIVE TV BY THE GAME SHOW'S ANNOUNCERS, HUEY, DEWEY, AND LOUIE.

THAT'S US!

WE'LL BE RIGHT BACK AFTER THESE MESSAGES...

UGH, NO MORE BISKWIT COMMERCIALS!

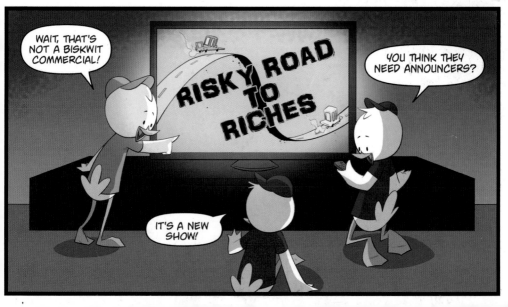

WAIT, THAT'S NOT A BISKWIT COMMERCIAL!

RISKY ROAD TO RICHES

YOU THINK THEY NEED ANNOUNCERS?

IT'S A NEW SHOW!

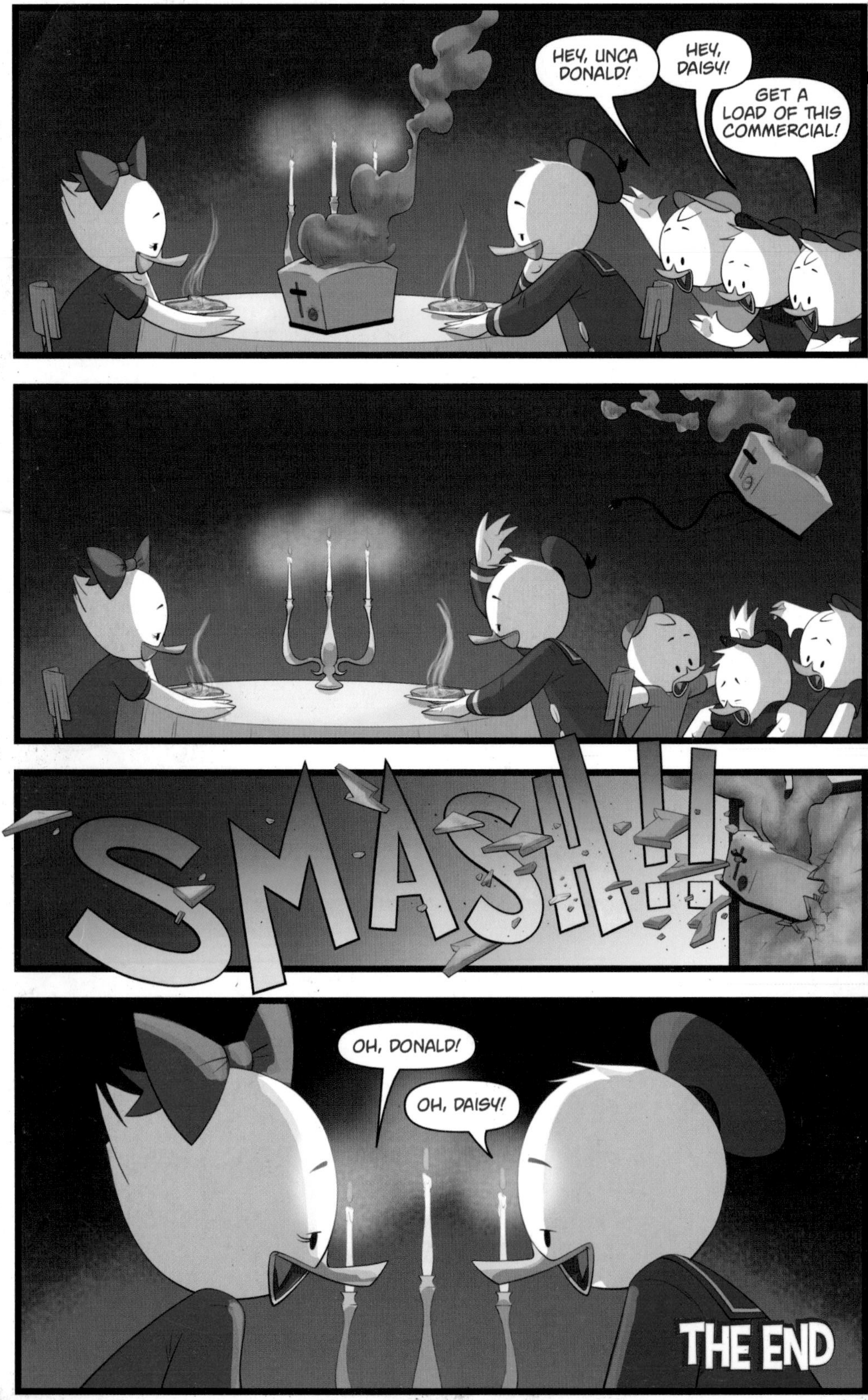
HEY, UNCA DONALD!
HEY, DAISY!
GET A LOAD OF THIS COMMERCIAL!
SMASH!!
OH, DONALD!
OH, DAISY!
THE END

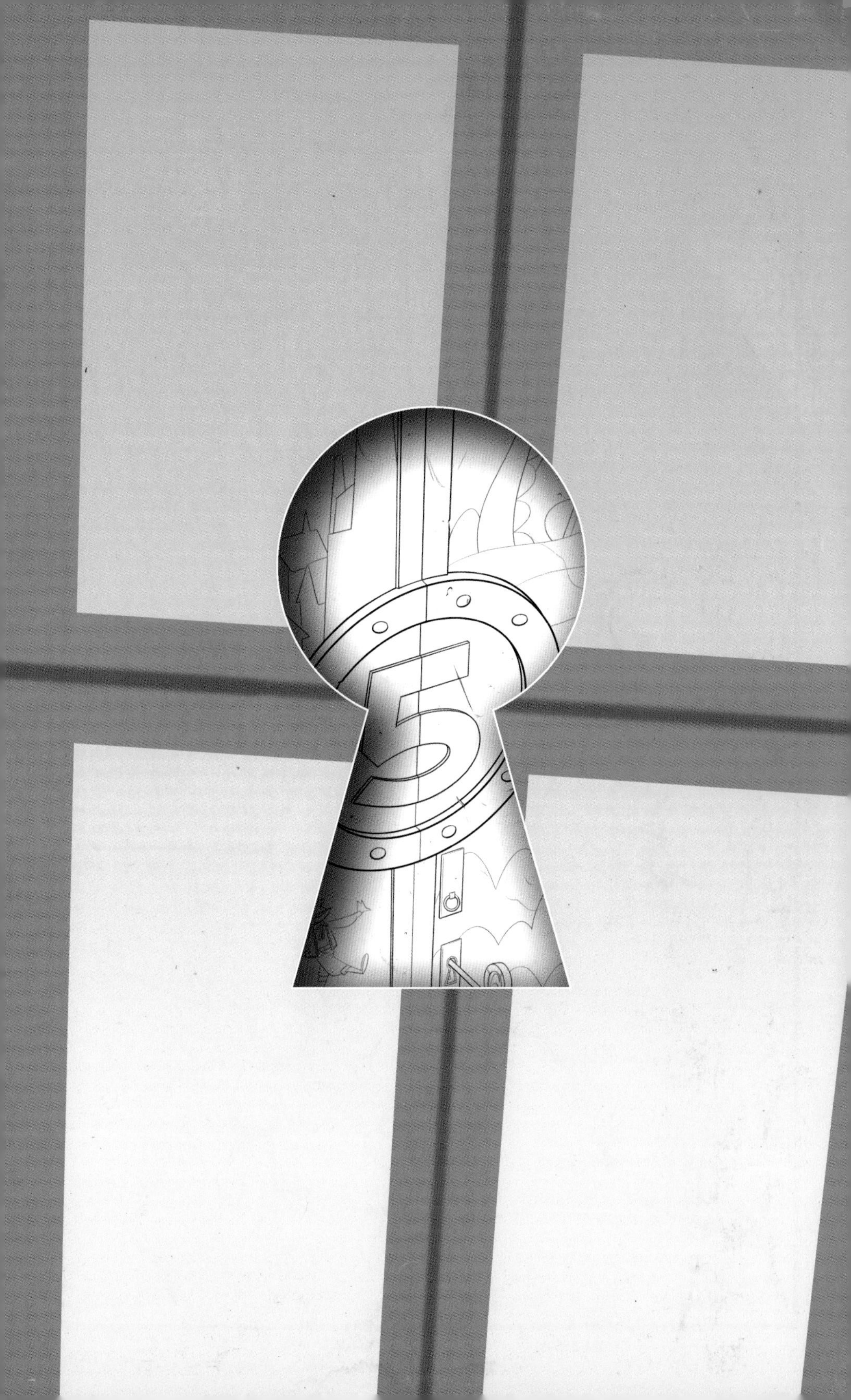
5

PENCIL SKETCH

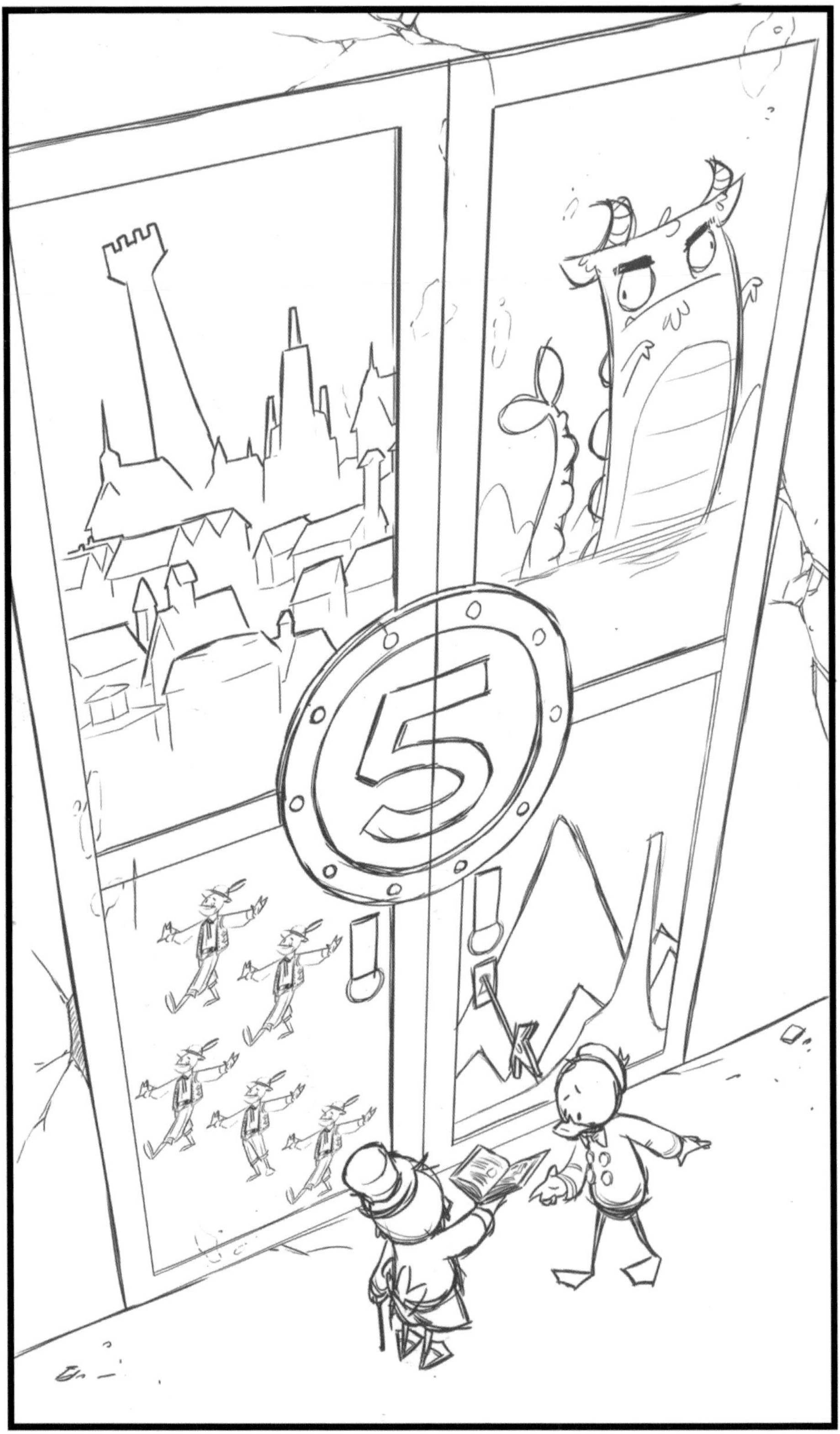
5

INKS

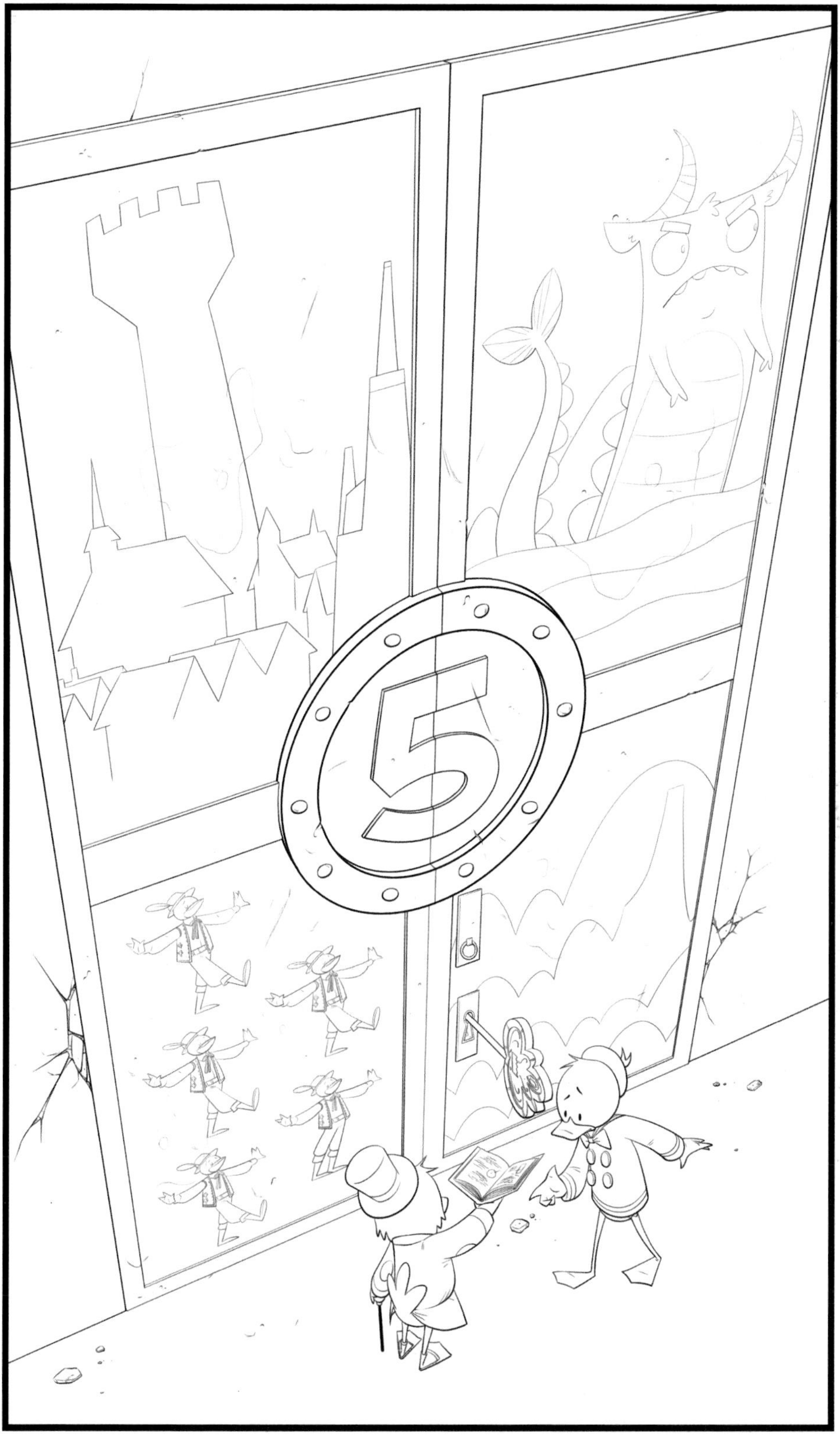

5

FINISHED COLORS

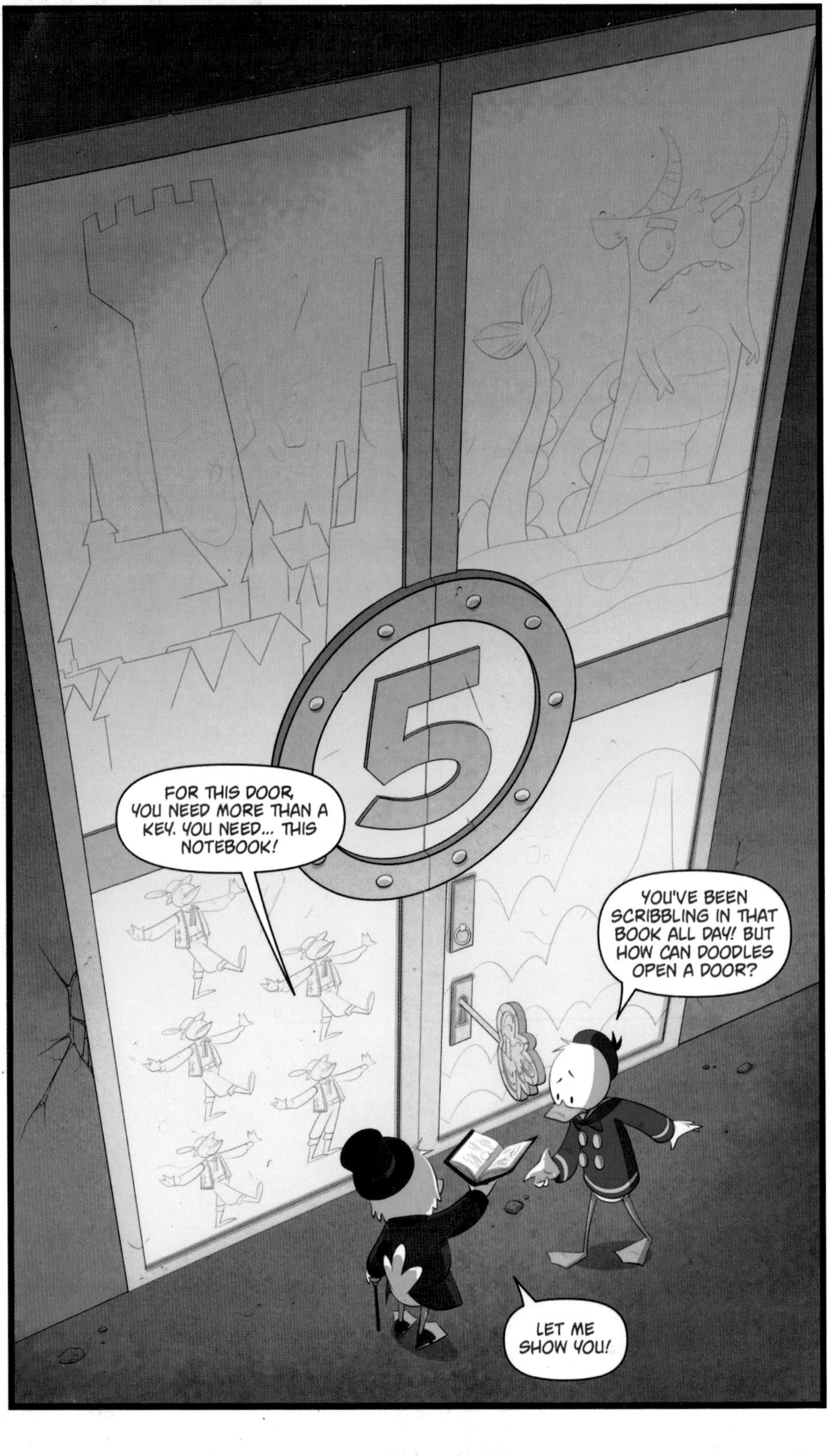
5
FOR THIS DOOR, YOU NEED MORE THAN A KEY. YOU NEED... THIS NOTEBOOK!
YOU'VE BEEN SCRIBBLING IN THAT BOOK ALL DAY! BUT HOW CAN DOODLES OPEN A DOOR?
LET ME SHOW YOU!